Still Waters

SHIRLEE McCOY
Still Waters

Steeple
Hill®

Published by Steeple Hill Books™

STEEPLE HILL BOOKS

Steeple
Hill®

ISBN 0-373-78510-0

STILL WATERS

Copyright © 2004 by Shirlee McCoy

Printed in U.S.A.

To Ed and Shirley Porter,
who taught me to believe in myself and to trust in
God. You get to be first this time, Dad!

To Rodney,
who believed even when I didn't. Ten years!
Want to try for another fifty?

To Willetta Ruth Pothier,
who shared her middle name and her love of books
with me. I love you, Nana.

And to Darlene Gabler.
Friend, confidante, endless source of story ideas.
This one's for you, Gal!

Chapter One

"Tiff, come on. Just a mile more." Brian McMath's voice echoed through the early-morning fog a moment before he appeared. Brown eyes keen, he watched as Tiffany approached, then resumed his own quick jog as she drew up beside him.

"You're doing great." Brian's words were followed by a glance in Tiffany's direction. She had little doubt he had taken note of her slick skin and damp clothes. *He* hadn't broken a sweat.

"I really...don't think...I can make it."

"Of course you can. It's only a mile. We've already done three."

"That's...one more...than I've been...doing. I've got...to stop." With a groan of relief, Tiffany did just that. Muscles quivering, she leaned forward, rested her hands on wobbling knees and struggled to catch her breath.

Brian stopped beside her and despite Tiffany's desperate need for oxygen she didn't miss the quick glance he cast at his watch. Nor could she mistake the pinched look around his mouth for anything other than the impatience it was. She forced herself upright. "Look Brian, I know you're anxious to finish the run. Why don't you go on ahead? I'll meet you at the diner."

"No, we agreed we'd do the jog together this morning. Just take a few deep breaths. I can wait another minute."

If Tiffany hadn't been so out of breath she might have laughed. As it was, she shook her head and tried to speak without panting every word. "It's going to take more than a minute for me to recover. Go on ahead."

Brian hesitated a moment and Tiffany knew he was torn between the desire to stay with her and the need to maintain his Saturday morning routine. In the end, routine won over affection and he nodded. "All right. If I get moving I'll still have time for breakfast before prayer meeting."

Tiffany smiled to hide her disappointment. Though she hadn't expected him to, a small part of her had hoped Brian would walk to the diner with her. "I shouldn't be more than fifteen minutes behind you."

Brian nodded absently and leaned forward to plant a kiss in the region of Tiffany's ear. "See you then." With a jaunty wave, he was gone, swallowed up by the fog.

"Don't worry. I'll be fine." Tiffany muttered the words aloud as she stretched the kinks from her strained calf muscles. Two ravens responded, cawing loudly from their perch on an unlidded garbage can a few feet away. With a sigh of frustration, Tiffany wiped sweat from her forehead and wondered how she had gone from spending Saturday morning with her boyfriend to talking to a couple of mangy-looking birds. As if sensing her thoughts one raven flew from the garbage can, his heavy body swooping close to the ground before he disappeared from sight. The other bird remained, its bright eyes following Tiffany's movements.

"I guess I'm not the only one being abandoned this morning."

The bird ruffled its feathers and cawed again before flying off to find its partner. Tiffany figured she'd better do the same and set off at a brisk walk.

The sun had already begun to burn away the fog and Tiffany reveled in its bright warmth and in the summer colors it revealed. She breathed deeply of rose-scented air, her pace unconsciously slowing as she caught sight of the lake. Eschewing the sidewalk, Tiffany made her way across an expanse of grass to Lakeview's public beach.

Smith Mountain Lake stretched out like blue-and-green dappled glass, the last vestiges of fog drifting across its smooth surface. Fishing boats speckled the water with color as die-hard fishermen cast lines and lazily reeled them in. In a few hours summer residents and vacationers would crowd the water and beach, bringing noise and activity with them, but for now the lake's tranquillity called to Tiffany.

Making her way across reddish soil and sand, Tiffany climbed onto the dock and walked to the end. The sun had yet to warm the wooden planks and she shivered as she lowered herself onto the smooth wood. With her feet dangling over the water, Tiffany stared out across the lake. For as long as she could remember, her soul had been stirred by its beauty, her mind awed by the power and artistry of the Creator who had made it. Often, in the earliest hours of the morning, she would come to pray and to listen. More often than not, she left feeling renewed and at peace.

Today, however, would not be one of those days.

The ebb and flow of the lake seemed to mirror Tiffany's

life—steady, placid, even keel. She supposed she should feel thankful that she could make the comparison, but somehow the knowledge stoked rather than soothed her irritation.

The past year had brought a boom in her computer maintenance business, a solid relationship with Brian and the loss of most of the thirty pounds she'd put on since college. It seemed to Tiffany that there wasn't a whole lot more she could want out of life, yet she couldn't shake the feeling that she was missing out on something important, something vital to her happiness.

With a disgruntled sigh, Tiffany rose to her feet. Discontent had been her unwelcome companion for more months than she cared to admit. She refused to dwell on it; refused to admit that the cause could be anything other than frustration with her failure to lose the last stubborn pounds of her postcollege weight.

Besides, Brian was waiting and if Tiffany didn't hurry, he'd be late to his prayer meeting. As Lakeview's newest physician, he had a reputation to uphold. Or so he'd told Tiffany on more than one occasion.

A motor purred to life in the distance. The deep throb of heavy metal music followed close behind, a hostile intrusion on the tranquillity of the morning. Surprised, Tiffany scanned the water and spotted a red speedboat as it rounded a curve in the lake. Several people stood in the helm of the boat, something large and black wiggling between them. She squinted, trying to make out the details, and decided they had either a large dog or a small horse on board. Whatever it was, it didn't want to be there.

Apparently the people in the boat didn't want it there, either. As they approached the center of the lake they heaved the struggling animal up and over the side. A terrified howl rent the air and was abruptly cut off as the dog hit the water. Shocked, Tiffany watched as the boat U-turned, disappearing the way it had come.

In the wake of the retreating vehicle the dog sank beneath the water, then surfaced again. Though it was quite a ways out, Tiffany figured the animal could make it to shore. At least she hoped it could. Still, she couldn't bring herself to abandon it. She stood on the dock, watching the dog's progress and silently cheering it on.

It only took a minute to realize the dog couldn't swim. His head bobbed for a moment, slid beneath the surface of the lake, then popped back into view. Tiffany watched as his paws paddled frantically against the water, the black head sinking again and again. Unwilling to let him drown, she kicked off her shoes and dove into the water.

Sheriff Jake Reed bit back a curse and slammed on the brakes, bringing his truck to a screeching halt yards from where the woman had disappeared into the water. Adrenaline lent speed to his movements as he threw open the truck door and raced across the grassy slope to the dock. He'd seen rescue attempts like this one before; seen good-hearted people trying to save a life only to find themselves in trouble.

Or worse.

Jake had no intention of letting that happen this time. Not if he could help it. He ran across the dock, shouting a warning to the woman as he went. She didn't pause, just continued her swift, steady progress toward danger. Jake marked her location, and dove into morning-cool water. The rhythm of the swim came slowly, Jake's muscles protesting the cold. He ignored the discomfort and forced himself to greater speed, the urgency that propelled him forward warning him that time was running out.

Tiffany circled behind the thrashing animal, grasped him

under the forelegs and attempted to tug him toward shore. He strained against her hold, the force of his movements pushing Tiffany beneath the surface. Coughing, gasping for breath she struggled back up for air only to be pushed down again. Darkness swirled behind her eyes and she fought against it, pushing against the dog, against the water, and against the strange lethargy that made her want to sink deeper into the lake's cool embrace.

Then something snagged the back of her shirt, pulling her up and over. She gasped and choked, coughing up water and sucking in air as an arm snaked around her waist and tugged her upright.

"Don't struggle. I've got you."

The deep voice penetrated Tiffany's panic, pulling her from the edge of darkness. She let herself go lax; let herself lean against the hard chest of the man who held her. Tiny shivers coursed along her spine as she struggled to calm her frantic breathing.

"Are you okay?" The words rumbled against Tiffany's hair and she nodded, forcing herself to respond though she barely had the energy to move.

"I'm fine."

"Good. Let's get back to shore."

"What about the dog?"

The man stilled, his arm tightening a fraction around Tiffany's waist. She thought for sure he'd lecture her, tell her how foolish she was. Instead he sighed. "Do you think you can tread water for a minute?"

"Yes." Tiffany hoped she sounded more confident than she felt.

"Good. I think we can use my belt to tow the dog in, but if he tries to use you as a raft again we let him loose and he fends for himself."

"All right."

The arm around Tiffany's waist slid away and she slipped deeper into the water, barely keeping herself from going under. A few yards away, the dog splashed and wailed, his heavy body sinking again and again. Tiffany shuddered as she watched, picturing her own struggle just moments before.

Water lapped at her back, but Tiffany didn't have the energy to turn and face her rescuer. Instead she waited, her movements clumsy and disjointed as she tried to stay afloat. When a hard arm wrapped around her waist, she sighed with relief, leaning into the support that was offered.

"Okay. We're set. Hold this."

A belt slithered over Tiffany's shoulder and she grabbed it, eyeing the thin leather skeptically. "Do you plan to lasso him?"

"No. I'm hoping to use it as a tow line. If we can get the mutt to bite down on it, we might be able to haul him in."

"Okay."

"Call the dog. See if you can get him closer. Then toss the belt out."

Tiffany did as she was asked, whistling and calling the panicked animal. Somehow he seemed to sense her intent and moved toward them, velvety brown gaze fixed on Tiffany. With a whispered prayer she tossed out the belt, reeled it back in and tossed it out again. The third time the dog surged forward, biting down on the belt and tugging with enough force to pull Tiffany against the arm that held her. She swallowed down a fit of coughing and held on tight. "Got him."

"Good. You hold the belt. I'll do everything else."

Tiffany didn't argue. She didn't have the energy to. Instead she allowed herself to be tugged toward shore.

Moments later cool lake water was replaced by warm air, and Tiffany was unceremoniously dumped onto prickly grass and sand. Coughing, still trying to ease her frantic breathing, she rose onto wobbly knees. A few feet away the dog stumbled onto shore, shook water from thick, black fur and collapsed onto the ground.

"Looks like the dog will be fine. How about you?"

Tiffany pushed tangled hair from her eyes and turned to face her rescuer. He knelt beside her, dark hair glistening with moisture. Even on his knees he looked tall. Broad-shouldered and strongly built, the man had a presence about him that Tiffany felt sure made people take notice when he entered a room.

He seemed familiar, though Tiffany wasn't sure where she'd seen him before.

"Are you all right, ma'am?"

A blush heated Tiffany's cheeks as she realized she'd been staring. Flustered she turned away, focusing her gaze on the dog. "Yes, I'm fine. Thanks."

"You're lucky."

"I know. Thanks for coming to the rescue."

"No problem. Did you get a look at any of the kids in the boat?"

"No. They were too far away. I think there were four or five of them, though."

"That's the impression I got as well."

"I don't understand why they'd throw the dog into the lake. It's cruel."

"People are cruel sometimes."

Tiffany couldn't argue the point. Instead she shrugged, gesturing to the dog. "Well, at least he's okay."

No thanks to her own foolish efforts. Tiffany's face heated again as she thought of the reckless impulse that had sent her diving into the lake. If not for the man kneeling beside her she might not be alive to regret her foolishness. Tiffany shuddered and turned to meet his assessing gaze.

Jake eyed the sodden, pale-faced woman beside him and bit back the recriminations that hovered on the tip of his tongue. No doubt she was doing a fair job of berating herself. He didn't need to add wood to the fire. Instead he stood and ran a hand through his hair. "I'll call animal control and have them bring the dog to the SPCA."

"Animal control? Forget them, I'll take care of the dog. What we need is the police. Why aren't they ever around when they're needed?"

"Actually, ma'am, I'm the police." Jake offered the woman a hand, clasping her slender fingers and pulling her up as he introduced himself. "Jake Reed. County Sheriff."

Heat stained her cheeks, bringing color back to her too pale face. "I'm so sorry, Sheriff Reed. I thought you looked familiar, but without a uniform—"

"Don't worry about it."

"I hope I didn't offend you."

"Not at all. This has been an unsettling experience. I don't blame you for being upset."

"Being upset isn't a good excuse for being rude. I *am* sorry." She tried to smile the apology, but it fell flat, the curve of her lips not reaching her eyes.

Eyes, Jake noticed, that were amazing. Deep green, shimmering with flecks of gold, and fringed by thick, dark lashes, they were striking against the woman's alabaster skin. For a moment he felt caught in her gaze, compelled to keep looking. Then she spoke and the spell was broken. "I hope you find the people responsible. They need to be held accountable for their actions."

"I agree, Ms....?"

"Oh, I'm sorry. Tiffany. Tiffany Anderson."

Tiffany. Jake had known one other Tiffany in his life. She had been petite and blond. A cheerleader, if he remembered correctly. The woman before him was more substantial. Long-limbed and well curved. Womanly in a way that some might consider out of style. Personally, Jake preferred it to the boyish look of today's fashion models. Not that it mattered. He wasn't in the market for any kind of woman.

Relationships were for people with the time and patience to indulge in them. Jake had neither. He'd learned that the hard way and had no intention of repeating the mistake. He'd get the dog and Tiffany Anderson home safely and get back to the first day of his vacation. The sooner he did both, the better. "Do you need help to your car?"

"No. Thanks. I walked."

"How about a ride home?"

At his words, Tiffany's eyes widened. "Home? Oh, no! Brian's waiting for me at the diner."

"Brian?"

"My boyfriend. I was supposed to meet him for breakfast."

"Becky's Diner, right?" It was the only diner in town, one Jake had become familiar with in the year since he'd moved to Lakeview.

"Yes. Poor Brian. He must be worried sick."

Jake didn't comment. Another lesson he'd learned young—people who *should* care, often didn't. He didn't say as much to Tiffany, just nodded and pointed to his truck. "I can give you a lift. The dog can ride in the back if you can get him to move."

Worry eased from Tiffany's face and her mouth curved into a half smile. "Thanks. That would be great."

She wiped a hand across her forehead, brushing away

moisture that dripped from her hair. Jake's gaze followed the movement, his eyes tracing the arch of Tiffany's brow, the curve of her cheek, and the stubborn point of her chin. She had an interesting face, one made almost beautiful by velvety skin and a dash of freckles across her nose.

Maybe she'd seen him before, but Jake was sure he hadn't seen *her.* If he had, he wouldn't have forgotten.

"Do you think he'll come if I call him?" Tiffany's voice pulled Jake from his thoughts and he forced his gaze away from the alluring woman beside him.

"He looks pretty comfortable, but it can't hurt to try."

Tiffany let out an ear piercing whistle. "Come here, dog. Here doggie, doggie."

The dog lifted his head, but didn't stand. Jake figured the mutt was more interested in resting than moving. "Tell you what. You get in the truck. I'll take care of the dog."

"Maybe if I knew his name I—"

"Trust me. The dog isn't going to budge, no matter what you call him. Come on. Your boyfriend's waiting."

And so was Jake's vacation, but he decided not to mention *that* as he ushered Tiffany to the pickup truck.

Tiffany sat in the cab of the old Chevy and wondered how her day had gone so bad, so fast. All she'd wanted was an hour with Brian. A quick morning jog so they could touch base and discuss a few things that were on her mind. Instead she'd gotten a near death experience and a chance to ride in the sheriff's pickup.

Tiffany grimaced, imagining Brian's face when she walked into the diner, soaking wet and escorted by an officer of the law. At least the man wasn't wearing a uniform. Not that it would matter. People in Lakeview knew one another. And they liked to talk. A lot.

With a sigh, Tiffany glanced out the window. The dog and

the sheriff were having a standoff. One determined to move toward the truck, the other just as determined to stay put. Finally Jake leaned down and grasped the dog under its belly, lifting him from the ground with an ease that surprised Tiffany. She watched as he walked toward the truck, his stride long but unhurried, as if the hundred-pound dog were no weight at all. She supposed that had something to do with the bulging muscles of his biceps and the wide, toned breadth of his shoulders. As if sensing her gaze, Jake glanced in Tiffany's direction, his blue eyes dark and unreadable. Tiffany's heart did a little flip of awareness before she had the presence of mind to turn away.

Physical strength, stunning good looks—those things might appeal to some people, but not to Tiffany. Brian's lanky runner's frame and boy-next-door looks were pleasant but it was his dedication, faith and intelligence that had drawn Tiffany to him.

If the sparks didn't fly when her eyes met Brian's—well, that was to be expected. They weren't living a romance novel and they weren't teenagers experiencing the bliss of their first love. Brian was everything Tiffany had asked God for—more—and she was thankful. Really.

"All set." Jake appeared at the driver's side door and slid into the truck cab, his shoulder brushing Tiffany's as he buckled his seat belt and started the engine.

It didn't take long to drive to Becky's Diner and neither Tiffany nor Jake felt compelled to speak during the short ride. Tiffany wasn't sure of the reason for the sheriff's silence. Hers was due to fatigue and worry. She eyed the parking lot as Jake circled it for the second time. Cars were crammed close together, bright sunlight reflecting off their hoods. Even the overflow area was packed tight with vehicles, a result, Tiffany knew, of summer's arrival.

During the hot months of June, July and August, seasonal residents and tourists flocked to Smith Mountain Lake for recreation. The small, tight-knit community Tiffany had grown up in swelled to twice its size, and the diner's normally adequate parking lot filled to overflowing. Most times, Tiffany didn't mind the inconvenience. Today she was in a hurry, and prayed a parking spot would open soon.

As Jake circled the parking lot for the third time, Tiffany's gaze wandered across the rows of cars. Where was Brian's Saturn? He'd picked her up at home this morning and driven to the diner—the starting and finishing point of their four-mile run. Now his car was gone.

"I don't see Brian's car. I hope he didn't go looking for me."

"Want me to go in and ask for him?" Jake spoke as he maneuvered the Chevy into a vacated parking space.

"No. I'll go in myself. Do you mind waiting with the dog? I'll get him when I come back out."

"No problem. But if you're planning to go in the diner you might want to put this on." He reached behind the seat and pulled out a blue jacket, thrusting it into Tiffany's hand.

His expression revealed nothing of his thoughts, though his gaze drifted down to rest briefly on Tiffany's wet shirt. She followed his gaze with her own, gasping in surprise as she realized the extent of the damage. Smudges of dirt and grass stained the front of the shirt and a jagged tear rent the hem. Worse, the material clung to her like a second skin. Hastily pushing her arms through the sleeves of the jacket, Tiffany zipped it to her chin and tried to ignore the fine trembling in her hands. Her lake ordeal had left her exhausted and she couldn't wait to get home.

She pasted a smile on her face and turned toward the sheriff, ready to make light of the moment and be on her way. Instead she froze, flustered by the intense stare of the man beside her. He didn't smile, didn't offer any encouragement, just held her gaze, his face set in an expression that shouted *stay back*.

Tiffany imagined him using that expression on criminals. Imagined him forcing a confession by the sheer force of his gaze. She swallowed back nervous laughter and pushed open the truck door. "I guess I'd better get in there. Thanks for the jacket. And for saving me. And the dog, too. I mean...I'd better go find Brian."

Without a backward glance, Tiffany hopped out of the truck and headed for the diner.

Chapter Two

Jake watched her go, a smile tugging at the corner of his mouth. It surprised him a little, the pulling of muscles and crinkling of eyes, the spontaneous response to simple pleasure. The past year had been short on smiles. Those that *had* graced Jake's face felt forced and unnatural.

Now he was close to grinning thanks to Tiffany Anderson and her rambling, embarrassed banter. Not to mention her shuffling run as she moved across the parking lot, the sleeves of his jacket falling down over her hands. He'd thought her hair to be brown, but now realized he'd been wrong. It was red—a bouncing, shouting array of gold and fire.

He wondered if she had a temper to match, then forced his mind away from the question. He didn't want to know about Tiffany. Didn't want to find out who she was, what made her tick, or why she would risk her life for a dog.

He'd done it once—searched for the answers to a woman's heart. The result had been two years of bitter feuds and cutting silences. In the end, he and Sheila had divorced. He'd thrown himself into his work. She'd thrown herself into the bottle. Jake had blamed himself. Now he avoided relationships, preferring a life of solitude to a life of regret.

Jake ran a hand through his hair and eyed the closed door of the diner. Too much time had passed. Tiffany should have returned by now. The dog whined as if he, too, were growing impatient. Determined to get on with his day, Jake stepped out of the truck and checked on the dog, who lay panting loudly in the morning heat. No doubt he was thirsty.

Jake figured he could get the dog some water in the diner. Then he'd find Tiffany Anderson and politely ask her to remove the mutt from the back of his truck.

If he could find Tiffany. *If* she hadn't scooted out the back of the diner and left the dog to him. Jake winced at his own cynicism. Ten years patrolling the most squalid areas of Washington, D.C., had taught him everything he needed to know about human nature. Not that he'd had much to learn. He'd cut his teeth on lies and faithlessness. Where Jake grew up, a promise made was a promise broken and the only person he could trust was himself.

Forcing his mind away from the past, Jake pushed open the door of the diner and walked into warmth and chaos. The sun shone through huge storefront windows, bathing the room with light. Jukebox music and eager conversation filled the dining area as waitresses shuffled order pads and balanced food-laden trays. The heady aroma of bacon and sausage wafted through the room and Jake's stomach rumbled in response. Once he found Tiffany and got rid of the dog, Jake figured he might just start his vacation with a stack of pancakes and a side of home fried potatoes. Taking a seat at the counter, he gazed around the room searching for a head full of rioting curls.

"Looking for Tiffy?"

Jake turned to greet Doris Williams, the current owner of Becky's Diner. "Tiffy?"

"Tiffany Anderson. She said you brought her here from the lake. I thought maybe you were looking for her."

"Yeah. She leave?"

"She's in the bathroom. Crying, I'd say. Not that she's the mopey kind, mind you. But a girl counts on her man being there for her when she's down. When he's not, it's disappointing."

Jake's mind spun at the turn in the conversation but he nodded anyway. "Yes, I suppose it is."

"No supposin' about it." Short and thin, with wiry salt-and-pepper hair and skin the color of toasted pecans, Doris was known for her harsh tongue and soft heart. She would go to her grave denying it, swore she'd never committed a charitable act, but the residents of Lakeview knew the truth and loved Doris for it.

Jake had been hearing stories of her timely interventions since the day he'd moved to town. In the twelve months since then, he'd seen for himself the extent to which Doris would go to make a single mother feel comfortable taking leftovers from the diner's kitchen, or to talk an out-of-work father into accepting free meals for his children. He'd also seen that when Doris needed a hand with something, the townspeople were quick to go to her aid. Jake wasn't about to break with tradition.

Which he supposed was good, as it seemed Doris wanted something from him. Shifting in his chair, Jake met Doris's watchful gaze and tried not to fidget beneath her scrutiny.

"Well?" Coal-black eyes flashed as short-nailed fingers beat a tattoo against the counter.

Jake cleared his throat. "Well, what?"

"What are you going to do about Tiffany? Dr. Brian has gone off to the men's prayer meeting and left her here. *Someone's* got to give her a ride home."

The tone of Doris's voice left little doubt that the someone was going to be Jake. Pushing aside his exasperation, Jake resigned himself to the task. "You said she was in the bathroom?"

"Yes. Drying her shirt, she said. But I know better. Knock on the door loud and get me if she doesn't come out. I'll fetch her for you."

"Right." With a last wistful look at a tray of pancakes being carried to the dining room, Jake headed for the rest rooms. His belly could wait. Duty called.

"Pull yourself together!" The whispered words did little to stanch the tears that dripped down Tiffany's cheeks. She mopped at the offending moisture with a wad of toilet tissue, blinked hard and sniffed. It wasn't far to her house and any other morning she would have enjoyed the walk. But Tiffany was tired. She was wet. The hair she'd so carefully braided that morning fell around her face in straggly curls.

And Brian had left her to fend for herself.

Not that she could blame him. After all, he was leading the prayer meeting and it wouldn't do for him to be late. Still, it would have been nice if he'd come looking for her. Or barring that, waited until she'd shown up. Tiffany didn't think it was too much to ask that Brian be as concerned about her well-being as he was about his meeting. Unfortunately, if she'd had to count on him to rescue her, Tiffany would still be floundering in the lake.

The thought brought fresh tears and Tiffany grabbed another handful of tissue, rubbing hard at red-rimmed eyes. The tissue broke apart and dotted her face with tiny bits of white. Irritated, she used the sleeve of Jake's jacket to rub the residue away. Walking back through the dining room looking like the before ad for allergy relief medication would be embarrassing enough; she didn't need toilet paper stuck to her face as well.

Sniffing hard, Tiffany forced back more tears and reached for her purse. The one blessing in the whole fiasco was that Brian had remembered to leave it with Doris. Rifling through its contents Tiffany pushed aside car keys, house keys, lip balm and a pack of gum before she realized she'd left her wallet at home. She didn't have enough change in the bottom of her bag to get the diet soda she wanted. With the kind of day she'd been having, the knowledge didn't surprise her. Nor did it surprise Tiffany when someone knocked on the bathroom door. Having a few extra minutes to compose herself would have made the day just a little too easy.

"Just a minute." A last swipe with the tissue, a quick hand through hopelessly tangled hair and Tiffany was ready to face the world.

The corridor she stepped into seemed dark compared to the bright light in the bathroom and she didn't see the person standing against the wall until he spoke. "Doris told me you needed a ride home."

Praying the corridor was dark enough to hide her tear-ravaged face, Tiffany turned to face Jake Reed. "Not really. My house isn't far. I can walk."

"I don't mind giving you a ride home. Besides, how else are you going to get the dog there? I think he's too tired to walk."

Tiffany's heart clenched as she pictured the pitiful mountain of black fur and soulful dark eyes. She'd forgotten about the dog. "Is he doing okay?"

"He seems fine. Just tired. I came in to get him some water. It's getting hot out there."

"Yeah, and he *has* been through a lot. I doubt walking a mile in the heat would be good for him. Maybe I'll take you up on that ride after all." Tiffany seized upon the excuse Jake offered her.

"Good. Why don't you go out the back door there?" Jake gestured to a door at the end of the hall. "I'll meet you outside in a few minutes."

Tiffany attempted to smile her gratefulness, but knew her expression fell short of the mark. "All right. Thank you."

Jake watched her go and tried hard to convince himself he didn't care that she'd been crying; tried even harder not to notice the proud tilt of her curl-covered head or the unconscious grace with which she moved.

Dr. Brian was an idiot.

A flash of light illuminated the hall as Tiffany disappeared into the morning sunshine. The back door had been a good idea. Even the dim light of the corridor hadn't hidden the downcast turn of Tiffany's eyes or the dejected slump of her shoulders. Jake figured she was as uncomfortable with her tears as he was. He was glad she didn't have to show them to the world.

Not that she'd slunk away like a coward. She'd left with her head high and her chin lifted. Jake admired her grit. Turning away, he headed back to the dining room.

Doris was waiting.

"She still locked in the ladies' room? Got myself a key around here somewhere. Just hold on a minute and I'll get it."

"No need for that, Miss Doris. Tiffany went out the back way. She's waiting in the truck."

Doris stared hard, as if trying to ascertain the truthfulness of Jake's statement. Jake stared back, wishing he didn't feel like a school kid sitting in the principal's office. A moment passed with neither speaking. Then, apparently satisfied with what she saw, Doris nodded regally and stepped away. "Good. I figured I could count on you."

She reached behind the counter and grabbed a brown bag and a cup carrier, thrusting them both toward Jake, "Wrapped this up while you were fetching Tiff. The drink with the straw is diet. That's what Tiffany always orders. Now get outta here and get that girl home."

Before Jake could utter a word of thanks, Doris rushed away, weaving between tables and around customers with an ease born of years waiting tables for a living. She was a force to be reckoned with, a strong woman who had worked hard for a small piece of the American dream.

Pulling a soggy wallet out of his pocket, Jake took out several bills and placed them next to the cash register. Doris would complain later, but for now she was too busy to notice the money he'd left. Replacing his wallet, Jake moved toward the door. He needed to get Tiffany Anderson and the mutt home. Then, since he was up and about already, he'd see what he could find out about the morning's events.

There'd been a slew of misdemeanor offenses this summer—a bit of graffiti, stolen merchandise in a few main street shops, loud music in the early hours of the morning. Jake had a good idea the same teens causing the summer's mischief were responsible for throwing the dog into the lake. He'd ask a few questions, file a report at the office, and then, finally, he could begin his vacation.

The meteorologists were saying it would be a record-breaking day. Tiffany believed it. Already heat shimmered up from the pavement in waves of silver and black. The damp clothes she wore warmed quickly, the moisture evaporating as she waited for Jake to emerge from the diner. Part of her wanted to leap from the cab of the truck and run for home before he returned. The other part didn't have the energy to move.

She felt like a fool twice over. First for trying to save the dog and almost drowning herself in the process and second for expecting Brian to be waiting for her, only to find he had gone. Tiffany had been hard-pressed to face the sheriff in the shadowy hallway of the diner. Facing him in the bright sun would be even worse. She could feel her face reddening at the thought.

"Here. Doris sent this for you." Jake's voice startled Tiffany from her thoughts and she turned, reaching for a carryout cup being thrust through the open window.

"Thanks." Tiffany took a sip from the straw, smiling as the cool freshness of the soda hit her tongue.

"She sent these, too." A brown bag followed the cup through the window. "Go ahead and eat one. I'm going to give the dog some water before we take off."

Tiffany tried to ignore the aroma of vanilla and cinnamon that wafted through the truck as he moved away. Instead she concentrated on Jake, watching as he walked back to the diner and returned a few moments later with a plastic bowl. He smiled at someone who called his name, waved at someone else. All in all, the picture of an affable law officer.

But Tiffany sensed something else, a tension that lay behind the smile, a hardness around his mouth and jaw that warned of things better left hidden. Jake Reed played the part well, but Tiffany doubted his heart was that of a small-town sheriff. She'd heard rumors. Heard that he was a city cop. A man used to violent crime and hardened criminals. She'd heard he was ethical, tough-minded and fair.

What she hadn't heard was what had brought him to Lakeview.

"All right. We're set. Where to?" Jake slid into the driver's seat, casting a glance in Tiffany's direction.

"I live on Monroe Street."

Jake turned the key in the ignition and the Chevy sprang to life. "Mind if I have one of those?" He reached over and grabbed the bag out of Tiffany's hand, opening it up and lifting out a pastry.

Tiffany's mouth watered and she turned her eyes away from temptation.

"Want one?" Jake held the bag out toward her.

"No, thanks. I'm not hungry." The loud rumble of Tiffany's stomach belied her words. Jake lifted an eyebrow, his bland expression replaced for a moment by a flicker of something else. Amusement, no doubt.

"You sure?"

Tiffany nodded and turned away before she changed her mind.

"All right then. Let's get you home. You cool enough?"

"Pardon?" Tiffany had been so intent on ignoring the heavenly aroma still wafting through the truck that she missed Jake's question.

"Do you want me to turn on the air? It's warming up out here."

"No, thanks. I'm used to the heat."

"Yeah. Me, too."

"Did you grow up around here?" Tiffany seized on Jake's words. Anything to get her mind off the bag of pastries sitting on the seat between her and the sheriff.

"No. I grew up in D.C. It's hot and humid there in the

summer. Here on the lake the air doesn't seem quite so heavy."

"I visited D.C. my senior year of high school. It's a busy place. And you're right, the air did seem heavier."

"Probably pollution. Which way?"

Tiffany blinked trying to follow the turn in conversation.

"Left or right onto Monroe?"

"Oh, sorry. Left. I live near the old Sheffield place."

"I know where that is. Shouldn't take more than a minute to get there."

It took three. Tiffany watched the dashboard clock and counted every one, wishing away the gnawing hunger in her stomach. A pulse beat of pain worked its way behind her eye and she rubbed her forehead wishing the ache away. While she was at it she wished away the morning's disappointments, too.

Tiffany had prayed for years that God would bring her a life partner who shared her faith, understood her human frailties, saw her for who she was and loved her anyway. She'd believed, really believed, that God would bring that person into her life and that when He did, there would be no doubt in her mind that he was the one God intended her to spend her life with.

That wasn't how it happened. Oh, she figured Brian was The One. He met all the requirements she'd listed in her diary—he loved God, was faithful to His call, was smart, cared about others. The only question was, how much did he care about her?

The fact that Brian had not waited or worried when she failed to return to the diner said a lot to Tiffany. And none of it good. Though too practical to list it, Tiffany had always hoped that Mr. Right would be the knight-in-shining-armor type. The kind of man quick to step in when she needed a hand. Instead, it seemed Brian had more important things to do with his time.

Forcing her mind to stop such rambling thoughts, Tiffany tried to focus on the positive. Brian might not always run to her aid but that was because he knew Tiffany to be a competent self-reliant woman. He trusted her to take care of herself and that was a good thing. Right?

Later, when he called, Tiffany would explain to Brian how disappointed she had been to find him gone. He'd apologize and explain how important the men's prayer breakfast was to him. Tiffany had accepted months ago that Brian had high standards and rigid priorities. Though he loved her, Tiffany would never be first on Brian's to-do list. And that was okay.

Fantasies were fine as long as a person was willing to put them aside and face reality. And, in Tiffany's case, reality was a silent ride home with a stranger and a big black dog.

Stealing a glance at the grim-faced man beside her, Tiffany sighed. Reality was lonely.

Chapter Three

The forecast of record-breaking temperatures proved accurate and by late afternoon the thermometer had crept up to ninety-eight degrees. Tiffany wiped a bead of sweat from her forehead and eyed the picket fence that bordered her property. All but five of the pickets gleamed white. The others, scraped down to bare wood, wouldn't take long to finish. With any luck she'd have them painted before heat exhaustion set in.

"Good thing I saved this side of the yard for last. Just think how hot I'd be standing under the sun, huh, dog?"

The big dog lifted his head and thumped his tail in response before returning to the state of semisleep he'd been in since Jake had lifted him from the pickup truck several hours before.

Tiffany dipped her brush into the almost empty paint can she held and smoothed a coat of paint onto a bare wooden plank. The glide of paint against board, the warmth of the sun and the muted sounds of boats on water helped put the morning's fiasco into perspective. Good from bad, strength from weakness, blessings from curses—God made all things work for the good.

Tiffany may have been pulled from a lake, abandoned at the diner, and driven home by a taciturn sheriff, but at least she wasn't spending Saturday afternoon alone. Smiling, she glanced over at her companion. He'd made himself at home in the shade of a maple tree and hadn't budged, except to steal half of Tiffany's turkey sandwich.

Everything about the dog said "mutt." He had the shape and size of a Saint Bernard, the black coat of a Lab—if one didn't count the white paw and ear—and a shepherd's muzzle. Not a handsome dog by any standard, but the winsome expression in his brown eyes made him an adorable one. *And,* he was company.

"Almost done here, big guy. Then maybe we'll go inside and take your picture so I can make some posters. Someone must be missing you by now. We can take a run to the store and the diner later, put up the posters and by this time tomorrow, you'll be home."

The dog opened his eyes at the sound of Tiffany's voice and woofed quietly in response before rising to his feet and lumbering over. Tiffany patted his head and dipped brush into paint once again.

"Miss Anderson?"

With a startled cry, Tiffany whirled toward the voice. Splatters and speckles of paint flew from her full brush, landing on the grass, the dog and the front of Jake Reed's shirt.

The dog ran for cover. Jake stood his ground.

"Sheriff Reed! You startled me."

"Yes, I can see that."

Jake's gaze met Tiffany's and then dropped to his shirt where several fat, white globs of paint were beginning to run.

"I'm so sorry! Let me—"

"Not a problem. This is an old shirt anyway."

Before Tiffany could make use of the paint rag she'd been carrying in her pocket, Jake stepped to the side and gestured at a man and teenage boy. "Sorry to intrude on your afternoon but Mr. Bishop asked me to bring him by."

Hat in hand, thinning hair brushed to one side of his head, the man stepped forward. He looked familiar, blunt featured and hardened from years in the elements. Though they'd never been introduced, Tiffany recognized him as a farmer who lived several miles outside of town.

He spoke with a voice that sounded as dry and tough as the dirt he toiled over. "Miz Anderson, I'm James Bishop. My son Tom has something he needs to say to you." Stepping to the side he gestured to the teenager and watched as his son moved forward, eyes downcast. The boy mumbled something that Tiffany couldn't make out.

"You got cotton in your mouth, boy? Speak up. I ain't got all day and neither does Miz Anderson. Now say your piece. And say it so we can understand."

The young man's face colored, and Tiffany's heart went out to him. She tried to send a reassuring smile his way, but his downcast eyes prevented him from seeing it. When he spoke, his chin wobbled a bit, and Tiffany worried he'd break into tears and embarrass himself.

"I was one of the guys in the boat this morning. Sheriff Reed said you almost drowned saving the dog. I'm sorry."

"Oh, well—"

"Tell her the rest." James Bishop grunted out the words, then turned abruptly. Tiffany watched as Jake placed a hand on Bishop's, a shoulder that seemed weighted with fatigue and heartache. Despite his harsh words, Bishop was hurting for his son.

"He's my dog."

"Excuse me?" She'd been so intent on the drama of James and Jake, Tiffany had forgotten Tom.

"The dog. He's mine. I let those guys throw him in the water. I didn't know he couldn't swim. It was just a gag. You know, for fun."

The words rushed out. Eyes that had been staring at the ground now looked into Tiffany's. She'd expected hardness, rebellion, arrogance, but didn't find them. Instead, Tiffany saw sadness and uncertainty; a longing for understanding and acceptance, without any expectation of receiving it.

She refused to add to the young man's pain. "What's the dog's name?"

Surprise flickered in Tom's eyes before he dropped his gaze to the ground. "His name is Bandit. He's just a puppy. Not even a year old."

"Bandit is a good name."

"Yeah, it is. It may not be his for long, though."

Tiffany heard the hitch in the boy's voice, the hint of tears that refused to be shed. She wanted to offer comfort, but doubted Tom would accept it. "Why not?"

"We're taking Bandit back to the animal shelter when we leave here. Dad says a person cruel to animals doesn't deserve to own one."

Tiffany winced at the harshness of the words. Though she agreed with James Bishop's assessment, she couldn't help wondering if the punishment was too severe. Tom didn't seem to be a cruel boy. More a foolish one. And that, hopefully, would be remedied with time. "You don't need to bring Bandit to the shelter. I can keep him here."

The boy shrugged, an I-don't-care gesture, and kicked at a clump of grass at his feet.

"Well now, Miz Anderson, that's kind of you. Come on, Tom, let's go," James said as he walked to the edge of the lawn. Tom, too, turned to leave. Tiffany couldn't let him go. Reaching out, she placed a hand on his arm. He paused, shifting his gaze back toward Tiffany.

"Tom, how old are you?"

The boy looked surprised by the question but answered anyway. "I'll be seventeen in a couple of weeks."

"Perfect. I'm doing some renovations on my house. Lots of painting, sanding, refinishing and stuff. It's slow work. I could use an extra set of hands. Would you be interested?"

"You mean a job?" Hope flared briefly in Tom's eyes before he doused it.

Tiffany held her grin in check. "Yes."

"I don't know much about that kind of stuff."

"Neither do I, so we'll make a good team. Besides I can't pay a lot. Minimum wage, maybe a little more."

"I'm not sure...."

"You don't have to decide right now. Talk to your father. See what he says, then give me a call. I work at home so just look up my business number in the directory. I'm listed under Anderson's Computer Technology."

"Tom! Come on. I got things to do."

The young man glanced at his father, but hesitated as if afraid that if he left, Tiffany would forget she had offered him the job.

Tiffany smiled reassuringly. "You better go. Talk to your father, okay?"

A slight nod was the only response she got before Tom shuffled to his father's side. The two moved away, walking with the same stoop-shouldered carriage and unhurried stride.

"The apple didn't fall far from the tree, did it?" Jake's voice drifted across the yard and Tiffany smiled toward him.

"No. Though I doubt they'd acknowledge their likeness at this time in their lives."

"Probably not. Too bad Tom's not living up to his father's example. James is a good man. A hard worker."

"Tom will be, too. He just needs some focus."

Jake raised an eyebrow and shrugged. "A lot of folks wouldn't see it that way."

"I'm not a lot of folks."

"No. You definitely aren't."

Tiffany wasn't sure if the statement was a compliment or criticism. She decided to ignore it. "Well, regardless of what other people think, I'm convinced Tom is a decent young man. As for being a hard worker, I'll find out soon enough. I offered him a job."

Something flared in Jake's eyes and was quickly extinguished. "Hopefully it will keep him out of trouble."

"That's the plan."

Jake nodded, his face set in an expression Tiffany couldn't read. "Good luck. Now, I'd better get the Bishops back home."

"All right. Goodbye."

"Bye." As quickly as he had come, Jake was gone and the yard fell into silence once again.

Letting out a breath she hadn't realized she'd been holding, Tiffany turned back to the fence. Jake seemed concerned about Tom working for her, though she had to give him credit for not saying as much. She couldn't help wondering if Brian would be as willing to hold his tongue.

Shrugging away the worry, she went back to work on the

fence, smiling as Bandit slipped out of his hiding place and plopped down on her feet. There were white splotches of paint on his midnight coat, and Tiffany wondered how difficult it would be to wrestle him into a bath. Probably very difficult.

Oh, well, he looked rather cute with white polka dots.

She reached into the pocket of her shorts and pulled out an animal cracker, then dropped it down onto the ground in front of Bandit. He inhaled it and looked up for more, the expression in his eyes so soulful, Tiffany had to laugh. "Getting a bit spoiled already, are you? That's okay, I'm enjoying your company so you deserve a treat."

She dropped a few more animal crackers down. "Hey, maybe Brian will stop by later. Add a little life to our paint party. What do you think?"

The dog woofed a response before dropping his head across Tiffany's feet. She stepped to the side and lifted her paintbrush, smoothing another coat over the picket. "You know, I think I'm going to like having a dog. Talking to you is so much better than talking to myself."

A soft snore was Bandit's only response.

"So Tiffany offered Tom Bishop a job and you don't approve." Ben Avery's words were muffled, his face half-hidden by the lid of the tackle box he was searching through.

Jake waited until his friend was upright in the bow of the boat before responding. "It's not that I don't approve. I'm just surprised. Tom's been in and out of trouble for years. I'd think Ms. Anderson would want to keep her distance. That would be the wise thing to do."

Ben chuckled as he pulled his fishing line out of the water and rebaited the hook. "Tiffany isn't known for making choices based on the world's wisdom. She makes them based on her heart."

"Yeah. I'm getting that impression. Maybe someone should talk to her."

"About what? About caring? About giving a chance to a kid who isn't going to get one from anyone else?"

"Chances are for people who earn them. Not for smart-alecky kids with chips on their shoulders."

"Everyone deserves a chance, Jake. You know that."

Jake sighed and ran a hand through his hair. "Yeah. I know. Unfortunately, experience has taught me that most kids like Tom don't respond well to second, third and fourth chances."

"But some do."

"The minority."

"That minority would be lost if not for people like Tiffany."

"And Will. Look what happened to him." Jake knew he sounded bitter. He *was* bitter. William Banks had been his partner for ten years. His best friend for just as long.

"He was a police officer. His situation was completely different than Tiffany's."

"Not so different." Jake cast his own fishing line, forcing his emotions down before he continued speaking. "Will was murdered by a kid he'd been mentoring for a year."

"I didn't realize that."

Jake shrugged and gazed out over the still water of the lake. "He devoted his life to kids like Tom. Volunteered at the community center when he had time. Tried to set an example of what a man should be. The thanks he got was a bullet to the chest."

"And you think the same thing is going to happen to Tiffany?"

"Who knows? I just hope she understands what she's getting herself into. All the affection, help and chances in the world can't change a kid who doesn't want to be changed."

"She's doing what she thinks is right. Living by the second greatest commandment—love your neighbor as yourself."

"I guess I can't argue with that."

"You can't argue with *anything* I say. I'm your pastor."

Jake shook his head and scooped up a handful of water, sending it flying toward his fishing companion. "Yeah, well, I'm *your* sheriff. So watch yourself."

Ben just smirked and leaned back against the vinyl seat. "Don't make me sic the ladies' auxiliary on you."

"You wouldn't dare."

"No? Don't bet on it, friend."

And Jake wouldn't. He knew Ben Avery to be as tenacious as a bull terrier, and twice as wily. Seven months ago Ben had spotted Jake amidst his congregation. From that moment on, his mission had been to befriend the town's new sheriff. Evening visits, phone calls—Ben had slowly but surely infiltrated his way into Jake's solitary existence.

Something Jake would be eternally grateful for.

He sighed and rebaited the hook on his line. The gentle swell and sway of water rocked the boat's hull, the lulling movements helping to ease away some of Jake's tension. Gold-and-pink clouds dotted the horizon, the sunset slowly fading their color to silver and gray. Around the boat tiny insects buzzed in clouds of annoying energy, and every few minutes a fish or frog splashed its presence.

Jake enjoyed it all—the hum of life, the slow drifting pace of the day. Though his week's vacation had started off rocky, it had improved as the day wore on.

Had Tiffany's day gotten better? Was she still painting

the white picket fence? Or was she off somewhere, offering friendship to another lonely soul? Maybe rescuing more hapless creatures? If so, who would rescue her? Certainly not her boyfriend. *Dr. Brian.* The man sounded like a loser.

"So, who's Dr. Brian?" The question was out before Jake knew he was going to ask it.

The speculative gleam in Ben's eyes made him wish he hadn't. "Interesting."

"Dr. Brian?"

"No. You. We've been out here for an hour and in that time we've discussed Tiffany Anderson saving a dog, Tiffany Anderson offering a job to a kid, and now you want to discuss Tiffany Anderson's boyfriend."

"I don't want to discuss him. Doris mentioned the name this morning and I wondered who he was."

"Dr. Brian McMath is a family practitioner. Good doctor."

"That's it?"

"And he's Tiffany Anderson's boyfriend."

"Not a very good one." Jake wanted to pull the words back but it was too late. Ben's gaze settled on him once again.

"According to who?"

"According to me. He was supposed to meet Tiffany at Becky's. By the time we got there he'd gone to prayer meeting and left her to find her own way home."

"I guess Brian has his priorities."

"Shouldn't Tiffany be one?"

"That's for Tiffany to decide."

Jake bit back a comment that wasn't fit to be spoken and forced himself to let the topic go. "True. And it's not my business, anyway."

"No?"

Jake was saved from responding by the beep of his pager.

He checked the number and shook his head. "Looks like there's more trouble. I'm going to have to call it a day."

"I thought this was your vacation." Ben reeled in his line, and started the boat's motor.

"It is, but I told dispatch to keep me informed. There's been too much petty crime this summer, and I've got a feeling things are going to escalate."

"So what's happened this time?"

"Some windows smashed at the middle school. I want to go interview the neighbors. See if anyone saw anything."

"Any hope of that?" Ben spoke as he maneuvered the boat into the dock.

"Not much. Whoever's causing the trouble is being careful not to get caught. That won't last for long, though. Sooner or later he'll get cocky and make a mistake. Then I'll slap him with every punishment available under the law."

"Sounds harsh, Jake. This is Small Town, U.S.A. Not the big city. People here will expect you to be lenient. Especially if it's kids involved."

"Not kids. A gang. I've dealt with enough to know the signs."

"Still—"

Jake held up his hand, forestalling the words. "Like I said before, giving kids second chances just gives them the opportunity to commit more crimes. I won't do that. No matter what people here expect."

"Understood, friend. So let's get moving. We don't want to miss all the excitement."

"We?"

"Sure, what better way to get people to tell the truth than to have a pastor along? Besides, we rode here together, remember?"

Jake hesitated. In D.C., he wouldn't have considered

taking a civilian along on a police matter, but here in Lakeview things were different. That was one of the reasons he'd taken the job as sheriff. *One* of them. "All right. Let's go."

Chapter Four

Tiffany rubbed at the tension in her neck and tried to ignore the loud conversation going on in the living room. Brian and his parents were discussing Lakeview's summer crime wave. Though she was as interested in the welfare of the community as anybody, Tiffany figured five play-by-play descriptions of the broken windows at the middle school, the sheriff's quick response to the crime scene, the dusting for fingerprints and the interviewing of witnesses was overkill. She shook her head at her own irritation and vowed to try to be a more pleasant hostess.

Or maybe she'd just keep hiding in the kitchen until the McMaths left.

The fact was, Tiffany needed a break from her Sunday afternoon routine. If the aches in her arms and legs hadn't told her that, the image reflected in the gleaming surface of the toaster she was cleaning would have. Deep lavender smudges shadowed the area under her eyes. Dull, reddish curls escaped the confines of the chignon she'd scraped her hair into that morning. And her skin, pale on the best of days, looked like the underside of a toad—greenish-white with a shiny glow. She had spent most of the night tossing and turning and it showed.

Turning away from her reflection, Tiffany used a damp cloth to wipe the counter. Then, with quick, efficient movements, she unplugged the coffeepot, placed the last mug in the cupboard, and turned to inspect the kitchen. Every surface gleamed, including the floor which Tiffany had scrubbed within an inch of its old-linoleum life. A haphazard housekeeper, Tiffany accepted her cleaning frenzy for what it had been—avoidance.

Cleaning the kitchen had been a good excuse for escaping the living room and Brian's parents. Though the Mc-Maths had always been kind to Tiffany and she enjoyed their company, somehow their presence at lunch every Sunday afternoon had become a habit. A habit only Tiffany seemed to be getting tired of.

Worse, she couldn't remember the last time she and Brian had spent any time alone together and that, along with a whole list of niggling worries, had kept Tiffany from sleeping. Now she was tired, frustrated and annoyed. She needed some time to herself. Time to think about Brian and their relationship. Or lack of one. What she did *not* need was a three-hour discussion on Sheriff Reed and his dedication to his job.

The loud conversation quieted, and floorboards creaked. A moment later, the McMaths called their goodbyes and Tiffany responded in kind, glancing out from the kitchen and waving, before retreating to her spot beside the kitchen sink.

Brian stepped into the room, a smile on his face and questions in his eyes. "Lunch was great. As usual. Thanks."

"I'm glad you enjoyed it. Did you put the leftovers out on the porch for Bandit?"

"Yes, but I still don't think it's a good idea for a dog to eat table food. You'll spoil him."

"I don't think a dog can be spoiled."

Brian shrugged in response, the silence in the room stretching out as he surveyed the clean floor and gleaming counters. "You were being a Martha today."

"What do you mean?"

"A Martha...you know, busy cleaning instead of talking to your guests."

Tiffany felt her cheeks redden at the veiled criticism and bit back an angry retort. Taking a deep breath, she tried to steer their conversation back to safer ground. "Your parents didn't seem to mind. And your mom came in to chat with me for a while. She's really enjoying that quilting class she's taking."

"Yeah, and I guess she's pretty good at it. She said one of the quilts is going to be on display at a regional folk art show. Maybe I can get some time off and we can go see it."

Tiffany didn't respond. Instead she reached for a teacup, filled it with water, and placed it in the microwave.

"Is that decaf?"

Startled by the question, Tiffany glanced down at the tea bag she'd taken from the cupboard. "I don't know. I think so."

"If you're not sure, you probably shouldn't drink it. Caffeine can increase appetite. You're doing so well on your diet. I'd hate for you to blow it."

"I think I'll be fine." Jerking open the microwave, Tiffany dropped the tea bag into the heated water, turning her back to Brian in the process. The last thing she wanted was a lecture about healthy eating.

"Tiff, something's bothering you. Why don't you tell me what it is?"

Tiffany shrugged and turned to face the man she had pinned so many dreams on. "I'm upset about what happened yesterday, Brian. I'm afraid of what it says about us."

Brian's brow furrowed, a puzzled expression replacing his concern. "I apologized for leaving you at the diner."

Tiffany met Brian's gaze, then looked down into her teacup, watching the water turn brown as she tried to think of words that would express her concern as well as her disappointment. "Yes, you did but that doesn't change what happened."

"Okay, I thought we'd settled this last night but I guess we didn't." Brian ran a hand through his hair. Tiffany was sure he glanced at his watch while he was at it. "Why don't we go in the living room and figure out what's going on here?"

"Fine." Tiffany led the way down the hall and into the large room she used for company. Two overstuffed chairs and a love seat created a cozy U around the room's fireplace. Tiffany dropped onto the love seat and took a sip of her tea as Brian made himself comfortable in one of the chairs.

When he spoke he did so with an air of weariness that made Tiffany wish she had waited another day or two before starting this conversation. "Look, I'm not happy about what happened, either. I sat at the diner, alone, waiting for you. I was almost late for my meeting because you took a detour by the lake."

"I almost drowned, Brian."

"I know that. And now you're taking responsibility for a huge mutt and a juvenile delinquent. I don't understand how you could even consider letting Tom work for you."

Anger rose swift and vicious, sending blood pumping hard through Tiffany's veins. She swallowed it down. "Tom is not a delinquent. He's a boy who's getting into trouble because he has too much time on his hands. His mother abandoned him years ago, his father drives trucks because their farm is going under. The kid is alone more than he's with someone. No wonder he's having problems."

"Everyone in town knows the boy's situation. It *is* sad but it's *not* an excuse for poor behavior."

"You're right, it isn't an excuse. It *is* a reason. Tom needs something constructive to do while his father is away. The job I'm offering him will fill up his time and keep him out of trouble."

"Or bring the trouble to you. Come on, Tiffany, even you can't be so naive as to think giving the kid a job is going to change him."

Anger surged again and this time Tiffany let it have its way. Rising from the couch, she stretched to her full five foot eight inches, and glared at Brian who rose to face her. "I'm a thirty-three-year-old woman who built a computer support business from the ground up. My company is pulling in a profit every year. If I were as stupid and naive as you seem to think I am, I would never have accomplished what I have."

"I never said you were stupid."

"Stupid. Naive. It's all the same when I'm being treated like a child."

Brian's eyes widened in surprise, his lithe form tense and stiff with anger. Silence stretched between them, thick as morning fog. Then, as suddenly as the argument had begun, it was over. Tension eased out of Brian's shoulders and he ran a hand through his short blond hair. "I'm sorry for calling you naive. I'm just concerned."

Tiffany sighed and shook her head. "But not concerned enough to wait for me at the diner."

"Tiff..."

"Nothing you say can change the fact that your prayer meeting was more important to you than I was. And if that's the case, I don't think we have a future." Tiffany paused for a moment, gathering the courage to say what she had to. "And, if we don't have a future, then I don't see any reason to keep seeing each other."

"I think yesterday was more stressful for you than either of us realized. You're exhausted. Why don't I go home and let you rest? We can talk about this again when you're more yourself."

"That's probably a good idea."

"Want me to pick you up for evening service?"

"No. I'll drive my own car."

"You sure?"

"Yes. Thanks, anyway."

"All right," Brian hesitated, unsure in a way Tiffany had never seen before. "We'll talk about this again. Soon."

"Right." Tiffany walked Brian to the front door and allowed herself to be pulled into a quick hug.

"We're signed up to help with the youth volleyball game before church tonight." Brian opened the door and stepped out into midday heat. "See you then?"

"Yes, but, Brian, I meant what I said."

Brian, already halfway down the porch steps, turned and nodded. "I know."

Tiffany watched as he drove away. Then stared out at her overgrown front lawn, wondering why it had taken her a year to realize that her relationship with Brian was no more than a convenience for either of them.

Only when Bandit nudged her hand and whined for attention did Tiffany shake herself from her thoughts. "Feeling lonely, big guy? Me, too. Don't worry, we can keep each other company while I work."

Tiffany stepped back into the house, shutting the door on the heat, and on her worries. She and Brian would have their talk eventually, but as far as Tiffany was concerned they had already said everything of importance. Now she had to get to work renovating the Victorian monstrosity she'd purchased with thoughts of children and grandchildren in mind.

Maybe Tiffany would never have the husband and family she desired, but at least she'd have a nice home to live in. Swallowing back the lump that formed in her throat, she grabbed the electric sander and set to work.

Five hours later Tiffany sat in her beat-up Cadillac, listening to the engine sputter and cough. A hand-me-down from her parents, the car had served her well for the past three years, and would continue to do so as long as she remembered to fill the gas tank. A task Tiffany would have performed had she not been running late.

Caught up in the job of stripping paint from the carved oak mantel on the living room fireplace, Tiffany had lost track of time. When the phone rang she had been too engrossed in her work to answer it. Luckily the answering machine had been turned up high, and even with the radio blasting into the room, she'd been able to hear Brian's message—another offer to give her a ride to church. If not for the timely phone call, she might still be removing layers of paint from wood. As it was, she was probably still wearing flakes of the stuff.

Worse, she was coasting on empty, the car giving one last sputtering sigh as the engine gave out. Using the car's forward momentum, Tiffany maneuvered to the side of the road and pulled to a stop. She resisted the urge to bang her head against the steering wheel, and focused instead on coming up with a plan of action. Most days she loved rural life, but at times like this, she would have been happy to be driving through the middle of the city, a gas station on every corner.

Unfortunately, Tiffany wasn't in the city and the church was six miles ahead; the nearest gas station ten miles back. That, and the fact that she'd left her cell phone sitting on the kitchen counter, made her options few.

Though summer added length to daylight hours, it also added heat. Tiffany was thankful for the first and worried about the latter. She'd make it to the church before dark if she didn't collapse from the heat first.

Of course, there was a chance someone would drive by and offer her a ride. Not much of a chance though, since Tiffany had bypassed Main Street and headed for church on one of the least traveled roads in Lakeview. Sighing in exasperation she opened the car door and stepped out into the heat. Waves of scorching air floated up from the pavement, curling around Tiffany's ankles and up her legs, hugging her body like a thick winter coat.

She was covered with sweat before she took a step.

Even sweating and stumbling along in high heels, Tiffany didn't mind the first mile. The second mile took more effort, and by the third, she would have given her life's savings for a drink of water. "Why did I take this road? Of all the roads I could have chosen, why the one that no one travels?"

But of course Tiffany knew the answer. She'd been running late and had hoped to make up for lost time by avoiding traffic and stop signs. She'd succeeded. There hadn't been a car or a sign for miles.

By the time Tiffany reached the crossroad two miles from

church, a pulsing pain beat behind her eyes and her stomach knotted with a familiar and dreaded nausea. With each step the pain grew sharper and soon Tiffany's desire for water was replaced by an overwhelming need to find a quiet, dark place to hide. Sinking down onto the thick roadside grass, she rested her head on her knees and prayed the migraine would pass quickly.

Jake's day had been pleasant until he spotted the abandoned car. He'd gone to church, had lunch at the diner and spent the afternoon exploring the back roads of Franklin County. Though he'd been living in rural Virginia for a year, the novelty of traffic-free travel hadn't worn off and Jake often took the back roads for the sheer pleasure of not seeing another car.

Today was no different. Prompted by Ben Avery, Jake had decided to attend evening service and had picked a long, winding route to the church. He'd been enjoying the play of greens and browns in the fields that lined Old Farm Road when he saw the car.

Long, lean and old, the Cadillac was as easy to spot as a whale on the beach. Though abandoned cars weren't unusual, finding one on a little-used road was. Jake pulled over to examine the vehicle. The doors and windows were locked, the trunk closed tight, and the car empty.

Relieved, Jake got back in his truck and called in the tag number. His relief was short-lived.

Tiffany Anderson owned the car.

Jake figured a woman willing to risk her life for a dog, one ready to give a chance to a troubled teenager, might just offer a ride to a hitchhiker. He could picture Tiffany, red-gold hair swirling in a tangle of curls, smiling as she motioned for some not-so-helpless man to get into her car.

Jake examined the vehicle again, looking closely for signs of a struggle. He saw nothing that would lead him to believe Tiffany was in danger, but that did little to allay his concern. Images rose in his mind, images of other women. Women as compassionate and softhearted as Tiffany, who had been repaid evil for their kindness.

God willing, Tiffany hadn't met the same fate.

Jake forced his mind away from the memories that haunted him. This was rural Virginia, after all, not Washington, D.C. No doubt Tiffany had already made it safely to her destination. Still, there was no harm in making sure.

Jake hopped in his truck and headed in the direction the Cadillac was pointing. He'd driven close to five miles when he spotted a lone figure waving forlornly from the side of the road. Even the dim light of dusk couldn't hide the vibrant color of Tiffany's hair. Coasting to a stop, Jake stepped out into the heat and humidity. "I saw your car a few miles back. Need a lift?"

"Yes. I ran out of gas."

There was no life, no vitality in Tiffany's voice, and as Jake stepped closer, he realized the soft glow of health he'd admired the day before had been replaced by a sickly grayish hue. Lines of pain played around her eyes and she stumbled a bit as she moved toward him.

"Are you all right?"

"I'm fine. Just a headache."

Just a headache, but Tiffany's hands were shaking as she brushed a stray curl from her cheek. Jake's concern grew, and he grasped her arm, leading her to the truck. "You need to get out of the heat. Get in the truck. I'll drive you home."

"I need to go to church. I promised I'd help serve refreshments at the volleyball game."

"You need to go home. You're sick."

"I can't go home. I promised. And Brian's waiting for me."

"Like he waited for you at the diner?" The minute the words were out, Jake wished he could take them back. Tiffany's already drooping shoulders sagged even more and she shrugged away from his grasp, moving toward the truck with shuffling steps.

"I'm sorry. I shouldn't have said that."

Tiffany didn't respond. Her silence said more than words.

Watching her, Jake noted the deep shadows beneath her eyes and the perspiration beading her forehead. Tension pulled at the corners of her mouth and beat harshly in the hollow of her throat where her pulse pounded furiously. There was nothing Jake could say to ease Tiffany's pain; instead he gently moved her fumbling hands from the door handle and opened the truck door. "Hop in. I'll take you to the church. Grace Baptist?" Jake waited for Tiffany's nod of affirmation. "I was on my way there anyway."

Tiffany didn't look at Jake. She couldn't. For the second time in as many days, he'd come to her rescue and Tiffany's humiliation at needing his help almost outweighed the pain in her head. Even worse had been his words, they'd been like a knife twisting in an open wound. Not because they'd been spoken harshly, but because they were true.

Forcing herself to concentrate on the task at hand, Tiffany tried to slide into the raised cab of the truck. What had been easy while wearing shorts proved more difficult in the long, flowing sundress she wore. As she tried to lift herself into the cab the fabric of her dress caught under pain-clumsy feet and Tiffany pitched forward, banging her head against the door of the truck. Even before the pain could register, strong hands gripped Tiffany's shoulders and held her steady while she regained her balance. Then, as she reached to untangle her feet from the dress, Tiffany was lifted into the truck.

Flustered, she tucked the skirt of her dress neatly around her legs and tried not to look at Jake. The last time a man attempted to lift her, Tiffany had been eleven years old exploring an abandoned cabin with her first crush. Poor Danny Wilson. He'd been outweighed by twenty pounds, but had still made a valiant effort to boost her into a second-story window. They'd both ended up in a heap on the ground.

Thank goodness Jake had proven stronger than Danny. Tiffany had suffered enough embarrassment in the past two days without adding an attempt to crush the sheriff to the list. Blinking rapidly, she forced back the tears that threatened to spill onto her cheeks, then leaned forward to press a hand against the pulsing pain behind her eyes.

"Ready?" Jake slid into the driver's seat and Tiffany could feel his concerned gaze.

"Yes."

"You're sure you don't want to go home?"

She wasn't, but she nodded anyway.

"All right. Why don't you rest your eyes until we get there?"

Tiffany did as Jake suggested, keeping her hand pressed against her eyes and leaning her head against the window. When the truck engine roared to life, she winced at the sound, bracing herself against the jolting movement of the truck on rough pavement.

Light, sound, motion—they were too bright, too loud, too fast.

A gentle hand reached out and brushed aside curls that had fallen against Tiffany's cheek. "You're not up to a volleyball game. Why don't I drive to the church, run in and tell Brian you need him? He can give you a ride home."

The idea of spending time with Brian didn't appeal to Tiffany, but she didn't have the energy to think of an alternative. "That's fine."

The truck slowed as Jake turned into the church parking lot. Even through the closed window, Tiffany could hear people milling about, chatting and laughing as they made their way from parked cars. Usually she would have been eager to join the fellowship and fun but now the sounds were like lightning bolts, shooting pain into her skull.

As if sensing her discomfort, Jake spoke quietly, "I'll park in the overflow lot. It's quieter there."

The voices faded to a soft murmur, the bustle of the main parking lot replaced by the stillness of the side lot. A warm breeze carried the sweet scent of honeysuckle into the truck as Jake opened the door. "Sit tight. I'll be back in a minute."

When the door closed with a gentle click, Tiffany unbuckled her seat belt and drew her knees up to her chest. Imagining Brian's face when Jake asked for his help did little to comfort her. Tiffany had been dating Brian for almost a year, had imagined herself married with a house full of children, had even convinced herself that God wanted Brian to be her husband. Only now did she realize that in all her daydreams she had never pictured Brian in the Victorian monstrosity she owned. Nor could she see him with a crowd of boisterous children.

Her friends, her family, even the kids in the Sunday school class she taught thought Brian and Tiffany were a perfect match. Apparently the world was filled with fools. And Tiffany was the biggest one of all.

One tear escaped. Another joined it, sliding down Tiffany's cheeks and dropping onto her dress. Would Brian come for her? Did he care enough to leave the game and take her home?

Tiffany wanted to believe he would. Wanted to believe that what she'd dreamed of and longed for was more than just a fantasy. Somehow though, she doubted it.

Chapter Five

Jake hurried toward the church, the sound of laughter and good-spirited competition drawing him around the corner of the building. A volleyball net had been set up and teams of teens were going after the ball with more enthusiasm than skill. It didn't take long to locate the doctor. Everyone seemed to know him, and all were eager to point Jake in the right direction. Seated on a plastic lawn chair, his short, blond hair combed neatly to the side, Brian McMath held himself erect, surveying the net and players with a look of amused tolerance that set Jake's teeth on edge. Even from a distance, Jake could see the fastidious crease in the doctor's khaki pants and the neat, even column of numbers he'd written on the white board he held in his hand.

The doctor's finicky appearance and staid expression were a direct foil to Tiffany's vibrancy and spirit. How the two had ended up together was a mystery. Not that it was any of Jake's business. He just hoped the good doctor didn't try to fit Tiffany into a mold of his making. Jake had grown up watching a vibrant woman beaten down. He'd hate to see it happen to Tiffany.

"Dr. McMath?"

"Yes?" McMath looked up, his eyes wary.

"I'm Sheriff Jake Reed," Jake offered his hand as Brian put down the white board and stood to face him.

"Sheriff Reed," Brian's handshake was firm, his expression curious, "Nice to meet you."

"Thanks. Sorry to interrupt your scorekeeping but I gave Tiffany Anderson a lift from Old Farm Road. Her car ran out of gas on the way here."

"Really? I wonder what she was doing traveling on that back road. I've told her a hundred times not to take that route."

"I guess she didn't listen."

"Yeah, well, that's pretty typical of Tiffany."

Jake didn't like Brian's tone, or his words. "She's an adult. I guess she's capable of deciding what road to drive on."

"If she were capable of that, she wouldn't have needed a ride here. Where is she, anyway?"

Jake had to bite down on the urge to shove his fist into the doctor's face. He'd met plenty of men like Brian McMath, and he hadn't liked any of them. "She's got a headache so she's waiting in my truck."

"A migraine?"

"She didn't say, but it looks like she's in a lot of pain."

"She must have been out in the heat too long." The crowd cheered and Brian's gaze drifted from Jake to the game. Picking up the white board, he made a quick notation before turning his attention back to Jake. "I guess this means she won't be helping with the refreshments."

Jake's jaw clenched, his hands curled into fists. "I guess not."

"Well, thanks for letting me know. I'll ask one of the girls to fill in." Brian turned back to the game. "Tell Tiffany I hope she feels better."

As quickly as that, Jake was dismissed. He stood still for a moment, wondering if Brian McMath was as poor a physician as he was a friend. He doubted it. Men like McMath were good at prioritizing. And, if Jake didn't miss his guess, patients were much more important to Brian than a girlfriend would ever be.

Swallowing back his frustration, Jake turned away from the doctor and the game. Tiffany would be upset. Letting her see his anger would only make things worse. He made a quick circuit of the church, burning off some steam as he went, and approached his truck quietly, hoping that Tiffany had dozed off.

She hadn't. Hunched over her knees, curly hair tumbling around her shoulders, Tiffany looked defeated. She glanced up when the door opened, her eyes pools of dark ink in the fading light. In the space of a heartbeat, Jake knew she hadn't expected Brian to be with him. There was no question in her eyes, only acceptance. "Did you find Brian?"

"Yeah. He was keeping score."

Tiffany nodded, wincing at the movement. "I guess he's pretty busy."

Jake remained silent, afraid if he opened his mouth, he'd ask why Tiffany even cared what the jerk did.

"I'm sure I can find someone else to give me a ride."

"Forget it. You're already in my truck. I'll give you a ride." Jake heard the harshness in his voice and regretted it.

"I don't want to be a bother."

Taking a deep breath, Jake reined in his emotions and

gentled his voice. "You're not. I'm happy to help out. Now, fasten your seat belt and relax. I'll have you home in a few minutes."

Tiffany wished the earth would open and swallow her. First the lake, now this. If her head hadn't been pounding so badly she might have said something witty and flip. At least she could have tried to salvage a little dignity. As it was, she couldn't think past the pain, and she figured anything she said would end up sounding whiny and pitiful.

She held her silence and fastened her seat belt.

She expected Jake to start the truck. Instead, he leaned toward her, his shoulder pressing against hers as he opened the glove compartment. Tiffany tried to ignore the warmth of Jake's arm and the clean, fragrant scent of shampoo that lingered in the air after he moved away.

"I've got some Tylenol here and a bottle of water in the back of the truck. You want to take a couple of these?"

Tylenol wouldn't touch the pain, but Tiffany grabbed the bottle anyway. She struggled with the lid for a moment, feeling her face burn with heat as the bottle slipped and slid beneath her fingers.

"Here," Jake reached over and removed the bottle from Tiffany's fumbling grasp, "Let me do it. How many do you want?"

"Three, for now."

Jake raised his eyebrows but poured three pills into Tiffany's waiting hand. Then he slid open the truck's back window, reaching through it to a large cooler that sat pressed up against the cab. When he handed the bottle of water to Tiffany, the coolness felt heavenly in her hand and she couldn't resist pressing the ice-damp plastic against her throbbing eyes.

It took a moment for her to remember she wasn't alone.

When she did, she looked over at Jake. He watched her, his expression unreadable. "You've had a rough couple of days."

The compassion in his voice made her want to lean in close and lay her head against his shoulder. Instead she popped the pills in her mouth and gulped a mouthful of icy water. "Yes, it has been difficult."

"Hopefully a good night's sleep will make things look better."

Tiffany doubted it, but she tried to smile anyway.

Jake watched her for a moment, opened his mouth as if to speak, then changed his mind. Shoving the keys into the ignition he started the truck. "All right. Let's get you home."

Tiffany's house reflected the cheerful warmth of its owner. Or so Jake thought as he paced through her hall. A golden-oak floor gleamed in soft overhead light, and quilts of various sizes and colors hung against cream-colored walls. At one end of the hall a curved stairway led to the upper level of the house, its intricately carved banister the same golden tone as the floor. At the other end a two-paneled door opened into Tiffany's kitchen and dining room. On either side of the hall, doors opened into even more rooms.

Jake had been in enough Victorian-era homes to recognize the Queen Anne architecture. The small room to one side of the front door had once served as a receiving room. Now it contained a sewing table and a hodgepodge of colorful fabric. A door on the opposite side of the foyer opened into the parlor where Jake had led Tiffany when they'd returned. Despite the oversize dimensions of the room, it felt cozy and comfortable. Tiffany had chosen bright colors to accent the dark pine floor. A throw rug of red and gold lay centered in front of the fireplace. Twin recliners and a matching love seat surrounded it, their heavy cream brocade rich and luxuriant against the dark floor. Jake knew if he glanced in the room he would see Tiffany curled up on the love seat, resting against gold-and-red pillows.

Though she had said he should go home, Jake hadn't felt comfortable leaving her alone. He'd heard that migraines were debilitating, but watching Tiffany had given new meaning to the word. She'd been withdrawn during the ride home, leaning against the seat with her hands pressed against her eyes. Only twice had she spoken, once to ask Jake to turn off the radio and once to tell him to stop the truck. That time his response had almost come too late. He'd barely coasted to a stop when Tiffany yanked open her door and jumped out. By the time he reached her she was kneeling at the side of the road vomiting into a clump of bushes. Jake knew Tiffany would be embarrassed later, but she hadn't argued when he wet a pile of napkins with bottled water and used them to cool her hot face.

Nor had she protested when they arrived at her house and he insisted on following her inside. Jake doubted she had even noticed his presence until he asked if he could get her something. Tiffany had motioned toward the end of the hall and said something about medicine before she retreated to the parlor and collapsed on the love seat.

Finding the medicine hadn't been difficult. Tiffany's kitchen, though busy with color and texture, was well organized. Jake had bypassed white glass-fronted cupboards with their display of china, and had searched a small pantry near the refrigerator.

He'd found what he was looking for on the top shelf next to a first aid kit and an unopened box of Tylenol. The clear plastic bag contained a prescription bottle, a pamphlet of information about the drug Imitrex, and what looked to be an epinephrine kit. Jake had taken the bag and a glass of water to Tiffany, and watched as she took a pill from the bottle and swallowed it. He had wished he could do more. Maybe that's why he'd stayed.

Or maybe he just didn't like the idea that Tiffany's boyfriend had left her to fend for herself again. In Jake's estimation, a woman as easygoing and good-hearted as Tiffany deserved better than a lonely night, a debilitating headache and huge dog whining at her feet.

Speaking of which, where had the dog disappeared to?

Jake eyed the open door of the sewing room, and shook his head. He'd locked the mutt inside the room twice since his arrival. Though it seemed inconceivable that a dog who couldn't swim could open a door, the evidence was clear—what the dog lacked in swimming ability, he made up for in escape techniques.

At least he was loyal, escaping his prison and slinking into the parlor to lay his head on Tiffany's legs, rather than running around the house getting into mischief. Jake figured that's where Bandit was now, and he walked toward the room, ready to grab the mutt and put him outside.

Tiffany heard the soft creak of a floorboard outside the living room door and struggled to sit up. That involved pushing Bandit's head off her legs, and swinging those same legs off the love seat so that her feet touched the floor. Both tasks took all the energy Tiffany had, but at least the pain in her head had subsided to a dull throb.

"Feeling any better?" Jake walked through the door, his voice low.

"Yes, thanks."

"Mind if I turn on a light?"

"No, go ahead."

The overhead light burst to life and Tiffany blinked rapidly, adjusting her eyes to the brightness. When she looked up, Jake stood before her, his left foot gently nudging Bandit out of the way. "Move, Houdini."

"Houdini?" Tiffany glanced toward the dog, who watched her with dark, innocent eyes.

"Yeah, I locked that mutt in your sewing room twice. And he got out. Twice."

"You've got to be kidding me. He can't swim, but he can open doors?" Tiffany smiled and turned back to Jake, catching her breath in surprise when she realized he had lowered himself onto one knee and was staring intently into her face.

For a moment both were silent. Tiffany could feel each beat of her heart, could smell the same clean, soapy scent she had noticed in the truck. She could almost imagine she saw a look of admiration in Jake's eyes, could almost believe he cared about her and that his concern went beyond his duty as an officer of the law.

Then she remembered vomiting on the side of the road. "You didn't have to stay."

"No?" Jake's dark brows lifted, questioning the abruptness of her tone.

"I'm sorry. That didn't come out the way it was meant. I should have said, thank you for staying."

"I didn't mind. Your house is interesting. Queen Anne, right?"

Tiffany knew Jake's question was meant to put her at ease and she smiled gratefully. "Yes. You know something about Victorian architecture?"

"A bit. Visiting historic buildings was a hobby of mine when I lived in D.C. I've picked it up again here in Lakeview."

"Well, there are plenty of old homes to see in the area. And many of them have interesting histories. Like this one,"

Tiffany paused and gestured around the parlor. "It was built in 1876 for a doctor. He spent five thousand dollars to have it built to his specifications."

"Did he live here? Or just see patients?"

"Oh, he lived here. He and his wife raised seven children...." Tiffany's voice trailed off as she realized she was babbling on about something Jake probably had no interest in. "Sorry, I got off on a tangent."

"I was enjoying your tangent."

"Really?" Tiffany cringed at the hopeful sound in her voice. Being around Jake had turned her into a blathering idiot.

"Yeah, really." There was a smile in Jake's voice and Tiffany could feel her own smile forming.

"Well, most people don't. My family and friends all thought I was crazy to buy this old place. And I can't say I blame them. It was in pretty bad shape."

"Not anymore. You're doing a great job restoring it."

"Thanks, but with my computer business, I just don't have the time to do it all." Tiffany's gaze drifted to the half-stripped fireplace mantel. "I've got the kitchen, the hall and this room almost finished. And my bedroom upstairs. But there's still a lot to do."

"Is that why you hired Tom?"

"Yes, that was part of it."

"And the other part was that you figured he needed a place to spend his time?"

Jake's words made Tiffany's shoulders tense. After Brian's comments on her naïveté, she felt defensive about hiring Tom. But when she looked into Jake's midnight eyes, there was no condemnation, just interest and curiosity. Relaxing, Tiffany shrugged her shoulders and tried to think of the best way to answer Jake's question. "Wanting to give Tom a place to spend time helped me make my decision. But it was his remorse that made me certain he'd be a good employee."

"Remorse?"

"Yes. I could tell from speaking with him that Tom regretted what he had done. If he had any idea the dog would be hurt, I think he would have fought the other kids to keep it from happening."

"I'm not so sure of that. This isn't the first time Tom's made a poor decision, and there aren't many people in this town who are willing to forget that."

"There should be. We've been called to forgive as Christ forgave us. Besides, someone needs to help the Bishops. Things have been hard for them lately."

"It doesn't have to be you, Tiffany. Not when it might mean putting yourself in danger."

"I don't think there's any danger in giving Tom a job."

"I hope not. But be careful. I've seen things like this go bad before."

Jake spoke quietly, a shadow darkening his eyes, and Tiffany wondered what had put it there. She resisted the urge to ask him, telling herself she didn't know him well enough to pry. "I'll be careful. But like I said, I think Tom will be fine. He just needs someone to believe in him."

Jake was silent for a moment, his expression unreadable as he watched Tiffany. "You and your house make a good match."

Puzzled by the turn in conversation, Tiffany brushed at a stray curl and commanded her sluggish brain to respond. "How's that?"

"Both of you are interesting and unbelievably unique."

Tiffany wasn't sure Jake's words were a compliment, but at least he hadn't said they were both old and decrepit. "Thanks. I guess."

Jake laughed quietly, the sound deep and mellow. "See, that's what I mean. Most women wouldn't thank a man for comparing them to a house."

Tiffany smiled and leaned back against an oversize pillow. The long day, the comfort of Jake's presence and the effects of the medication she'd taken made Tiffany feel drowsy and warm. Her eyes drifted closed and she forced them back open.

"You're exhausted. I'd better go." Jake stood and Tiffany followed suit, forcing her aching body up from the couch.

"I'll walk you to the door."

"Are you sure you should be walking anywhere?"

"I'm much better. The headache is down to a dull throb."

Jake nodded and led the way out the door and into the hall. "Nice collection of quilts."

"Thank you. My mother and grandmother are both quilters. Some of these are theirs. Others I bought at flea markets and garage sales."

"Do you quilt?"

"When I can find time. Which isn't often enough. That quilt," Tiffany gestured to a quilt done in shades of blue and yellow, "is one of mine."

Jake stepped closer, examining the pattern. "This is my favorite. It looks like a bursting star."

"You're close. It's a broken star pattern."

"Looks pretty complicated."

"It wasn't one of the easiest quilts I've made but I enjoyed doing it."

"Your love of the craft shows. The work is detailed and exact. I'm impressed."

"Thank you."

Jake continued studying the quilt for a moment before he turned away. "I'd better leave you to your rest."

"Thanks again."

"No problem. Good night."

"Good night."

Jake pulled open the front door and stepped out into the night. "Tiffany?"

Something about the way Jake said her name sent Tiffany's heart skittering in her chest. "Yes?"

"I'm pretty sure Tom is going to take the job you offered him. If he does and you have any trouble, give the station a ring. I'm on vacation for a week, but they know how to reach me. Tell the dispatcher I want to be called."

"All right."

Without another word, Jake walked down the porch steps, climbed into his truck and drove away.

Tiffany watched as the taillights of the Chevy disappeared. Then she closed the front door and leaned against its heavy wood. With Jake gone the house seemed silent and lonely, the cream-colored hallway with its bright quilts too empty. There should be children upstairs giggling and whispering secrets to one another, and toys scattered across the floors. Instead there was silence and a neatness that came from living alone.

Dating Brian had put Tiffany's dream of marriage and a family within her reach, and she knew that if she backed down, if she allowed their relationship to continue, she could have all the things she wanted so desperately.

But at what cost?

She deserved to be more than an inconvenience, more than a trophy displayed or put aside with equal measure. She deserved to be waited for and worried about, not left alone.

As if sensing Tiffany's mood, Bandit lumbered out of the living room and nudged her hand. "All right, boy. Enough of these morbid thoughts. Ready for some dinner?"

The big dog thumped his tail, woofing a response, and Tiffany made her way into the kitchen and to the mudroom behind it. She wanted to let go of her worries, wanted to let God take care of filling her life, but what if doing that meant living alone? What if it meant never getting married, never having children, never being anything but Tiffany Anderson, computer whiz?

The thought depressed Tiffany, but she knew she'd rather that than accept a relationship based more on convenience than affection. With a sigh, she poured food into Bandit's bowl and went into the kitchen to make a cup of tea. The clock read nine-thirty. Church would be over. Brian finished his work with the youth. No doubt he'd call and apologize.

And when he did, Tiffany would be ready to tell him exactly what she thought, how she felt, and why he didn't need to call her again.

Teacup in hand, she sat at the kitchen table and waited for the phone to ring.

Chapter Six

A week later, Tiffany sat in her turret room office eyeing the silent telephone. Seven days had passed and she was still waiting for Brian to call. Not because she wanted to speak to him, but because she wanted closure, a firm and final end to the relationship. Sure, *she* could call *him*, but to what end? Obviously Brian had moved on.

Tiffany rolled her shoulders against the tension there and glanced out the window. She could see Tom, bent over the porch railing, carefully sanding away old paint. The sound of sandpaper brushing softly against wood drifted through the window, easing the silence of the empty house. It was nice to have someone around. Even if that someone was a rather closemouthed teenager.

Closemouthed, but efficient and hardworking.

Tiffany smiled, and stood to gather some papers. She didn't regret hiring Tom. He worked with an eye to detail and tackled the job with determination. Though the porch was large, stretching across the front of the house and around both sides, Tom had set a grueling pace for himself and didn't seem at all daunted by hot weather or layer after layer of stubborn paint. No doubt he'd accomplished more in the five days he'd been working for her than she could have in two months.

The sweet scent of lilac and honeysuckle drifted on the air, inviting Tiffany to enjoy the day. Unfortunately, she didn't have time. With a sigh of regret, she grabbed a stack of work orders from her in box, placed them in her briefcase, rebraided her hair, and stepped to the window.

"Tom?"

"Yes?" Tom stepped closer, paint flecks clinging to his clothes and a layer of dust coating his dark hair.

"I've got a couple of network jobs today. I doubt I'll be done before five."

"Okay."

"Do you need a ride home?" Not quite seventeen, Tom had a driver's license but no car. His father dropped him off in the morning but often didn't finish his truck deliveries until late in the evening.

"I think so."

"Okay. If I'm running late I'll give you a call. There's soda in the fridge. You know where the snacks are, so help yourself."

"Thanks." Tom scuffed a worn sneaker against the porch floor and looked uncomfortable. Like his father, he was a man of few words and even fewer smiles.

Tiffany figured it was going to take a lot longer than a week for him to warm up to her. In the meantime, she'd just keep feeding him. Though Tom rarely ate the snacks Tiffany purchased, he had yet to turn down the lunches or dinners she prepared. Tiffany didn't know how long it had been since he'd eaten a home-cooked meal, but the first time she'd offered him dinner he had eaten with such gusto that Tiffany began making him meals every day. If nothing else, he would leave her employ with some meat on his bones. Smiling at the thought, Tiffany grabbed her purse and briefcase and headed out the door.

It was past five when she returned home. The heat of the day had yet to give way to evening coolness, and hours of driving in an unairconditioned car had zapped Tiffany's energy and turned her crisp linen suit into a sticky mass of wrinkles. Luckily she'd stopped on the way home and bought a chicken sandwich and some fries for Tom. She didn't have the energy to cook. Or to eat, for that matter.

A featherlight breeze blew against her skin as she stepped from the car, evaporating some of the moisture from her face and loosening tendrils of hair that clung in sticky clumps to her neck. The sound of Tiffany's return brought Bandit lumbering around the corner of the house. A few flecks of paint clung to his black fur and he panted heavily as he approached.

Concerned, Tiffany leaned down and patted the dog's head. "What's wrong, boy? You haven't been outside all day, have you?"

She glanced around, hoping to find Tom. It wasn't like him to leave Bandit outside in the heat. "Tom?"

The trim and railing on the front and sides of the porch had been stripped of paint and Tiffany could see Tom had finished his work for the day. As usual he had carefully cleaned up his supplies, the ladder leaning against a side wall the only sign he'd been working.

Uneasy, Tiffany made her way to the backyard, calling Tom again as she walked. The backyard was as silent and empty as the front. She glanced around, noting a bucket and a coil of hose sitting near the mudroom door. These disturbed her more than the emptiness of the yard. Tom never left supplies out.

The mudroom door was unlocked, the room cool. As Tiffany moved toward the kitchen, Bandit squeezed by and stood on his hind legs, lapping up drops of moisture from the utility sink.

"You have been out a while, haven't you?" As she spoke, Tiffany filled Bandit's water bowl and scooped out some kibble for him to eat.

"Tom?"

"We're in here."

Brian's voice was an unexpected, and not entirely welcome, surprise. No doubt he wanted to discuss their relationship in person. Though why he hadn't called ahead, Tiffany didn't know. Sighing, she attempted to brush wrinkles from her skirt as she made her way to the living room.

Brian stood beside the love seat, hovering over Tom like a malevolent scarecrow guarding a field of corn. Tom, sullen and angry, sat hunched over his knees, staring at the floor. He looked up when Tiffany entered the room but glanced away when she smiled in his direction.

"Hi, guys. I hope you haven't been talking about me." Tiffany's attempt at humor fell flat. Tom continued to stare at the floor, while Brian eyed him with contempt.

"I didn't notice your car out front, Brian. I'm surprised to see you."

Brian's attention shifted to Tiffany, his dark eyes flashing with frustration. "I jogged from the diner. I wanted to drop off the Sunday school materials for next week. I didn't get a chance to pick them up last Sunday since I worked my shift at the clinic."

"That was nice, but—"

"When I arrived, Tom was fooling around in your office."

Tiffany's gaze darted to Tom. His body was taut, his cheeks tinged red with anger or embarrassment. The rebellious turn of his lips made it difficult to tell which. "Is that true, Tom?"

Brian spoke before Tom could answer. "Of course it's true. I caught him going through some of your papers. He'd knocked a few things off your desk while he was at it."

"I did not." Tom's voice was sullen and defensive.

"Oh, come on. I came in the house, heard noise in the office and found you rifling through Tiffany's desk."

"I wasn't going through her papers—"

"You were!"

Tom jumped up, fists clenched. "You don't know what you're talking about."

"Are you calling me stupid, boy?"

"Don't call me boy." Tom stepped toward Brian, violence in every line of his body.

"Wait!" Tiffany's near shout cut through the argument, silencing the feuding pair. "Why don't we all sit down and try to cool off?"

Brian shrugged and sat in a chair as Tom lowered himself back onto the love seat. Tiffany sat down next to him. "Now, Tom, why don't you explain what happened?"

"I made a mistake and was cleaning up after it. I'm sorry."

Brian shot Tiffany an I-told-you-so look, before picking up a magazine and leafing through it. Though he pretended indifference, Tiffany could see the tense set of his shoulders and the white-knuckled grip he had on the magazine.

Trying to ignore him, she turned her attention back to Tom. "What do you mean, you made a mistake?"

The angry flush on Tom's cheeks deepened and his

glance slid from Tiffany to the floor. "I was working on the side of the porch near your office, finishing up the trim. I thought if I sprayed everything down today it would dry and I could start painting tomorrow. I put all the stripping stuff away and got out the hose. I was just washing everything down, but Bandit came out and he was barking at the hose, chasing the water and stuff." Tom paused and Tiffany nodded encouragement.

"Well, I got kind of carried away and I didn't realize the window was open and I sprayed right into your office. So I ran inside to see what got wet. I was drying some of your papers when *he* walked in."

There was little doubt who *he* was. Brian looked up from the magazine he'd been leafing through and caught the tail end of Tom's withering look.

"Hey, don't look at me like that. You didn't tell me you were cleaning up a mess in there."

"You didn't ask."

"Well, you could have volunteered the information. Not that I'm sure I believe you. The fact is—"

"Tom," Tiffany cut in, staving off another argument, "I brought a chicken sandwich and some fries for you. They're on the kitchen counter. Why don't you go eat? I'll drive you home as soon as Dr. McMath and I finish talking."

Relief smoothed the anger from Tom's face and he leaped to his feet, half running from the room. Tiffany listened as his footsteps pounded softly on the oak floor of the hallway. Only when the thud of the door announced his entrance into the kitchen did Tiffany turn to Brian.

With his brown eyes hard and angry, and his mouth set in a grim line, he seemed almost a stranger. His words, when he spoke, were clipped and to the point. "I told you this was a mistake."

"I don't agree."

"Tiffany, let's be realistic for a minute, okay? Tom is trouble."

"Tom is diligent, polite and eager to do a good job at the work I've given him. I don't see how that equates to trouble."

"Of course you don't. You're blinded by your soft heart."

Tiffany bristled at the comment but Brian didn't seem to notice. Placing the magazine on the floor, he stood and began pacing the room. "Look, why don't you just admit you're in over your head? Tom was going through your desk, probably looking for something to steal. I saw him with my own eyes."

"I believe his explanation."

Brian shook his head at Tiffany's words, pausing his pacing long enough to glare at Bandit who had entered the room and curled up on the throw rug. "You believe anything a person tells you."

"I'm getting a little tired of these veiled criticisms, Brian."

"I'm not criticizing. I'm warning."

"I'm a grown woman. I don't think your warnings are necessary."

"Well, I don't think the little snit you've been in lately is necessary, either."

"What are you talking about?"

"This whole idea that you're breaking up with me. Over what? Being left at the diner?"

Tiffany felt anger burning bright and hot. "Was I ever the woman of your dreams, Brian?"

"Dreams? What are you talking about?"

"Was I the woman of your dreams? When you envisioned a lifetime spent with someone—building a home, having children—was I the one you saw?"

"Of course. We were talking marriage. Who else would

I have pictured spending my life with?" Brian stopped pacing and looked at Tiffany, exasperation at her questions obvious in the frown that marred his brow.

"Maybe because your dream woman is what you think I can be. Not what I am."

"I don't see the difference."

"There is one. Which me did you want to spend your life with? The me who is slender, in shape, has perfect hair, perfect nails? The one who never argues and always says the right thing. Or the real me? The one who isn't perfect and never will be."

Brian ran a hand through his hair and shook his head. "This is ridiculous. I don't have time for it right now."

"I didn't think you would."

"Look, we'll talk about it later." Brian turned and moved toward the door, impatience written in every movement.

Tiffany swallowed against the lump in her throat and said what she knew she had to. "There isn't going to be a later."

The words stopped him and he turned to face Tiffany again, his eyes reflecting disbelief. "So, you were serious. You really want to end what we have."

Tiffany nodded, struggling to hold back tears.

"Why?"

"Because we don't *have* anything. I'm not sure we ever did. We're not right for each other, Brian. I'll never be first in your life and I can't accept being less."

"God is first in my life. You know that."

"God is first in my life, too, but after Him, it's been you. For a year I've tried to line my life up so you could be part of it. What have you done to fit me into yours?"

"That isn't fair. I have responsibilities. I can't just drop what I'm doing every time you get yourself into some foolish situation."

The words hurt. Tiffany had wanted denials. Instead she'd been spoon-fed another criticism. "Like I said, we're not right for each other."

For a moment she thought Brian would argue; almost hoped he would. A nod of his head revealed his intentions before his words cut the silence. "Maybe you're right."

Without another word, Brian strode from the room and out of her life. Tiffany watched him leave, all her dreams scrambling into line behind him.

Jake pressed on the gas pedal and tried not to speed as he closed in on Lakeview. With less than three miles to go, he could hardly wait to unpack his bags and settle back in. Though his four-day sojourn to Maryland had been pleasant, visiting William's widow had been difficult, their reunion bittersweet. A grim reminder that Will was no longer around to laugh, joke and argue with.

Jake had spent too much time remembering his friend. Remembering the way Will had lent support during Jake's divorce seven years ago. And how, two years later, he'd stood beside Jake at Sheila's funeral. Those had been hard times for Jake. Times when guilt had eaten at his gut and made him question his worth as a person.

Will had been a steadfast rock during the most turbulent times of Jake's life. His enthusiasm for life and his love for God a shining example of Christianity. It was that more than anything that had led Jake to the Lord. Two years ago he'd become Will's brother in Christ.

And now Will was gone. Cut down by a gang member's bullet.

Jake's hands tightened around the steering wheel, his jaw clenched against anger, pain and frustration. God help him, he couldn't forgive or forget what the fifteen-year-old kid had done. Despite the fact that he knew he needed to.

Will's wife had seen the hard edge of Jake's pain. She'd prayed with him and for him, her own pain a sweeter, softer version of what Jake felt. There was no anger in her. Only acceptance.

Would that Jake could feel the same.

Maybe with time and distance, he would. Jake gunned the engine, as if he could move more quickly from the pain and anger he felt, and rounded a curve in the road.

"Whoa!" Braking hard, Jake swerved around a figure kneeling in the middle of the road. The truck squealed in protest before coming to a stop, inches from the huddled form.

Hands shaking with adrenaline, Jake opened the door and jumped from the truck. "What's going on? Are you okay?"

"Yeah. Sorry."

The voice sounded familiar and Jake moved closer, trying to identify the person. "You would have been more than sorry if I'd been driving a little faster."

Reaching down, Jake grasped the young man by the arm and hauled him to his feet. Face puffy, one eye already swollen—it was clear Tom Bishop had been on the wrong end of someone's fist. "Looks like you had a disagreement with someone."

The kid shrugged, shaking off Jake's arm and wincing at the movement.

"I don't suppose you want to tell me what happened?"

The silent, surly expression on Tom's face was the only answer he seemed willing to give. Jake understood the sentiment. He'd been in enough scrapes and trouble as a teenager to know what it felt like to be on the wrong side of the law. And to know he wasn't going to get any answers.

He placed a hand on Tom's shoulder and steered him toward the truck. "All right. Get in. I'll give you a ride home."

Tom resisted for a moment, holding his ground against the pressure of Jake's arm. Then, as if suddenly out of energy, his shoulders sagged and he slid into the Chevy.

"Buckle up."

Tom did as he was told, snapping the belt together as Jake closed the door and walked to the other side of the truck.

"Thought you were working for Ms. Anderson." Jake snapped his own seat belt closed and started the engine.

"Yeah. So?"

"So, if you're supposed to be working and staying out of trouble, what are you doing a mile outside of town looking like the stuffing's been beat out of you?"

"I *am* working and staying out of trouble."

"That doesn't answer my question."

Tom's only response was to stare out the window.

Jake knew the drill. Pushing for an answer would make the kid clam up more. He held his silence and waited. They passed the diner, the corner deli, and the bank, and still Tom didn't speak. They had just reached the outer limits of the town when he caved. "Some friends offered me a ride home."

Jake glanced sideways at Tom who sat looking out the window, acting for all the world as if he hadn't spoken. Jake waited.

"See, I was working and then Dr. McMath showed up and he was giving me a hard time. So I was waiting on the porch, you know, until Tiffany got done talking to him. Some of the guys drove by and saw me and offered me a ride home."

"So how did you get to the opposite side of town kissing dirt?"

Tom's shrug didn't surprise Jake, the fact that he kept talking did. "We had a sort of disagreement."

"Want to tell me about it?"

"No."

There was silence again, as Jake's mind raced with possibilities, none of them pleasant. Though most of the townspeople thought of Tom's friends as mischievous pranksters, Jake knew better. He'd seen enough gangs to know what one looked like; had spent five unforgettable years as a member of D.C.'s antigang task force. He'd seen the violence, the hate, the fear. And more, he'd seen the camaraderie, the loyalty and the inability to escape the steel embrace of the gang hierarchy. If Tom's "family" had turned on him, there had to be a reason. A good one.

An image of Tiffany Anderson floated through Jake's mind. He didn't believe in coincidence. Didn't believe that Tom's beating, just days after he started working for Tiffany, could mean anything else but trouble for the woman who'd hired him. "This is about Tiffany, isn't it?"

Tom tensed, his reaction saying more than words that Jake was right.

"Keeping quiet won't do you any good. I'll drop you off at home and drive the streets of Lakeview until I find some of your buddies—"

"You don't know who they are and you won't find out. You wouldn't even have found out I was on the boat the other day, if it weren't for Miz Camden spying out her window and recognizing me."

The words were defiant, but lacked conviction, and suddenly Jake wondered if Tom wanted to tell him. If somehow the young man hoped to be forced into spilling the whole story. If so, Jake could accommodate him. He swung onto the dirt road that led to the Bishop farm, and braked hard in front of the house, turning toward the teen and crowding into his space. "Ms. Camden is the best thing that ever happened to you, kid. Because of her, you were caught before you got in real trouble. Because of her you got offered a job by a lady who had no reason to trust you, but did anyway. And now what? You're going to repay Tiffany by letting your friends ruin her property, hurt her business or worse?"

"They wouldn't—"

"They would!" Jake growled the words, and sliced his hand through the air with enough force to rock the truck.

Tom cringed away, his good eye opened wide. Fear hollowing out his features.

Jake had seen the look before. Knew it well from his years playing hardball with tougher, meaner kids than Tom Bishop could ever hope to be. He leaned even closer, his words barely a whisper. "Get this through your head, Tom. The gang you're hanging with doesn't care about you. They don't care about anything but the next deal. The next score. The next crime. They'll drag you down and walk on top of you. Then leave you to rot in jail while they waltz away."

"No—"

"Yes. I've seen it happen over and over again." Jake paused and watched as Tom took a deep shuddering breath. "You've got a chance, Tom. A person who believes in you enough to give you a fair shot. That's more than most kids like you get. You can screw it up. Or you can make it work for you. But let's get one thing clear. If anything happens to Tiffany. If she's hurt, if her house is vandalized, I may not know where to find your friends, but I *will* know where to find you."

Jake settled back into his seat, waiting for Tom to make a decision. Outside the truck, evening shadows danced over the Bishops' house. Gray with age and neglect, it stood like a faded Southern beauty—strong and graceful, despite its years. If times had been better, Jake knew the house would have been painted white, the yard cared for and green with life instead of being left to mud and weeds and ruin.

Perhaps then Tom would have had more of a chance.

Jake bit back a weary sigh and turned to the teen. "Go. You've got nothing to say, and I've wasted enough time."

Tom scrambled to open the door, shoving it hard and leaping out onto dry earth. Then he paused, the bruises on his face vivid and ugly. "You're just like everyone else. You hear the stories about me and you think I'm running wild, looking for trouble. Well, I'm not. Maybe I've made mistakes. Maybe I've done some things wrong. But I know what's right. Tiffany trusts me. She leaves her door unlocked for me when she goes on jobs." Tom's voice hitched, his breathing coming harsh and fast. "I'm not gonna screw that up. Not for a bunch of rich boys who've got more money than sense."

"What'd they ask you to do?"

"Steal credit card numbers off client invoices."

"Give me some names."

Tom snorted. "You think I'm nuts? They already beat the crap out of me."

"Once they're locked up they won't have another chance at you."

"Right. Their rich daddies will have them bailed out in an hour. Then where will I be? Forget it. I told you everything I can. Now leave me alone!" He whirled and ran to the house, flinging the door open and slamming it shut with a force that echoed through the air.

Jake thought about going after him, thought about pushing for more answers, but the hitch in Tom's voice when he spoke about Tiffany had hinted at a softness in the young man that Jake hadn't suspected.

Or hadn't been looking for.

Tiffany had seen it. She'd seen promise in a kid everyone else had given up on. Jake could only hope she wouldn't live to regret her compassion.

With a last glance at the old farmhouse, Jake put the truck in gear and headed back to town. There wasn't a lot he could do with the information Tom had given him, but Jake planned to write up a report anyway. And while he was at it he'd ask a few of the deputies to keep an eye on Monroe Street. The odds were, the gang wouldn't have the guts to try to steal the credit card numbers on their own. But Jake never played the odds.

He'd file the report today. Tomorrow he'd pay Tiffany a visit.

Chapter Seven

Tiffany hung up the phone and breathed a sigh of relief. Tom was at home. She'd been worried for nothing. Which meant she could now do what she'd wanted to do since Brian walked out the door an hour ago.

With a pint of Ben & Jerry's in one hand and a newspaper in the other she headed out to the old gazebo. A century old, paint faded to gray, it stood in a back corner of Tiffany's yard, hidden by bushes and shaded by towering pine trees. A rickety swing hung from the gazebo's eaves, its rusty chains and chipped paint more eyesore than antique. Still, it offered a view of the lake and the setting sun, and provided Tiffany with the perfect place to think and to dream.

Or to cry.

Sniffing hard, Tiffany wiped at a stray tear and settled onto the swing. The ice cream looked soft and half-melted from the heat, but Tiffany didn't have the heart to take a bite. She eyed the container with regret. "I finally decide to go off my diet and I'm too depressed to eat. Figures."

Bandit whined in sympathy, rising from slumbering repose to press his wet nose against Tiffany's hand. She sniffed back more tears and patted the dog on his nose. "I hate crying. It never does any good and I always look terrible afterward."

The dog pressed harder against Tiffany's hand and she responded, rubbing the warm fur of his neck and smiling slightly at the soft thump of his tail. At least one of the men in her life was easy to please.

Scratch that.

The *only* man in her life was easy to please.

Blinking hard, Tiffany forced back another round of tears. Crying *was* a waste of time and she was done with it. Besides, she'd made the right decision. Brian might be a wonderful person but that didn't make him Mr. Right.

Or did it? Tiffany couldn't stifle the doubts. She knew Brian wasn't right for her, but there weren't many single Christian men in Lakeview. And even less who were over thirty. Perhaps Tiffany's expectations were too high. Why else were all her friends married and having children while she wallowed in singlehood? Unless, and Tiffany was afraid to even think it, God didn't intend for her to get married.

Though she knew there were men and women called to remain single, Tiffany had never felt like one of them. Her desire had always been for a husband, children, a family and a home. Now that Brian was out of her life, those dreams seemed far from achievable.

Shaking her head, Tiffany pushed aside regrets, shoved down even more tears, and reached for the newspaper she'd carried outside earlier. The sun dipped low on the horizon, kissing the lake with pink and gold, and sending long shadows across the pages Tiffany held. She squinted at the words but the effort of reading in dim light made her head hurt.

She was tired anyway. Too tired to concentrate on faded newsprint and too tired to move from the creaking swing. Pushing aside the wilted container of ice cream, Tiffany stretched out across the length of the swing and closed her eyes.

She tried not to think about Brian, about marriage or about the children she might never have. Instead her mind conjured up other worries. What would her friends and family think when she broke the news? Maybe she'd just call her mother and sisters and let them tell everyone else. That would at least spare her from the words of surprise and pity. Not to mention the head shaking and tongue clucking. Some people would be appalled. Others sympathetic.

And Tiffany didn't want any of it.

Turning onto her side, she opened her eyes and stared into the fading light. She had choir practice in another hour, but for now there was no harm in staying put. Trailing her fingers over the wooden seat, Tiffany felt for Bandit's warm fur and patted him gently.

"Just another minute, boy. Then I'll get you some dinner."

Bandit rumbled a soft reply and they both fell silent.

Jake's phone rang at quarter past two in the morning, the time shining from the lighted alarm clock as he reached for the bedside phone. "Yeah?"

"Sheriff Reed?"

"Speaking."

"This is Mary, at the station."

"What's up?"

"Tiffany Anderson's mother called about an hour ago.

Apparently Tiffany didn't show up for choir practice tonight and she's not answering the phone. Josh drove over to the house to check things out and he asked me to give you a call."

Adrenaline pumped through Jake's blood and he came fully awake, his heart thumping harshly in his ears.

"You did want to be called if anything happened at the Anderson house, right?"

"Yeah. Right. Have you heard from Josh?"

"No, but I expect he'll be calling soon."

"Okay. Give me a ring when you hear from him."

"Will do."

Jake was out of bed, pulling on faded jeans when the phone rang again. "Sheriff? Mary, again. Josh called. He said Ms. Anderson's car is parked outside the house. No lights on inside the residence and no answer when he knocked."

"Any sign of trouble?"

"No. The doors are locked. The windows secure. Could be she's gone out with friends."

"Could be."

"You want me to tell Josh to enter the house?"

"No, tell him to go on with his patrol. We can't enter the house without cause and we've got no reason to believe Ms. Anderson is in trouble."

"Will do."

"Call me if things change." Jake hung up the phone and tried to relax, but his mind refused to let go of the information Mary had relayed.

Jake didn't know Tiffany well, but what he did know told him she wouldn't needlessly worry people who cared about her. If that was true, she'd never have missed choir without calling her mother.

That, more than anything, had Jake pulling on clothes

and strapping on his gun belt. He tried not to imagine the kind of trouble she might have gotten into. Tried not to picture her hurt, or worse, as he drove his truck to her house. Though intelligent and spirited, Tiffany seemed to attract trouble like food attracted flies. That being the case, Jake figured anything might have happened to her.

The gas-guzzling Cadillac stood sentry in front of the aging Victorian, its faded paint gleaming softly in the moonlight. A quick search of the house's perimeter revealed no signs of forced entry and no hint of trouble.

Jake listened intently, eyeing the corners of the yard, waiting for a sound that would betray another's presence. When he heard nothing, he stepped onto the porch and approached the front door. A quick test of the knob proved it was locked and Jake used the knocker to rap loudly against the old wood. No flurry of activity or sudden light followed, nor did Bandit rush to the door barking.

Either Tiffany had gone out and taken the dog with her, or someone had done something to both of them.

The sudden crash and crackle of leaves to his right had Jake swinging toward the sound, his heart hammering and his hand on his service revolver. Tense and ready, he waited, his eyes scanning the darkness, until a large shadow moved around the corner of the house. A soft bark of welcome broke the stillness and Jake relaxed his stance, letting his hand drift back to his side. "Well, at least one of you is okay."

The dog approached, licking Jake's hand in greeting.

"I don't suppose you can tell me where Tiffany is?"

Bandit's ears perked at Tiffany's name and he gave a short bark before leaping off the porch and heading into the backyard. Jake felt like a fool, but he followed the dog anyway. Though the moon brightened the yard, Bandit's dark fur was difficult to spot and it took a moment for Jake's eyes to distinguish the dog's shape from the shadows of trees and bushes that shaded the ground. Feeling like an actor in one of the old Lassie movies, Jake hurried to catch up with the slow-moving animal.

Bandit made his way across the well-trimmed lawn and into an overgrown area of tall pine trees and neglected bushes. Jake followed, pushing his way through brambles that caught at his clothes and scraped his skin. Was it possible that Tiffany had collapsed in the midst of this overgrown jungle? Or had she been dragged there?

Jake's hands tightened into fists, his heart pounding a slow, heavy warning. Things happened. Even in places like Lakeview, Virginia. Things that defied common decency, that made grown men blanch and shudder. Things that broke the heart and hardened the soul.

Jake had seen them all. Had left the city to cleanse himself of the filth and evil that seemed to cling to him, clogging his senses with the smell of rot and decay. He needed time to heal and to grow in the new faith he'd learned from Will.

He needed to find Tiffany alive and healthy. Anything else might just destroy him.

Tiffany stood at the door of the church sanctuary, listening for the first strains of the bridal march. Yards of white silk cascaded to her feet, a long train of the same material flowing behind her. In her hands she held a bouquet—hyacinth and mums, mixed with tiny orange and red rosebuds.

Perfect.

Heart overflowing with happiness, she gazed down the aisle, longing to meet her beloved's eyes. A dog barked....

A dog? Tiffany's heart pounded as she came out of a sound sleep. The hard wood under her shoulder and hip told her where she was before the moonlight and darkness did. She hadn't meant to fall asleep, but judging by the look of things, she'd been sleeping for quite a while.

The moon shone bright through the broken and missing boards of the gazebo's roof, casting strange shadows. Tiffany shuddered, sitting up and peering into the gloomy depth of the trees that surrounded her. Bandit barked from somewhere to the right, and Tiffany started, her heart leaping to her throat as the dog crashed out of the trees, leaped onto the gazebo and skidded to a stop at her feet. He barked again, the warning coming as the sound of breaking branches filled the air.

Something was crashing through the trees. Something big. Visions of bears and cougars, wolves and monsters flashed through Tiffany's mind as she scrambled for a weapon. There were two—the newspaper and the soggy pint of Ben & Jerry's. Neither packed the force of a two-by-four, but given the situation, they would have to do. At least she had surprise on her side. Grabbing the ice cream, Tiffany readied herself for attack.

Seconds later a tall form emerged from between towering pine trees. Tiffany pulled back with her pitching arm and let the ice cream fly. A muffled exclamation gave evidence of a successful hit but Tiffany didn't wait to find out where the ice cream had landed. Pivoting hard, she jumped off the gazebo's raised platform and headed into the trees just as Bandit decided to join in the fray. Four legs tangled with two and Tiffany went down hard, breath whooshing from her lungs with enough force to leave her gasping for air.

Bandit's howl mingled with the pulsing of blood in her ears and, above both, the sound of footsteps crunching across dry pine needles. *God help me!* The prayer screamed through Tiffany's mind as she struggled frantically to untangle herself from the dog, the shrubs and her own clumsy feet. Her efforts yielded results a moment too late. Moonlight disappeared behind the tall figure of a man as Tiffany struggled to her knees.

"Don't come any closer. I'm armed." The words emerged as a trembling squeal and Tiffany cleared her throat, ready to scream.

"Hopefully not with more ice cream. I'm sticky enough." A callused hand reached out and grasped Tiffany's arm, hauling her to her feet.

"Jake?"

"Yes. Are you all right? You hit the ground hard."

"I'm fine."

"Good. Let's get out of these trees."

Out in the open yard, the moon cast a soft glow, illuminating the surrounding area and giving Tiffany a clear view of the ice cream dripping from Jake's forehead. "I guess I hit my target."

She tried to control the laughter that bubbled up in her throat but a shaky chuckle escaped. Then another, and another, until peals of laughter rang through the night. Clutching at her sides, Tiffany gasped for breath and struggled to control herself. "I'm...sorry...it's not funny...."

"Guess it depends on which side of the flying ice cream you were on." The soft rumble of Jake's laughter joined hers. "You've got quite an arm. I suppose softball is one of your many talents?"

"Actually nothing quite so noble. I spent my senior year pitching balls at a target, practicing to dunk the school's principal."

"Dunk?" Jake put a hand on Tiffany's arm as he spoke and began steering her toward the house.

"Yeah. Every June the school held an end-of-the-year

picnic. Mr. Beally would climb up into a dunking booth and dare us to hit the target. No girl had ever succeeded. I wanted to be the first."

"Were you?"

Tiffany eyed the ice cream dripping from Jake's hair, and smirked. "What do you think?"

"I think I am in as much need of a towel as Mr. Beally was."

Jake's laughter shivered along Tiffany's nerves, warming her. "I really am sorry. Bandit's bark startled me and when I heard you coming through the trees, I panicked."

"No problem. Sometimes it's safer to act first and ask questions later."

"Well, in this case, I wish I'd waited." Tiffany unlocked the mudroom door and stepped inside, flicking on the overhead light as she walked into the kitchen.

Jake stepped in behind her. "Three in the morning is a strange time for visitors. You made the right decision."

Startled, Tiffany glanced at the clock. "Good grief! I've missed choir practice."

"That's why I'm here. Your mother called the station. When you didn't show up, she got worried."

"Why didn't she call me?" Tiffany paused and shook her head. "Never mind, I'm sure she did. And my dad's on a business trip with the only working car, so she couldn't drive over. She must be frantic."

Jake nodded. "The dispatcher said she was pretty upset."

"I'd better call her." Tiffany reached for the phone but Jake's hand on her arm stalled the motion.

"Do you mind getting me a towel first?"

"Oh. Yes. Sure." Embarrassed that she'd forgotten, Tiffany reached into a drawer and grabbed a clean dishcloth. "I can't believe I did this to you. I'm so sorry."

Gently extracting the cloth from her fingers, Jake motioned to the phone. "Relax. I wash up pretty well. Go ahead and call your mom. Let her know you're all right."

"Good idea." Tiffany grabbed the phone and dialed her mother's number. As she suspected would happen, the phone was picked up on the first ring. "Hi, Mom."

"Tiffany? I'm so glad you called, I've been worried sick. Are you okay?"

"I'm fine. I just fell asleep and lost track of time."

"You didn't hear the phone ring? When you didn't show up for choir practice I phoned your house. Several times in fact. What's going on?"

Tiffany recognized the edge creeping into her mother's voice. Her initial worry over, Patti Anderson wanted answers. "I fell asleep out on the gazebo swing and didn't wake up until Sheriff Reed came by to check on me."

"What were you doing out on the swing? You told me that was your worry spot. Is something going on that I should know about?"

Tiffany glanced at Jake who had wet the dishcloth and was using it to clean ice cream from his head. "It's a long story, Mom. Why don't I call you back at a decent time and fill you in?"

"I've been up for hours worrying about you. Another few minutes isn't going to hurt me. Besides, you know I never sleep well when your father is away."

Tiffany glanced at Jake again. He'd finished with the cloth and was scratching the back of Bandit's ears. Tiffany lowered her voice and stepped out into the hall. "Okay, something has happened and it upset me so I went out and sat on the swing to think."

"This isn't about Tom Bishop, is it? Rumors are flying all over town about that young man working for you."

"No, Tom is doing great. It's Brian I have a problem with."

"Brian? You're kidding. I thought you two were as thick as thieves."

"Yeah, so did everyone else."

"Did you have an argument? Is that what this is about?"

"We didn't argue. Exactly. It's more like I suddenly realized Brian isn't the kind of man I want to be married to. And if he isn't worth marrying, he's not worth dating."

Silence, heavy with unspoken thoughts, stretched across the phone line.

Tiffany rushed to fill it. "I know this is a surprise and I know you're probably disappointed. I am, too. But staying with Brian would mean accepting less than what I think God wants for me." Tiffany felt the lump forming in her throat as she said the words.

"I'm not surprised. I'm relieved."

"What?" Tiffany was so shocked she forgot to keep her voice lowered. "What do you mean relieved? You love Brian. You said he would make a great husband."

"He will. But not for you. I realized soon after you started dating Brian that he would never value you the way he should. Your father felt the same way. We've been praying about it."

"I wish you had filled *me* in." Tiffany heard the whining sound of her voice and winced.

"Really? Do you think you would have listened? You're an adult with your own life. I stopped trying to tell you how to run it a long time ago," Patti hesitated, then continued. "Well, mostly I don't tell you how to run it."

Tiffany grinned at her mother's admission. Though she tried to keep quiet about her daughters' lives, Patti had been known to give a bit of advice when she felt it was needed.

"Tiffany, if I hadn't thought you would make the right decision about Brian I would have talked to you about it a long time ago. But, as your father is always saying, we didn't raise a fool. I figured sooner or later Brian would wear on your nerves and you would dump him."

"What if I hadn't?"

"It was your decision to make. I wouldn't have interfered. The person you marry is someone you need to choose on your own. Without me sticking my nose into it."

"You're right, Mom. You usually are."

"Chalk it up to age and gray hair. So, now that you aren't dating, maybe you can get together with your old Mom. I've been dying to try that new Chinese restaurant in Rocky Mount but you know how your father hates to try new things."

"I'd love to." Tiffany paused before asking a question she desperately wanted an answer to. "Mom, I dated Brian for a year and didn't realize there was a problem. How did you figure it out so quickly?"

"Oh, that's easy. He didn't spend enough time wooing you."

"*Wooing* me?" Laughter bubbled up around the tears Tiffany had been holding back and a wet gurgly sound of amusement escaped. "Come on, Mom. I'm not the kind of woman men court with roses and candy."

"What kind of nonsense is that? Of course you are. Besides, candy and roses are nothing. I'm talking time, affection, love letters. You know. Like your dad when we were dating."

"I'm afraid Dad is one of a kind."

"True, but you'll find your own one-of-a-kind guy. You just have to be patient."

Tiffany sighed but didn't argue. Her mother had been married since the day after she turned nineteen. She had no idea what it felt like to be over thirty and single. "Maybe so."

"There's no maybe about it. God has someone special waiting for you. Now, when are we going for Chinese?"

"Pick a night. I'm free for the foreseeable future."

Her mother laughed. Tiffany didn't think it was all that funny.

A few minutes later, she said good-night to her mother and went back into the kitchen. The room was quiet and empty. Tiffany tried to tell herself she wasn't disappointed at Jake's departure, but when a whisper of sound drifted from the mudroom her heart did a little tap dance of pleasure.

"Jake?"

"Your dog seemed hungry, I found his bowl and filled it with kibble."

A soft snuffle and crunch let Tiffany know Bandit was enjoying his meal. "Poor Bandit. I meant to feed him before I left for choir. He must have been starving."

Jake raised a dark eyebrow, a half smile curving his lips. "I doubt you have to worry about that. The dog is built like a tank."

Tiffany shrugged, feeling Jake's gaze as she grabbed the ice cream-coated dishrag and rinsed it in the sink. Though Jake's words and actions were casual, Tiffany couldn't help wondering if he'd heard what she was saying to her mother and retreated to the mudroom to get out of earshot. Blushing, she tried to think of something to say.

Jake watched as Tiffany rinsed the dishrag for the third time. A black smudge ran the length of her cheek, looking suspiciously like smeared letters. Leaning closer, Jake made out the word *he*. "Newspapers don't make very good pillows."

"What?" Tiffany looked up from the dishcloth, her green eyes wide with surprise.

Jake took the wet cloth and rubbed it against her cheek, trying not to notice the gold flecks in Tiffany's eyes, or the freckles sprinkled across her nose. "See? Ink." Jake lifted the cloth so Tiffany could see the dark stain on its edge.

"You've got to be kidding. Can this day get any worse?" Tiffany grabbed the cloth and rubbed at her cheek, replacing black with irritated red.

Jake couldn't help smiling at the picture she made, curly hair springing in every direction, green eyes flashing with annoyance. If he were a painter he'd want to paint her just like that. "Probably not."

Tiffany stopped scrubbing and looked at Jake, her eyes filled with suspicion. "Did you hear what I said to my mom?"

Jake had hoped she wouldn't have the guts to ask. He should have known better. "Which part?"

"What do you mean, which part?"

"The part about Brian McMath being an idiot? Or the other part about Brian McMath being an idiot?"

Tiffany's mouth dropped open, her eyes glistened, and for a moment Jake was afraid she was going to cry. Then, as if a dam had burst, laughter exploded in great, gasping breaths. "Sorry...the last thing...I...expected," Tiffany gulped back more laughter, "was honesty."

Jake fought his own laughter and wished, for the first time in longer than he could remember, that he had a different past. That he hadn't made so many mistakes, been touched by so much ugliness. But he had, and it had made him who he was—a man who knew that laughter and love lasted less time than it took to walk down the aisle and exchange vows. He pushed aside the regret and spoke as he walked to the back door. "Would you have believed a lie?"

"No. I guess not."

Tiffany walked up beside him, and Jake could see the

frown that marred the smooth skin of her brow. Perhaps she sensed his sudden withdrawal and wondered at it. He fought the urge to apologize, to reach out and smooth away the worry line. "Don't worry. I didn't hear anything that I didn't already know."

"That's supposed to make me feel better?" Tiffany grinned, her eyes beckoning Jake to join in.

And in that moment, Jake knew he needed to stay away from Tiffany Anderson. The banter between them was too easy, her smiles too hard to resist. Ignoring her question, Jake made a show of glancing at his watch. "It's late. Guess I'll be on my way."

Tiffany didn't seem to notice his eagerness to escape. Or if she did, she didn't acknowledge it. "All right. Thank you for checking on me. I'm sorry I had everyone so worried."

"No problem." Jake stepped out onto the front porch, the sight of a ladder leaning against the house reminding him of Tom Bishop's trouble. "I almost forgot. Tom Bishop had a run-in with some of his pals today."

"What kind of run-in?"

"The kind where their fists ran into his face."

"Is he okay?" Tiffany's concern was obvious even in the fading moonlight.

"He's fine but I don't trust that group of teens. They wanted access to your account information. I guess they were trying to get credit card numbers off the invoices."

"I never would have thought of that as a potential problem but some of the invoices do have credit card information."

"Tom put a stop to them for now, but I wouldn't put it past them to try again. I've got some officers doing regular patrol along this street until the summer crowd leaves. But take precautions anyway. Keep your windows and doors locked."

"I will. Thanks for the warning."

"I know you don't want to hear this, but having Tom around might bring trouble your way. You should consider letting him go. At least for the summer."

"That's not a possibility."

Jake could see from the set of Tiffany's chin that her decision was final. He wanted to argue. Wanted to tell her in detail exactly what happened to people who trusted too much. But that wasn't his right, so he bit back the words and nodded. "Be careful then."

"I will."

"Good." Stepping down from the porch, he surveyed the early-morning world and tried to convince himself that he didn't mind leaving Tiffany alone in her oversize house. The descending moon wove a spell of shadows across the yard. Night sounds had quieted as the moon moved toward the horizon and it seemed the world was holding its breath, waiting for dawn to streak across the sky.

"It's beautiful, isn't it?" Tiffany's words drew Jake's attention and he turned toward her, saw the dreams in her eyes, heard the yearning in her voice, and wanted to share it all.

"Beautiful?"

"Yes. The way night ends. Sometimes, when I can't sleep I come out here and watch. First, the world grows silent and then, like a special surprise, glimmers of light shoot up from the horizon and a new day is born. Each time I see it, I feel as if my soul has been touched by God's hand."

Jake knew he should leave. The moment felt too intimate, the thoughts too personal. Yet Tiffany seemed unfazed by her own revelation, unperturbed by the piece of her heart she had just revealed, and Jake's feet refused to follow his brain's command. Instead of leaving, he remained rooted to the spot, watching the farthest piece of sky until a faint tinge of light streaked into the darkness.

He might have stood until daylight chased away night if Tiffany hadn't yawned and broken the spell that seemed to hold him in place. Turning to her, Jake tried not to imagine what it would be like if he didn't have to leave. "You're tired. You better get to bed."

"Good night, Jake."

"Good night." Stepping off the porch, Jake made his way to the Chevy. He didn't look back.

Chapter Eight

Sunday morning dawned bright and beautiful, and despite prayers to the contrary, Tiffany felt fine. No fever or migraine, no flat tire on the Cadillac, no natural disaster. Absolutely nothing to keep her away from church. It wasn't that she didn't *want* to attend service. She did. She just didn't want to face the speculative looks and knowing glances that sitting without Brian would garner.

And of course there were other things to consider. Like the possibility that she would run into Brian. Or worse, Jake. Even now Tiffany blushed when she remembered the way she'd waxed poetic in the early hours of Tuesday morning, her voice droning on about darkness and daylight. She had to give Jake credit—he hadn't laughed. Hadn't even smiled. He had just looked at her, his face solemn and still, while something flickered and faded in the depth of his eyes.

He probably thought she was a nut and Tiffany couldn't

blame him. She had managed, in the short time she'd known him, to almost drown herself, run out of gas on a deserted road, splatter Jake with paint, and cover him with ice cream. Not a very auspicious start to a new friendship.

Not that Jake had offered her anything but the help she needed. She hadn't seen him since Tuesday. Nor had she seen Brian. Strange that Jake's absence seemed to leave a greater emptiness than the one left by a man she'd dated for a year.

Refusing to think of the reason for that, Tiffany pushed thoughts of Jake and Brian aside. She had a Sunday school class to teach and no matter how much she might want to avoid the knowing looks of friends and acquaintances, Tiffany couldn't shirk her duty.

Twenty minutes later Tiffany wished she had stayed in bed with the covers pulled over her head. The whispered condolences and words of support were bad enough, but when Brian walked by, Lisa Jenner clinging to his arm, Tiffany wanted to sink beneath the floor. Her closest friends closed rank around her, forming a barrier against Brian and the woman fawning at his side. Though Tiffany tried to explain that the breakup had been her idea, her friends just smiled benignly and continued to pat her on the back.

Tiffany tried hard to keep her smile in place, but then she noticed the huddled group of men standing along the wall and her smile slipped. Boyfriends, fiancés and husbands of the women surrounding her, they waited in companionable silence for their concerned counterparts.

Abruptly Tiffany stepped back from the crowd of women and raised her voice so it could be heard above their tsks of sympathy. "Thanks for your concern, everyone, but I think service is about to start." Tiffany waved her friends away, a smile pasted to her face, watching as they moved toward their partners. Some linked hands, others twined their arms together. There were smiles and whispered conversations. Secret looks that passed from one to another. And down the hall, just entering the sanctuary, Brian leaned close to Lisa and said something that made her smile.

Tiffany had never felt so alone in her life.

Jake's morning had been going pretty well until he walked into the church and saw Brian McMath. The doctor hadn't wasted any time finding Tiffany's replacement. The blond woman he was escorting through the church clung to his arm like a flea on a dog's behind. Jake had watched with narrowed eyes as the woman maneuvered the doctor down the hall and past a huddled group of women. A flash of red-gold curls shone through the crowd at the same moment a look of triumph passed briefly over Brian's date's face. Pale pink fingernails dug slightly into the gray suit McMath wore, marring the line as the woman staked her claim to the doctor.

Jake tried to ignore the two and tried even harder to ignore the group of women who were slowly dispersing, each walking off with a boyfriend or husband, until Tiffany stood alone in the middle of the hall. Organ music drifted from the sanctuary as the call to worship began but Tiffany didn't seem to notice. Her eyes were downcast, her hair falling softly against her cheeks and down over her shoulders blocking Jake's view of her face. Then she looked up, her shoulders straightening, and Jake could see the flash of fire in her eyes.

A grin twitched at the corner of Jake's lips. He'd seen Tiffany in a variety of embarrassing, uncomfortable and downright upsetting situations, and her reaction had surprised him every time. No wilting flower, she refused to be brought low by the circumstances she found herself in. Jake figured it was one of the few things they had in common.

Fighting the urge to go to her, he watched as Tiffany smoothed a hand down the front of the lilac sundress she wore. The material hugged her waist and fell in a gossamer cloud to her ankles. As she moved to the sanctuary door the fabric floated around her legs, making Jake think of wild-flowers tickled by a breeze. He imagined he could hear the gentle brush of fabric against skin. Imagined how that same material would wrap around his pants-clad legs if he were walking beside her.

With a muffled exclamation, Jake turned abruptly from Tiffany's retreating form. He refused to think about what would never be. Frustrated with his errant musings, he stalked to the sanctuary door and walked in several paces behind Tiffany.

Tiffany chose her seat carefully. Knowing from experience the back pew usually remained empty, she slid across the smooth wood surface and tried not to look around. It wasn't that she cared if Brian had a new girlfriend, though she supposed she probably should. She just wished he had waited a few more weeks to find one. Then the church wouldn't be buzzing with the story that he had broken up with Tiffany in order to date Lisa.

Running a hand through her loose curls, Tiffany pretended she didn't care that half the congregation was sneaking peeks at her. Though the church community wasn't small, its members numbering just over four hundred, she had grown up with most of the people who attended and they all felt as if they were part of her life, even when she didn't want them to be.

Tiffany lowered her head and tried to ready her heart and mind for the service but the sick knowledge that she was alone while all her friends sat with their significant others nudged its way into her thoughts again and again. Forcing herself to relax, Tiffany focused on the organ music. The melody was a familiar one and she could feel tension easing from her neck and shoulders.

Then she smelled the perfume. Feminine and flowery, it drifted on the air as a scuffle of movement told Tiffany someone had claimed the pew in front of her. She opened her eyes, ready to smile at the newcomer and caught sight of blond hair pulled into a sleek chignon and manicured fingernails tinged a discreet pink.

Before Tiffany could close her eyes and pretend ignorance, Lisa turned toward her. "Tiffany. So nice to see you. It's been a long time."

"Yes, it has."

"I was just commenting to Brian that the shade of purple you're wearing suits you. Wasn't I, Brian?"

Brian nodded, his eyes meeting Tiffany's for a moment before he turned his attention to the empty pulpit.

Tiffany tried on a smile that felt more like a scowl. "Thank you. I love lilac."

"Yes, well, with your coloring, it's surprising you'd choose such a pale shade but it does enhance your eyes."

Tiffany bit her lip and didn't respond.

"Oh, look, there's Maggie Morrison. I've got to go tell her about last night." Lisa smiled pointedly at Brian before turning back to Tiffany. "Excuse me, won't you?"

The organ music prevented Tiffany from hearing the conversation between Maggie and Lisa, but from the blonde's wolfish grin and gestures in Brian's direction, Tiffany figured she could guess what it was about. When Lisa shot a knowing glance her way, Tiffany decided she'd had enough. Reaching for her purse and Bible she got ready to move.

A hand covered hers, preventing Tiffany from retrieving her belongings. "Don't give Goldilocks the satisfaction."

Startled, Tiffany looked up into Jake's blue eyes and watched as he slid into the pew beside her. He didn't look happy. "I—" Tiffany was prevented from commenting by Ben Avery's arrival at the pulpit.

Settling back against the pew, Tiffany glanced in Jake's direction. Jaw set, eyes staring straight ahead, he seemed as approachable as a polar bear on the hunt.

But he'd been right. Leaving the sanctuary would have played into the act Lisa had been putting on. And that was the last thing Tiffany wanted to do.

As Pastor Avery's rich baritone filled the sanctuary, Tiffany straightened her skirt and relaxed for the first time in hours. Music, announcements and prayer gave way to the sermon and she forgot Brian and Lisa, forgot that the entire church thought she'd been dumped, forgot everything but the truth of the words Ben spoke and the warmth of the man sitting beside her.

When the last hymn had been sung, Tiffany turned to Jake wanting to share her enjoyment of the sermon. "What—"

"Tiffany?" Lisa's Southern drawl was unmistakable.

In most people, Tiffany found the drawl charming. In Lisa it was annoying. Gritting her teeth she turned to face the woman. "Yes?"

"Brian and I were hoping to speak to you for a moment."

"Sure, what's up?"

"We had the most wonderful dinner last night. Didn't we, darling?" Lisa didn't wait for Brian's answer, though a glance his way told Tiffany that he agreed. He had certainly never looked at *Tiffany* that way. "The General's Club House, I'm sure you've heard of it. Wonderful lake views and fantastic food. So romantic, you know."

Tiffany didn't. Brian had never taken her there. But she wasn't about to say so. "How nice for you."

"Yes. Anyway, we discussed the Sunday school class you were helping Brian teach. So kind of you to help out, but—" Lisa paused, her gaze flicking from Tiffany to a point beyond her shoulder and back again.

Tiffany felt, rather than saw, Jake move behind her. She'd thought he had left and couldn't decide if she was pleased that he had stayed or embarrassed that he could hear the conversation.

"—Well, we're just not sure you'll be needed in the class anymore."

Tiffany focused her attention back on Lisa's words. "Are you trying to say you want to teach the class with Brian?"

"Well, yes. If you don't mind. It just seems more appropriate. You understand." Lisa laid a proprietary hand on Brian's arm.

"Sure." Tiffany's disappointment was keen but she tried to mask it. The young men and women in the teen class had a zeal Tiffany didn't often see in adults. Their enthusiasm and dedication to the things of God had astounded and humbled her at times. But it looked like that was over for the time being.

"Great. I am so excited about the opportunity. Brian thinks I'll be a great role model for the young ladies. I plan on giving mini courses on fashion and modesty. And of course, *I* understand the importance of supporting a husband or boyfriend in his chosen career."

"Are you implying—" A hand landed on Tiffany's shoulder, squeezing lightly, and cutting off her words.

The low timbre of Jake's voice rumbled next to her ear as he spoke. "I'm sure you'll be wonderful, ma'am. Now, if you'll excuse us, Tiffany and I are teaching the four-year-olds this morning."

"We are?"

"Well, I am. I was hoping you might be willing to lend a hand. The Sunday school coordinator called last night and asked me to teach the class. Seems the teacher is on maternity leave." Jake didn't look at Tiffany as he spoke. Instead he smiled at Lisa and Brian, acting for all the world like he wanted Tiffany to help.

She suspected otherwise. "Jake, I—"

Tiffany was going to say she didn't think helping him was a good idea but he cut her off before she could utter the words. "I don't have much experience with kids. I could really use the help."

Tiffany doubted Jake *ever* needed help, but a smug grin flirted at the edges of Lisa's mouth, as if the woman knew Jake was just trying to help Tiffany save face. "Of course, I'll help. I love kids."

At least she loved her nieces and nephew. Though, if pressed, she'd admit she had never actually dealt with a large group of youngsters. Shrugging, she followed Jake's lead, saying a quick goodbye to Lisa and Brian before walking out into the hall.

She hurried to keep pace with Jake, a nervous flutter starting in the pit of her stomach. She wasn't sure which was worse, having to face a room filled with preschoolers, or having to spend an hour with a man who obviously didn't want her around. Before she could make up her mind, Jake rounded a corner and opened a door, disappearing into the room. Squaring her shoulders, Tiffany followed him inside.

Jake hadn't been lying when he said he didn't have much experience with kids. He usually avoided them like the plague. Not because he didn't like them, but because he didn't know what to *do* with them.

Ten minutes after entering the preschool class, Jake realized he had nothing to worry about. The kids knew what they wanted and made it pretty clear. He had little ones climbing his legs, hopping on his back, begging for horsy rides, and asking him to read books. He let them have their way for a few minutes then corralled them all onto an area rug to begin the Bible lesson.

He tried to keep his gaze on the story or on the kids, but it kept drifting to the back of the group where Tiffany sat, swirls of lilac material spread around her legs, two children cuddled in her lap. When the story was over, she set papers and crayons out and supervised the activity page, moving among the children with an ease and grace Jake found alluring.

He should never have asked her to help but watching McMath's blond friend preen in front of Tiffany had set Jake's teeth on edge. When he'd first seen Lisa and Brian slide into the pew in front of Tiffany, he'd told himself to ignore the situation. But then McMath's new girlfriend had made a point of engaging Tiffany in conversation. Before he could think better of it he was next to Tiffany, telling her not to get up and leave.

Things had gotten worse from there. His plea for assistance with the four-year-olds had taken the wind out of Lisa's sail but it had also put Jake in a position he'd wanted to avoid—namely, close proximity to a woman he'd be better off avoiding.

Even now, as he helped towheaded twins build a block tower, his gaze kept wandering to the corner where Tiffany sat, a child in her lap, another three behind her watching as a fourth tied Tiffany's hair into what was supposed to be a braid. All of them were giggling.

A picture of Tiffany, a baby in her arms, a toddler cuddled to her side, filled Jake's head and he shoved it ruthlessly aside. He'd made a mistake with Tiffany. A big one. Somewhere along the line he'd let his guard down, had forgotten to keep his distance. Now he was paying the price.

Being with Tiffany reminded him of all the things he used to want, but had learned he couldn't have—marriage, children, a family. He'd tried for those things with Sheila, hoping he could make a better life than the one he'd had growing up. Within months she'd complained that he worked too hard, was gone too much. That his commitment to his job came before his commitment to her.

Maybe she'd been right.

In the end it hadn't mattered. She'd partied hard while he was gone. When he was home they argued. Finally the effort to keep things together had been more than the effort it took to go their separate ways.

"Mr. Jake? Mr. Jake?" A small hand tugged at his, forcing Jake away from the past.

"What is it, sport?"

"Is it snack time yet?"

Jake glanced at the clock, wishing its hands would move a little faster. "Yep, I believe it is. Come on everyone, it's time to eat."

Chapter Nine

Children scrambled for their chairs and Tiffany moved forward to lend a hand. Together they handed out snacks, pushed in chairs and settled disputes. At times, Jake could feel Tiffany's gaze and he knew she wondered about his silence.

"Amazing how quiet they get when they're eating, isn't it?" Tiffany's green eyes were focused on him now, her warm smile a gentle offering of friendship.

"Yes." Jake let his own face relax into a smile, hiding his turbulent emotions. It wasn't Tiffany's fault circumstances had brought them together time and time again.

"Thanks for inviting me to help out. I've taught junior high and high school. But this is a new experience for me."

"That makes two of us."

"Well, if that's the case, I wouldn't know it. You're a natural with the kids."

Jake nodded his thanks, letting silence drift between them

again. Tiffany fidgeted beside him, tugging at a wisp of hair that fell against her cheek as she watched the children devour their cookies. Finally she turned back toward him, her eyes filled with questions Jake had no answers for. When she spoke her words were blunt and to the point. "Look, I'm sorry if this situation is uncomfortable. I know you were just trying to help me save face earlier."

"That wasn't the only reason I asked for your help."

"No? Well, you're certainly competent enough to do the job on your own."

"Maybe, but I didn't know how things would go until I got here. I was afraid there might be thirty of these little monkeys."

One of the children giggled at Jake's words and Tiffany smiled in response. "Well, you seem fine with fifteen. If it will make you more comfortable I can leave now."

Jake knew he should take her up on the offer. "Is that what you want to do?"

"Not really. I'm enjoying myself. Besides if I leave this room there will be twenty people out in the hall waiting to tell me how sorry they are for me."

"Why? What is there to be sorry for?"

"Couldn't you tell? Brian dumped me for Lisa. Or at least that's the way the story's being told."

"Sounds like a gossip mill."

"Well, the church is like my extended family. I guess they feel that means they can spread news about me." Tiffany rubbed a hand against her temple. "Even if it isn't quite true."

"Have you told anyone what really happened?"

"Sure, but they just keep clucking their tongues at me and giving me reassuring pats on the back."

"I'd think they'd assume you dumped the guy. Not the other way around."

Tiffany's eyes widened with surprise, a deprecating smile curving the edges of her lips. "Thanks, but half the church remembers when I was a chunky, awkward preteen. I think they just can't imagine I'd let a prime catch like Brian get away. Especially not at my age."

Before Jake could respond, a squeal of alarm sounded from a little girl whose juice had tumbled to the floor and Tiffany rushed to clean up the mess. A moment later a hand tugged at Jake's and a blue-eyed boy demanded to be taken to the bathroom. Jake wasn't sure if he was relieved or disappointed that his conversation with Tiffany had ended.

Tiffany grabbed a handful of napkins and mopped up the puddle of juice. The distraction was timely, saving her from revealing more about her sorry situation than Jake wanted to know. She shouldn't have pushed for conversation. Jake had a right to his silence and certainly had no obligation to talk to her. Still, she missed the easy companionship they'd shared the few times they'd been together. Always before, she'd felt as if he were an old friend returning after a long visit. Their conversation had flowed smoothly from topic to topic, their silences unstrained. Now she could feel the tension radiating from Jake. Had felt it from the moment she'd walked into the room and, for the life of her, Tiffany could not understand why Jake had asked for her help.

Tiffany told herself she wasn't hurt by his behavior. After all, they weren't even friends. Just acquaintances who seemed to bump into one another more often than most. Still, it rankled that he would ask for her help and then ignore her. Perhaps she *was* as expendable as Brian's quick recovery from their breakup seemed to indicate.

With a sigh, Tiffany mopped up the last of the juice and threw the soggy mass in the trash can. Jake had disappeared with several of the boys, taking them, Tiffany supposed, on a potty break. When they returned a few minutes later, a dark-haired little boy approached Tiffany, a yellow rose thrust out in front of him.

"Miss Tiffany, this is for you."

Tiffany reached out for the flower. "Oh, my, where did you get this?"

"We finded it on our way to the bathroom."

Tiffany turned to Jake who shrugged and smiled.

"Really, well, thank you. I think this is the prettiest rose I've ever been given." It was actually the only rose she'd ever been given, but Tiffany didn't think anyone needed to know that.

Mission accomplished, the little boy bounced off to the puzzle table. Tiffany watched him for a moment before walking over to Jake. "You guys *found* this?" Tiffany waved the rose in the air between them.

"You could say that."

"Tell the truth. Where did you get it?"

"Let's just say I have friends in high places."

"Friends?"

"Friends with access to last week's pulpit flowers."

Now that he mentioned it, the rose did seem a trifle worn, the edges beginning to wilt just a little.

"Ben had last week's flowers in his office. I happened to spot them on the way to the bathroom and asked for the rose."

"It's beautiful. Thank you." Tiffany didn't ask what the occasion was, but Jake answered the question anyway.

"It's droopy, but it's the best I could do on short notice. I figured you could cut off the stem and wear the rose in your hair when you leave. When people ask about it, you can tell them you got it from the guy you dumped Brian for."

Jake's grin invited Tiffany to share in the joke and she smiled in return. "Now, Sheriff, I can't believe you're telling me to lie in God's house." Tiffany stretched out her vowels, doing an imitation of Lisa's thick Southern drawl.

"Well, now Miz Anderson, I wouldn't call it lying. More like stretching the truth a bit."

Jake's deep chuckle warmed Tiffany and her heart did a little flip in response. "More than a stretch, I'm afraid." Sighing, she lifted the flower and inhaled its delicate aroma. "Though I have to admit, I'd be tempted to do it if I wasn't sure people would be begging me for a name."

"Don't let all this get you down. By next week you'll be old news."

Tiffany knew Jake was right but she couldn't shake the melancholy mood that had suddenly come over her. Afraid her voice would give away her feelings, Tiffany just smiled and nodded.

"Want me to get rid of that for you?" Jake gestured to the rose, apparently deciding it should be disposed of now that the joke was over.

Tiffany didn't plan on giving it up. "No, I'll take care of it."

"All right. Parents should be coming in a few minutes. I'm going to get these kids cleaning up."

When Jake turned away, Tiffany grabbed a napkin from the table, soaked it in leftover apple juice, and wrapped it around the cut end of the rose.

The flower might be wilted and old but it was hers. Who cared that the man who gave it to her did so as a joke? At least when her nieces were old enough to ask, Tiffany could tell them honestly that once upon a time a handsome prince had given her a rose. Of course, they might not believe her, old maid that she'd be. That was why Tiffany planned to press it and put it in her scrapbook.

Then she'd go on with her life. Forget about Brian and

Jake. Maybe even men in general. After all, thirty-three was too old to be worrying so much about love.

"I guess you haven't had any trouble with Tom or his friends?"

Jake spoke from across the room, and Tiffany shoved the rose deep into her purse before she turned to face him. "None at all. Tom's been working hard. He's a great kid."

"I'm glad it's working out." Though Jake's voice sounded pleasant enough, his eyes had gone hard. The darkness Tiffany had sensed in him when they'd first met suddenly was close to the surface.

"What's wrong?"

"I'm not sure I trust him. And I know I don't trust his buddies."

"I don't think Tom's been hanging out with anybody lately. He told me his dad's been taking him on weekend runs, and during the week he's at my house."

"That still leaves the evenings."

"Jake—"

"Just be careful. I've got a bad feeling about things."

Tiffany nodded, surprised at the force of Jake's words. She knew there'd been trouble in town in the past few weeks, but she hadn't considered herself to be in danger.

Now she wondered if she should.

The first parent arrived at the door, preventing her from asking questions. But even as Tiffany said goodbye to children and parents, she thought about Jake's words. About his certainty that something was going to happen.

"Don't look so scared. People will think I've been intimidating you." Jake spoke close to her ear as the last child walked through the door.

"I'm not scared. I was just wondering why you're so convinced I'm going to have problems with Tom's ex-buddies."

"Just a feeling. Call it instinct."

"Have you ever been wrong?"

"Not often."

"Well, I can't fire Tom. I won't."

Jake saw the heat in Tiffany's eyes, and knew he couldn't change her mind. "I've still got patrols running your street. So don't worry. Just be cautious."

"I will." She ran a hand through her hair and turned to survey the room. "You've got everything cleaned up. I guess we can go."

"I guess so. Thanks for helping."

"No problem."

"I might stop by and speak with Tom later this week. He working every day?"

"Yes."

"All right. See you then." Jake stepped out into the hall, and turned to wave goodbye. Then caught his breath as he met Tiffany's gaze. There was warmth in her eyes, and promises.

"Let me know when you're stopping by. I'll make sure I'm there. That way Tom won't try to escape when he sees you coming."

Jake nodded and turned away. He didn't have the heart to tell Tiffany he'd changed his mind. That he'd track Tom down at home instead. When he didn't stop by her place, she'd assume he'd forgotten, or that he was too busy.

But the fact was, Jake couldn't risk it. Couldn't risk spending time with a woman who made him feel things he'd thought long buried. He'd been through one bad marriage. Had proven himself too emotionally distant to sustain a relationship. One woman had suffered for it. He wouldn't let the same happen to Tiffany. If that meant staying away from her, if it meant turning his back on her offer of friendship, so be it.

He'd rather rebuff her now than hurt her later.

With that in mind, Jake walked out of the church and headed home.

By Friday, Tiffany was sick to death of sympathy phone calls and unannounced visits. Even her closest friends seemed convinced she'd been dumped, and had called and stopped by with enough frequency to make Tiffany cringe each time the phone rang or someone knocked on the door.

That didn't mean she wanted to spend the evening alone. Unfortunately, all the friends who'd been so eager to offer sympathy and gather details, were busy. Probably with boyfriends, husbands or families.

Tiffany sighed and propped the fashion magazine up a little higher against the bedroom mirror before dabbing more gel onto her hands. The sleek, upswept hair the magazine model sported looked easy enough to duplicate. A dab here, a tuck there, a dragonfly barrette slipped neatly into place. What better way to spend a Friday evening than doing one's own hair?

She deserved a little pampering and had the whole evening planned out—hair, facial, makeup, manicure. According to the magazines she'd spent a small fortune buying, Tiffany would be model-gorgeous in no time.

Not that anyone would be around to notice her glorious transformation. Tiffany shrugged away the thought and ran gelled hands against her hair. The past week had been tiresome and tiring. Business had kept her busy, and Tom had seemed even more quiet than usual. That and the fact that Jake hadn't stopped by to speak with the teen made Tiffany wonder what was going on.

She suspected Jake had made a visit to Tom, just not at her house. The idea hurt more than it should. She barely knew Jake after all, and meant nothing to him. Nothing but trouble.

Tiffany sighed again and smeared more gel onto a wayward curl. It sprang back up, and she pressed it down again, eyeing the result critically. The style looked nothing like the picture in the magazine.

She reached for the gel again, pausing when a flash of headlights illuminated the bedroom window. Patrol cars had cruised by her house every few hours for the past five days. Most of the officers didn't bother driving up the driveway. Henry Simmons did. Tiffany had no doubt it was his car that flashed its lights across her window.

Slightly rotund and two inches shorter than Tiffany, Henry had introduced himself the first night of his patrol. His shy smile and green eyes had a hopeful, puppy dog expression that reminded Tiffany of Bandit. Hat in hand he'd explained that since he and Tiffany were both alone for the time being he thought they might spend some time together. Shocked, Tiffany had mumbled something about not being ready for another relationship.

Though Henry had accepted her answer, he'd come to her door every night for three nights running. And now, with Friday night looming empty before her, Tiffany wondered if she should have been more welcoming. After all, a dinner out didn't constitute a dating relationship. And maybe, just maybe, she would have found Henry a likable companion, someone with whom she might consider a long-term relationship.

Tiffany snorted at the thought and Bandit, sleeping on the carpet at her feet, raised his head to look at her, his expression almost exactly mirroring poor Henry's. It wasn't that she thought Henry beneath her notice; it was more that Tiffany couldn't imagine dating someone so close to her father's age. Sighing, she glanced down at the magazine again. She would rather be home giving herself a makeover than out for dinner with a man she probably had nothing in common with.

Now, if Jake Reed had invited her...

Tiffany ended the thought before it could take root. She had even less in common with Jake than she did with Henry. Forcing her mind away from the men—or lack of men—in her life, Tiffany put another dab of gel in her hair and tugged it back ruthlessly.

She might be a failure in relationships, but she'd be darned if she would let her hair get the better of her.

An hour later she finally admitted defeat and moved on to the face mask—a strange cucumber and avocado concoction she'd bought online. Scooping up a liberal palmful, Tiffany smeared the green lotion onto her face. Leaning close to the mirror, she eyed the results. Though her hair shimmered with gel, it refused to lie in the elegant upswept style she'd been trying to achieve. Reddish curls popped out in every direction and stood at attention. Green sludge covered her face and dripped down her neck. The result of her makeover, Tiffany decided, was thus far less than becoming.

"May as well do my nails while I wait for this to dry. What do you think, boy?"

Bandit lifted an eyelid before returning to doggy dreamland.

"What color? Lush Raspberry? Blue Mist? No, I've got it—Neon Purple. That will go great with the green mask and red hair."

Tiffany smiled a little as she applied the first coat of sparkling purple polish. Allowing her youngest niece to pick out the color had seemed a good idea at the time. When the three-year-old grabbed for the brightest, most garish nail color available Tiffany had hesitated but Skylar's brown eyes, wide and lit with excitement, convinced her that purple would indeed enhance her wardrobe.

Humming softly under her breath, Tiffany applied more nail polish and wished she had thought to invite her nieces for a sleepover. At three, five and six, the girls were old enough to be active and engaging, but not quite old enough to completely fend for themselves. This made life difficult for Tiffany's sisters. Jenna, who was six months pregnant with her second child, and Valorie, who was still recovering from the birth of her third, would both have been happy for a break.

And Tiffany was sure *she* would have been happy with some messy, loud and adorable distractions from the funk she was in. Swiping another coat of garish nail polish onto her nails, Tiffany pictured her nieces, two blond-haired, blue-eyed replicas of Valorie and the darker-haired, brown-eyed little wonder that Jenna had produced. Somewhere in the labyrinth of her brain, Tiffany had stored pictures of the children she hoped to have one day. Red-haired imps with her own green eyes, little girls with pigtails, and boys with eyes the color of summer sky.

It seemed strange, now that she thought of it, that Tiffany had never pictured her children with Brian's dark eyes. She supposed that was another one of the little signs of incompatibility she had missed. Now, instead of worrying about eye color, she was beginning to wonder if she would have children at all. Though she knew women who had babies into their forties, Tiffany didn't think she wanted to be one of them. She'd always said if she didn't have children by the time she was thirty-five, she wouldn't have them at all.

Time was running out. Fast.

Slamming down the bottle of nail polish, Tiffany stood up

and stalked across the room. She refused to wallow in self-pity. If God didn't intend for Tiffany to have children, she would learn to love being childless. She hoped.

Determined to be cheerful, Tiffany rifled through her stack of CDs and pushed one into the player. Cranking up the volume, she sang along with the music as she sat down on the bed and began painting her toenails. She had just finished her right foot when Bandit jumped up from the floor and began barking ferociously.

Heart skittering in her chest, Tiffany leaped from the bed and shut off the CD player. Bandit's hackles were raised, his teeth bared, as he growled at the closed bedroom door.

"What is it, Bandit? What's the matter?" Kneeling beside the dog, Tiffany put her arms around his rigid back, and listened for sounds beyond the bedroom door.

For a moment all was silent, then a rustling sound whispered through the door. Cold with fear, Tiffany crept forward and pressed her ear against the wood, straining to hear above her heart's frantic pounding.

When the sound came again it was unmistakable—the same rustle of fabric Tiffany heard each time a visitor brushed against a hanging quilt. On normal occasions the sound put Tiffany at ease.

Now it filled her with terror.

Jake's words of warning shouted through her mind as the creak and groan of the floor at the base of the stairs confirmed her fears—someone was in the house.

Legs trembling, Tiffany stood, her mind racing for a plan. She hadn't had a phone jack installed in the bedroom, so she couldn't call for help. She could hide in the closet and hope the intruder would leave, but what if the person had a weapon? Or worse, decided to do real damage to the property and burned it to the ground. Old, dry wood burned easily.

Just the thought made Tiffany shudder. No way could she stay and wait things out. With careful, quiet steps she eased toward the closet and grabbed her softball bat. Then she pressed close to the door again, listening for the creak of wooden steps. When it didn't come she pushed open the door and peered into the hall. She'd left the lights off, hoping to discourage a visit from Henry, and she could see nothing but darkness.

Lord, help me get out of here.

She'd barely finished the prayer when the sound of shattering glass filled the air. A loud bang followed, then a thud as something fell or was thrown. Tiffany didn't wait to hear more. With one hand on Bandit's collar and the other holding the bat, she rushed down the stairs. She hit the landing at a run and careened the rest of the way down, her hold on Bandit loosening as she neared the front door.

He lunged, breaking her hold, barking and growling as he disappeared into the dark hall. A shouted obscenity followed. The dog's howl of pain an echoing response.

Frozen in place Tiffany commanded her trembling limbs to move. They responded with nightmarish slowness, carrying her forward just as a hulking figure rushed from the darkness and barreled into her. Knocked off balance, Tiffany lost her grip on the bat and tumbled sideways. She righted herself, prepared to fight but strong hands wrapped her arm in a cruel grip and twisted it back until Tiffany thought it might snap. Before she could even cry out in pain, she was shoved hard into the wall. Colors burst behind her eyes as her head smashed into the corner of an antique wall sconce. Stunned, dizzy, Tiffany scrambled to right herself, struggling to face her attacker.

He was gone. Or he seemed to be. The empty hall stretched to both sides of Tiffany, the front door gaping open. Tiffany's instincts told her the intruder had fled, but her mind conjured up vivid images of a tall, masked figure lying in wait, ready to attack her the minute she let down her guard. Though the office with its phone was only feet away, Tiffany couldn't bring herself to go into the room. Better, she thought, to use the cell phone she'd left in her car. At least then she could drive away if she needed to.

"Bandit?"

Relief poured through Tiffany as Bandit responded to her barely audible whisper, slinking out of the office and limping toward her. She grabbed him by the collar, patting a hand along his back and down his flank, checking for evidence of injury.

When she found none, she released her hold and stepped toward the door, reaching down to pick up the fallen softball bat. "Come on, boy. Let's get out of here."

She hesitated at the threshold, her eyes scanning the darkness beyond the door. Was the intruder lurking outside, waiting for her? Or was he hiding in the house, hoping to finish what he started? The thought spurred Tiffany to action, and she grabbed her keys from the coatrack, prayed that no one waited outside the house, and stepped out into the night.

Chapter Ten

Jake jumped into his patrol car and slammed it into drive, fury and fear making his hands tremble and his heart thunder. He'd expected trouble, but nothing as cocky as this. The dispatcher had said burglary in progress. Jake knew it was more than that. It was a message. One he heard loud and clear.

Tom's gang wanted him back. And they didn't plan to let Tiffany get in the way of that happening. By breaking into her house while she was home, they proved they had the upper hand. It was a scare tactic. An effective one.

Siren blaring, Jake sped down Monroe Street, and braked hard at the edge of Tiffany's driveway. The house was dark but for a single light in an upstairs window. Despite the darkness, Jake could see the open front door. Tiffany's Cadillac was a long, dark shadow near the front porch. According to the dispatcher, she was in the car waiting for help.

Pulling his gun from its holster, Jake stepped from the cruiser. Adrenaline pumped fast and hard as his eyes scanned the thick bushes that lined the porch. The perpetrator might be hiding there or behind one of the ancient oaks. Jake listened to the night, to the chirping crickets and the toads calling back and forth. Leaves rustled slightly as air shifted and in the distance a siren heralded the arrival of another officer.

Jake waited another minute but there was no hint of movement. No quieting of the night creatures. Gun in hand, he moved toward the house. As he approached, the car door opened and Tiffany called out. "Officer?"

"Stay in the car. Lock the doors and don't come out until I give you the all clear."

At the sound of his voice, Tiffany opened the door a little wider. "Jake? Is that you?"

"I said stay in the car and wait." His voice sounded harsh and cold, even to his own ears.

"Sorry." Tiffany closed the car door, but unrolled the window. "Be careful."

Jake heard the shakiness in her voice, could sense her fear, and wanted to comfort her, but now wasn't the time. He stepped away, moved up the porch steps and into the house.

It was empty.

Jake knew it before he checked every room. His instincts buzzed with the knowledge, his body relaxing in response. Still he walked through each room, checked each closet, searched every hiding place. He checked the basement and walked out to the garage.

"See anything, Sheriff?" Henry Simmons strode around the corner of the house, his face set in lines of worry.

"Some damage in Ms. Anderson's office. A brick through the computer monitor, dumped files, a broken chair. Nothing that can't be fixed."

"What are you thinking?"

Jake shrugged. "Same thing you're thinking."

Henry nodded. "Kids again."

"Right. Come on, we'll dust for prints. See if we can come up with anything."

Jake was glad for the other officer's presence as he dusted for prints and catalogued the damage. While he worked, Henry collected evidence, including the brick and a wood chisel that had been used to break the lock on the kitchen door.

Henry was a good officer. A competent one who'd been in law enforcement for almost as long as Jake had been alive. Unfortunately, he liked to talk. And tonight what he wanted to talk about was Tiffany Anderson.

"It's a shame. A cryin' shame. Poor woman living alone can't even feel safe in her own house."

"Hopefully the situation will change when fall arrives and the summer folk leave."

"Well, I have to say, I'm worried for Tiffany. That young woman needs a man around this big house. That's for sure."

The way Henry puffed up his chest, Jake knew who he thought should fill the position. Ignoring a stab of possessiveness he had no business feeling, Jake jotted down some notes and hoped Henry would tire of his pet subject soon.

"I wouldn't mind taking care of things around here for her if..."

Jake didn't let him finish. "I think we're finished here. Why don't you head out and finish up your patrol?"

The dejected look on Henry's face made Jake regret his abrupt words and he hurried to fill in the awkward silence. "You do great work, Simmons. We make a good team."

The older man nodded, the frown easing from his face. "Thanks, Sheriff. See ya."

Jake ran a hand through his hair and shrugged off his frustration, then walked toward the Cadillac. Tiffany waited, huddled in the back seat, one hand still clutching her phone, the other wrapped around Bandit. In the faint moonlight her face seemed unnaturally pale, her eyes dark and filled with fear.

Jake rapped on the glass and gestured for her to open the door. "The house is clear."

"Thank goodness." Tiffany nudged Bandit out of the car. "I was beginning to worry that you and Henry had been injured."

"We were just trying to get an idea of what happened in there." Jake offered a hand and helped Tiffany out of the car. The skin of her arm felt cool and Jake fought the urge to rub his palms against her flesh until it warmed.

"Is there much damage?"

"Not much. Let's go inside. You can relax while I ask you a few questions."

"That's fine." Fatigue laced Tiffany's voice and she pressed a hand against her temple, wincing a little.

"Headache?"

"Not too bad but I'll take something for it before we talk, if that's all right."

"Tell you what, you sit down. I'll get your medicine. We can talk when you feel up to it." Jake resisted the inclination to hold Tiffany's arm as they made their way into the house and down the hall.

The living room light was off and Jake switched on a table lamp as Tiffany lowered herself onto the love seat.

"Thanks." She glanced up and Jake saw the tension that marked her brow and the corners of her eyes.

He saw something else, too, something that looked like green goo covering her face—hairline to chin. Dry and cracking, it gave Tiffany the appearance of aged porcelain.

Her hair looked different, too, slicked back in some places and standing on end in others. Jake's eyes drifted to the terry cloth bathrobe that gaped over cow print pajamas. Tiffany's feet peeked out from the pants, her right toenails painted a garish, sparkly shade of purple that exactly matched the color of her fingernails.

Lips twitching, Jake looked away. What *had* she been doing to herself? Having no sisters and a minimal relationship with his mother, Jake knew nothing of women's exotic beauty rituals. Surely such things didn't include caking cucumber-colored paste on one's face.

"Don't even think about it."

"What?" Jake dared another look at Tiffany, then struggled to control his laughter.

"Don't laugh. This is *not* funny." Tiffany rubbed at her face refusing to meet his eyes. Her hands were shaking.

Sobered, Jake nodded his agreement. "You're right. It's not. Sit tight. I'm going to get your pills."

Tiffany watched him go, scraping a fingernail across one of her cucumber-encrusted cheeks. It figured Jake would show up tonight; he always seemed to be around at her most embarrassing moments. And she really couldn't blame him for almost laughing at her. She made a ridiculous sight. If she wasn't so tired, Tiffany figured she might be able to see some humor in the situation herself. As it was, she was just glad the entire ordeal was over.

Leaning her head against the cushions, Tiffany tried to halt the fine trembling of her muscles. Still, shaken by her ordeal, she felt absurdly grateful for Jake's strong, reliable presence.

"Here, take these."

Jake's deep voice interrupted her thoughts and Tiffany took the pill bottle and water he held out to her. "Thanks."

She glanced at Jake as she swallowed the medicine, expecting humor to be dancing in his eyes. Instead she saw anger and frustration barely contained beneath a facade of unyielding calm.

Tiffany wondered about the man beneath the surface. Wondered at the shadows and secrets she saw in his eyes. No doubt Jake's years as a city police officer had toughened him. But what else had made him the man she saw?

Though they had shared several conversations and Jake knew much about Tiffany's life, she realized she knew nothing about him. Not where he had grown up, or who his parents were, or why he'd come to Lakeview.

That she wanted to know those things worried her. A year ago she'd been curious about Brian McMath and look where that had brought her. Not to mention several curiosities during her college years...all ending with someone's heart broken. Usually hers.

Tiffany forced her gaze away from Jake. Forced her mind away from the questions that begged for answers. She'd learned her lesson. God would have to drop a man down through the roof of her house before she showed interest in one again. Especially one who seemed so determined to keep from being known.

"Do you think you're up to telling me what happened?"

At the sound of Jake's voice Tiffany choked on the water she had been swallowing. Coughing violently, she leaned forward and tried to catch her breath.

Jake's large hand thumped rhythmically against her back. "You okay?"

Finally catching her breath, Tiffany sat up and managed to nod. "Yes, I just swallowed the wrong way."

Jake waited another minute while Tiffany wiped at her watering eyes. "If you want I can leave and send someone out tomorrow to take your statement."

The thought of Jake leaving her alone in the house sent fear crawling up Tiffany's spine. It was an unfamiliar and unwelcome feeling. "No, I'd just as soon get it over with now."

"All right. Why don't you tell me how you knew someone was in the house?"

Tiffany described what had happened, giving as many details as she could remember, struggling to put facts in place of feelings and to describe what had been, not what she imagined had been.

Jake scribbled notes across a small pad of paper, asking questions here and there to clarify what Tiffany said, but mostly remaining silent. When Tiffany's story wound to an end, he slipped the notebook into the shirt pocket of his uniform along with the pen. "Good enough. I've taken some fingerprints. If you can come down to the station tomorrow, we'll get your prints and a list of the people who have been in the house in the past few days."

"Do you think whoever was here left his prints?"

"It's too soon to tell. The chisel had prints on it. Whether or not they belong to your intruder remains to be seen. Finding prints, unfortunately, doesn't mean we catch the bad guy."

Tiffany nodded. "I'm hoping you can match any prints you find." She didn't say that she wouldn't rest easy until the person was caught.

"I'm hoping for the same thing." Jake surveyed the room, his gaze resting on the windows. "In the meantime, a security system might be a good idea."

"You think he'll be back?"

"I'm not sure. I do think that the break-in had something to do with Tom. And I also think there's going to be more trouble before the summer is over. I'd hate for you to be part of it."

"Me, too." Tiffany shuddered at the thought of another intruder.

"I hate to bring it up again, but—"

"I can't fire Tom. It would ruin him."

Jake ran a hand through his hair and began pacing the room, frustration in every line of his body. "Look, I can't tell you what to do. I won't even try, but I'd be lying if I said I wasn't worried about your safety."

"I appreciate your concern, but I can't see why anyone would want to harm me. Besides, there hasn't been any violent crime this summer. Just a bunch of childish pranks. Tom's group of friends—"

Jake turned, his eyes blazing. "Gang, Tiffany. Not group. There's a difference. One is harmless. The other isn't."

"Still, they don't have any reason to harm *me*."

"You don't get it do you?" Jake's voice was low, his face cold. "They don't *need* a reason. You're here. You've stolen the loyalty of one of their members. They want revenge. Maybe a chance to get Tom back. Or maybe a chance to get back at him. Whatever the case, you're the way to do it."

Tiffany couldn't respond. Could think of nothing to say in the face of Jake's anger. Instead she grabbed her empty water glass and stood. "I need more to drink."

Before he could respond she fled the room.

Jake cursed himself for an idiot and followed her into the kitchen. He hadn't meant to be so harsh. Hadn't meant to sound as if anything that had happened was Tiffany's fault. She deserved better.

Tiffany stood facing the sink, her gaze fixed on some point beyond the window. He walked toward her, noting the fatigue and tension that bowed her shoulders. "I'm sorry. I shouldn't have been so harsh."

"It's okay."

Jake placed a hand on her shoulder, urging her to turn and face him. "No, it isn't okay. I'm frustrated. I spent most of the day trying to track down members of Tom's gang and didn't have much luck. I'm worried about you. About Tom. And about the safety of Lakeview residents. But it isn't your fault and I shouldn't have acted like it was."

"I understand." Her eyes held sympathy, compassion and forgiveness.

"You remind me of Will." The words were out before Jake knew he was thinking them.

"Will?"

"My partner when I worked in D.C. He was also my best friend."

"Was?"

"He was killed last year. A single bullet to the chest, fired by a kid he'd been mentoring for over a year. We were called in on a report of a robbery. Will saw the kid running from the scene, called for him to halt, but never pulled his gun. He believed in that kid. Believed he was redeemable. He's dead because of it."

"That's terrible. I'm so sorry."

Jake was, too, but he didn't have the heart to talk about it anymore. "Look, I know you want to trust Tom. I won't tell you not to. Just be careful. Don't take any chances."

"I won't."

"Good. And get that security system. The sooner the better."

A shadow darkened Tiffany's eyes, and she nodded. "I will, not that it'll do me any good tonight."

"You'll be okay. Bandit will let you know if there's anyone prowling around."

"I'd rather have a housemate. Or better yet a husband.

The Incredible Hulk type. Big muscles. Bad temper. No one would dare come near me."

Jake laughed, the sound bursting past the tension and frustration he felt. "You'd really want a big, ugly monster living with you?"

"It'd be better than being alone." Though Tiffany's voice was light, Jake could sense the truth behind her words.

"Being alone isn't so bad. There's lots of benefits to it."

"Like what?"

"Like freedom to do what you want when you want. Never having to worry about someone else worrying about you. No one around to tell you what to eat or when to eat it. Watching TV until two in the morning, eating ice cream out of the carton, leaving dishes in the sink—none of those things are a problem when you live alone."

Tiffany smiled at Jake's assessment of single life. She had to admit she enjoyed her freedom. "True. Ice cream out of the carton tastes better, but living alone can still be tedious and lonely."

"I've found that some of the loneliest people live in houses overflowing with life."

"That's true. Besides, I'm not the marrying kind."

"No?"

"No. I don't think marriage and family are in God's plan for me." She'd meant to sound flip. Instead she sounded sad.

Jake was silent for a moment, his gaze so intent Tiffany felt the heat of embarrassment spread across her face. When he spoke, his words were gruff, almost grudging. "You're not going to be alone forever. You're the kind of woman that *should* be married."

"So, you think some people shouldn't be?"

"Without a doubt."

Jake's words were so emphatic, Tiffany couldn't help but

wonder if he was thinking of himself when he spoke them. She was tempted to ask him but decided against it. "Well, I'm probably one of them."

"No. You're the marrying kind. You just have to be willing to wait on God's timing."

"Great, so I might be 105, walking down the aisle with Bandit the fourth limping along behind me."

Jake laughed. Not just a chuckle, but a full-bodied, warm laugh that shivered up Tiffany's spine and sent her heart racing. "I doubt it. But at least in the meantime, you won't be completely alone."

He gestured to the mudroom, where Bandit had appeared. "Looks like the mutt has been doing his Houdini routine again."

They both watched as Bandit made his way across the floor and curled up near Tiffany's feet. She reached down and scratched him behind the ears. "I suppose having him around *is* some consolation. How'd you get in here, boy?"

"Probably the mudroom door. Which reminds me, I need to rig some kind of lock to keep the door secure for the night. Why don't you go rest while I take care of it?"

"I'll be fine."

"The migraine is gone?"

"It's negligible. If I catch them before the pain gets intense, the medicine usually works quickly."

"Do you have any tools?"

"Yes, there's a small box under the sink."

Jake quickly located what he needed, grabbing a hammer and a handful of nails from the toolbox. "How about plywood? Or, better yet, a couple of two-by-fours?"

Tiffany's lip twitched at the thought of her door barricaded shut. "You're not serious? You don't think that's overkill?"

"It's up to you, but the lock is completely destroyed and the entire mechanism needs to be replaced. I couldn't get the door to latch shut properly when I tried earlier. I can probably get it to close, but rigging a replacement lock won't be any more effective than the one you had before."

Tiffany pictured a masked intruder skulking in the shadows outside her house waiting for Jake to leave so he could break in and finish what he'd started. "There are some boards in the basement."

"Good." Jake opened the door that led into the basement—a dark, dank area of the house that Tiffany seldom entered—and disappeared down the steps.

Chapter Eleven

While Jake searched for the boards, Tiffany brewed some coffee and set out a plate of cookies. Then she went into the powder room and tried to scrub the mask off her face.

"I've got the boards." Jake's voice drifted out from the kitchen. "I'll just hammer a couple onto the door and wall. That should keep you secure for the night."

"Thanks." Tiffany dried her face and hurried out of the room, then followed the sound of hammering to the mudroom. Jake held a two-by-four in one hand and pounded a nail into the wood with the other. He glanced up as she walked into the room, his gaze drifting across Tiffany's partially scrubbed face.

She thought he would comment. Instead, he gestured toward the door. "A hard kick from the outside might be enough to loosen the board, so I'm going to hammer in a couple more, if you don't mind."

"Go ahead. I brewed some coffee. Would you like a cup?"

"Sounds good. I'll finish this first, though."

"Want me to hold one end of the board for you?"

Jake hesitated and Tiffany was sure he would turn down her offer of help. Then he shrugged and nodded. "That would make things a little easier. Thanks."

They worked in companionable silence, Tiffany holding the boards as Jake hammered. At times his shoulder would brush against her arm, or the warmth of his breath would fan her cheek. If Tiffany's skin tingled a bit, if warmth spread from each point of contact, she told herself what she felt was a reaction to stress and the sudden waning of the adrenaline that had been pumping through her system.

By the time the last board had been hammered up, her nerves were on edge. Backing away from Jake she tried not to acknowledge how much his presence affected her. "I'll go pour the coffee. Do you take cream or sugar?"

"Black is good." Jake looked up from the tools he was replacing, his expression so intense Tiffany was sure he knew the feelings he evoked in her.

She turned away, hurrying into the kitchen and busying herself with the coffee. Even then her mind jumped from thought to thought, her brain refusing to accept what her body was telling her.

Chemistry. That's what she felt when she stood near Jake. A deep, visceral response to his presence that was unlike anything she'd felt for Brian. She'd never worried that it was missing from their relationship, assuming that friendship and mutual respect were more important than gut-level attraction.

Now she wondered if she'd been wrong.

She both respected and admired Jake. The attraction she felt for him enhanced those feelings and she imagined if they were dating the combination would be powerful.

Was that *what romantic love was about?*

Hot coffee splashed onto the counter, overflowing from the mug she'd been pouring it into. Tiffany grabbed paper towels and wiped up the mess. Then took a sip of the scalding liquid, hoping the caffeine would jolt some sense into her.

She'd dated enough men to know that her reaction to Jake was unusual. But love? Even thinking the word in conjunction with Jake made her blush. She barely knew the man. Yet she couldn't help believing that with a little encouragement love was exactly what she would feel.

"The coffee smells good. Do you plan to share?"

Startled, Tiffany sloshed coffee from her over-full cup, and turned to face Jake. "Sure. Grab a mug and I'll pour you some."

He did as she suggested, then leaned against the counter, sipping the hot liquid. A shadowy beard colored his jaw, and fatigue pulled at the edges of his eyes. Still Jake seemed content to linger despite the late hour.

Tiffany didn't mind. It was nice having someone to keep her company. If that someone happened to be strong and capable of discouraging would-be intruders, all the better. Smiling a little at the thought, Tiffany slid the plate of cookies in Jake's direction. "Have a cookie."

Jake raised an eyebrow at Tiffany's tone. "You seem cheerful all the sudden." He grabbed a cookie and bit into it.

"I was just thinking how handy you are to have around."

"Yeah?" Jake grabbed another cookie.

"Yeah. You know how to use a hammer and you're good at scaring away the bad guys. Not to mention companionship potential. That's a heady combination. Someday you'll make someone a fine husband."

Tiffany had meant it as a joke but it was obvious from

Jake's expression he didn't find her words amusing. "I tried that before. It didn't work out."

"I didn't realize...I'm sorry."

"Don't worry about it." The words were terse, designed to cut off any discussion before it got started.

Tiffany knew she should take the hint, but curiosity got the better of her. "Did you manage to stay friends? So many people do, nowadays. I suppose that might make it easier."

"I doubt anything could make it easier." Jake ran a hand through his hair and took another sip of coffee, eyeing Tiffany over the rim. When he spoke again his voice was less harsh. "And no, we didn't stay friends. Maybe we were never friends to begin with."

"That's sad."

"Yeah. It is. Which is why I'm not planning to go down that road again."

"Did she?"

"Sheila? Get married again? No. She was a party gal. Liked to play hard and drink hard. Eventually that caught up with her. She was killed in a car accident a few years ago. Got drunk and ran her car off the road."

"How horrible."

Jake nodded. There was sadness in his eyes, and regret. Tiffany thought he might put down his coffee and leave. Escape her and the conversation she should have left well enough alone. Instead he reached for a third cookie.

"The cookies are good. Did you bake them?"

For a moment Tiffany considered ignoring the blatant change of subject, but the set look on Jake's face warned her to let it go. "Actually, I didn't. My mother did."

"Lucky you, having a mom who still bakes cookies for you."

"She is pretty great." Tiffany smiled, remembering her

mother's excuse for bringing the cookies. "She insisted she'd made them for my nieces and just thought I might enjoy a few."

"And you don't believe her?"

"No." Tiffany picked up a cookie and bit into it. "The girls hate raisins. As a matter of fact, I'm the only one in the family who likes them. Mom made these cookies for me. Guess she figured I could use some comfort food."

"Can you?"

"Not for the reasons she thinks."

"Meaning?"

"Meaning, she thinks I miss Brian." Tiffany finished the cookie and brushed crumbs from her hands. "I don't."

Jake's face softened, the lines of tension easing as he relaxed against the counter. Apparently he was more comfortable talking about Tiffany than he was talking about himself. "Really? According to at least six women who were chatting at the diner, you're pining away for McMath."

A bit of humor curled at the edges of Jake's mouth and Tiffany felt her own lips curving in response. "That's exactly what they were saying at the Cut'N'Dry when I was there earlier."

"You had your hair done today?"

Tiffany saw surprise in Jake's eyes as he surveyed the mass of lacquered hair plastered to her head. "Actually, no. I managed this" Tiffany reached up and touched her stiff hair "all by myself. I was at the Cut'N'Dry installing a new computer system. The owner wants to keep up with some of the fancy salons in Lynchburg."

"And the women just chatted about you to your face?"

"Of course not. They waited until I went into the back office. They just didn't realize how well their voices carried over the sound of the hair dryers."

Jake smiled, his gaze steady on Tiffany as she sipped coffee.

Flustered by his unwavering stare, Tiffany reached up and touched her hair. "I've got to get this stuff out of my hair before it sets permanently."

"I've been wanting to ask you about that all night." He reached out and rubbed a finger against the side of her face. "And this."

"This?" Tiffany tried to pretend the touch of his warm skin against hers had nothing to do with the sudden increase in her heart rate.

"The green stuff you had on your face." He lifted his finger, showing Tiffany a smudge of green. "I've been wondering if it's part of some female beauty ritual."

"More like cucumber and avocado. The jar said it would 'lift and tone and add elasticity.'" Tiffany ran a hand over her face, feeling the dry spots where bits of mask remained. "It didn't mention it would stick like glue. I think the only thing that will get the rest of this off is a hot shower."

Jake nodded, straightening to his full height. "Guess I'd better leave you to it."

The words sent fear shooting along Tiffany's nerves. Surprised by the intense emotion, she turned away from Jake, trying to pull herself together. Placing leftover cookies in the jar and rinsing out the coffeepot did little to still the frantic pounding of her heart. She'd never had cause to fear being alone, but now she questioned her safety. Someone had come into her sanctuary and ripped to shreds the contentment and security she had always felt there.

Jake saw fear in the brightness of Tiffany's eyes and the too cheerful way she tidied the kitchen. Despite his determination to keep his distance, he moved beside her and laid a hand over hers, stilling its motion as she moved to wipe the counter for the fifth time. "You're scared."

Tiffany didn't look at him, just ran a weary hand across her eyes. "I shouldn't be. But I am."

"You have a right to be afraid."

"I feel like a fool." Tiffany finally met Jake's gaze, her green eyes shimmering with unshed tears. "But I'm scared out of my mind. I keep thinking I'll get in the shower and when I come out, he'll be waiting for me."

"He won't be. Your house is secure."

"How can I know that? I thought it was secure before."

Jake understood her fear. He'd seen it many times in the aftermath of crime. "What you're feeling is a normal reaction to what happened tonight. I'd be worried if you weren't scared."

"Well, I suppose I should be thankful I'm not the only coward in the world."

It was as natural as breathing for Jake to lay a hand against the back of Tiffany's neck, kneading muscles gone tight with tension. "You're not a coward."

"I feel like one."

"You're exhausted. You can't rely on your feelings." Jake could feel Tiffany relaxing under his firm ministrations. "Look, go take a shower. I'll wait here until you're done and then we'll walk through the house together. Make sure everything's secure."

"Jake, I appreciate your offer, but I've taken up enough of your time in the past few weeks. I'll be fine."

"I may not be husband material, but I do know how to be a friend. Go take your shower."

For a moment Jake thought Tiffany would argue but in the end she nodded. "Okay. Thanks. I won't be long."

Fifteen minutes later Jake heard the soft creak of wood

and the faint thud of Tiffany's feet on the stairs. True to her word, she hadn't taken long. Jake stood and stretched, waiting for her to enter the room.

When she did, he caught his breath in surprise. Dressed in denim shorts and a well-worn T-shirt, damp hair curling around a face devoid of makeup, she shouldn't have been so attractive.

She was.

A light berry scent drifted on the air as Tiffany moved across the room. Her skin, still pink from the heat of the shower, glowed with health. When she spotted Jake, the tiny frown that creased her forehead eased and her eyes lighted with a smile seconds before her lips curved upward.

And Jake knew he was in trouble.

He'd never known a woman like Tiffany. She had a combination of strength, intelligence and persistence that might have been overpowering if it hadn't been tempered with compassion and love for those around her. And beneath all those things, hidden by layers of confidence, was an intense desire to be valued for who she was, to be accepted and to be loved. This vulnerability, as much as Tiffany's strength, drew Jake to her.

Strength and vulnerability. Jake had grown up believing one to be exclusive from the other. His father had the strength in their family, his mother the vulnerable neediness. Only after becoming a Christian and reading about the life of Jesus, had he realized a man could be both strong and gentle.

Perhaps if he had learned that sooner, he might have been a better husband to Sheila. As it was, the past lived too vividly in Jake's mind for him to ever risk a committed relationship again.

Especially not with someone like Tiffany. Someone who

deserved love, respect and commitment. Not emotional distance and little attention. Swallowing down regret, Jake grabbed his coffee cup and drank the last of the cold brew.

"Is something wrong?"

Jake shook his head. "No. Just gathering wool."

"I doubt that. You seem like the kind of person who's always thinking, planning ahead, laying out his next course of action."

Amused by Tiffany's assessment of his personality, Jake smiled. "That about sums it up."

"I thought so." Tiffany walked past him and sank onto a wood chair.

"Why?"

"My father is a thinker and planner, too. I can't count how many times I've seen him wearing almost exactly the same look you just had on your face."

"What look?"

"The look that says, 'There's a problem here and I plan to fix it.'"

Surprised by her insight, Jake didn't comment.

"So, want to share? You've helped me plenty, maybe I can give you a hand solving whatever problem you're having."

Tiffany's words were spoken with such sincerity and enthusiasm, Jake didn't have the heart to brush her off. "I'm just wondering who broke into your house." The statement was true, if not precisely what he had been worrying about.

He could tell by the look in Tiffany's green eyes she didn't believe him. "Oh, well, that is definitely something I can't help you with."

"Don't worry. I have a plan."

The words elicited a laugh from Tiffany, as they were meant to.

"Which begins with me walking through your house with you."

Offering a hand, he pulled Tiffany to her feet. Only when she turned to push in the chair did he notice the bluish purple lump behind her ear. Partially hidden by hair, it looked to be the size of an egg, round and hard and painful looking. Reaching out a hand, Jake smoothed damp curls away from the area and took a closer look.

"How did *this* happen?"

Jake's touch startled Tiffany and she turned to look at him, only to be forestalled by gentle pressure against the bruise on the side of her head. Wincing, she stopped moving and gritted her teeth against the pain. "I hit the wall sconce when the guy who broke in shoved past me."

"You must have hit it pretty hard. I thought you told me he just pushed by you." Jake's fingers continued to explore the swollen knot of flesh, the gentleness of his touch belying the anger in his voice.

Tiffany felt surprised by both. "He did. But he was in a hurry and I was in the way."

"A light shove doesn't do this much damage. No wonder your head hurt earlier." Jake gestured to the chair Tiffany had just pushed in. "Sit down. You need to put some ice on that."

Tiffany wanted to argue but she figured if Jake was as much like her father as she suspected, he'd just come up with reasons she should do as he asked. With a sigh of resignation, she lowered herself into a chair.

"Here." A plastic bag filled with ice was thrust into her hand and Tiffany dutifully applied it to the bruise. Jake hovered beside her shaking his head, a smile easing some of the anger from his eyes.

"What?"

"Nothing."

"You're shaking your head and smirking at me. I want to know why."

"I'm just in awe of your trouble-finding capabilities."

"I don't find trouble."

"You're right. You don't. It finds you."

"I can't help it. Trouble is the story of my life lately." The words were said on a sigh but Tiffany felt a smile tugging at her lips.

"No, I suppose you can't help it any more than I can." Jake's grin remained in place but it was joined by something that made Tiffany's heart beat faster and her mouth go dry.

"Can what?"

"Help it."

"Help what?" She must have hit her head harder than she thought. She had no idea what Jake was talking about.

"Help wanting to kiss you." Jake's grin was gone, his eyes once the color of summer sky had darkened to midnight.

For the first time in recent history Tiffany was speechless. "Should I take your silence for consent?" Before Tiffany could think of a response, Jake lowered his head and leaned in close. "You have lovely eyes. That's the first thing I noticed about you. Dark green eyes are very unusual."

"They are?" The words squeaked out of a mouth gone dry as the Sahara desert.

"Yes. And so are women who believe the best of people even when they don't deserve it. Women who care more for others than for themselves." Only a breath of air separated them, and Tiffany could see herself in the depth of Jake's eyes. "You are a uniquely beautiful woman in every way. Is it any wonder I want to kiss you?"

"Umm. No?"

Jake laughed, raising his hands to cup Tiffany's face. Her skin tingled where his hands rested, creating heat where none had been. "That's one of the things I find so appealing about you. Your ability to laugh at everything life throws your way."

The words, the touch, the steady gaze—they were entrancing. Tiffany fought the urge to lean closer, to close the tiny gap that remained between them. She told herself that she should pull away, stand up, make light of the intense moment.

But her body refused to cooperate with her common sense. Jake looked at her as no one else had, his gaze sweeping along the curve of her cheek, the line of her jaw, and resting on her mouth before returning to its journey. His fingers moved, too, curling into her hair and smoothing down its length.

Tiffany sensed that he struggled with his own indecision and she wondered which she wanted more, for him to lean in closer or pull away.

Then, on a sigh, Jake lowered his mouth to hers.

She had waited her whole life for this—the gentle warmth of Jake's lips against hers, the barely constrained passion that showed in the restless movements of his hands. When he finally pulled back, Tiffany felt abandoned and alone. Dazed, she looked up into his stormy eyes.

"I shouldn't have done that. I'm sorry."

Stunned by the kiss and hurt that he would so soon regret what had happened between them, Tiffany mumbled the first thing she thought of. "It's okay. I understand."

"You do?" There was humor in Jake's voice, as well as self-deprecation.

"Yes, it's late. We're both tired. We've had a traumatic experience—"

"*You* have had a traumatic experience."

"Well, yes, that's true but I'm sure the excitement—"

"The excitement had nothing to do with it. You did."

"Oh. I see."

"No, I don't think you do. I've admired you since the day you pulled Bandit out of the lake. The more I know of you, the more I want to know and if things were different, I'd be asking you to dinner. But I'm not the guy for you and I don't want to hurt you."

"You would never hurt me."

"I would."

"Jake—"

"God has someone special planned for you, Tiffany. I don't want to be in the way when he shows up."

Before Tiffany could comment, Jake stood up and moved away. "I need to go. Let's do a quick walk-through of your house."

Without another word, he strode into the hall.

Chapter Twelve

The following day Tiffany left the house early, hoping to conduct her business at the police station and be back home in time to meet with a locksmith and an alarm company representative later in the day.

It took three hours to be interviewed, fingerprinted and told she'd be called if there was any information about the case. The process would have taken half the time if Tiffany hadn't known most of the people that worked at the station. Each of them had to express anger at Tiffany's break-in and sorrow over her breakup. Usually she would have enjoyed the chitchat, but her nerves were on edge, her equilibrium disturbed by a culmination of the past few weeks' events.

And the kiss.

Tiffany willingly admitted to herself that Jake's kiss had left her shaken. Her early trip to the police station had as much to do with a desire to avoid him as it did with wanting to get home at a decent time. So why did her eyes stray while she chatted? Why did she look up every time a door opened? If, as she told herself, she wanted to avoid the man, why was she looking for him around every corner?

Unwilling to think about the answers to those questions, Tiffany left the station and stopped at Becky's Diner for lunch. She hoped the crowded diner would distract her from her thoughts but the hubbub of activity did little to soothe her feelings. The garden salad she ordered looked delicious, the lettuce crisp, the vegetables shiny and fresh. Tiffany ate alone, nearly choking on every bite, until she finally gave up and pushed the plate away.

She hated salad. She hated eating alone. She hated...

"You look fit to be tied. I can't recall ever seeing you look so angry. Something to do with last night?"

For a moment Tiffany's heart froze. Did the whole town know about the kiss? "Last night?"

Doris slid into the booth across from her, brown face creased with worry. "Heard there was trouble at your house last night."

Relieved, Tiffany tried to smile. "Not much. Just some vandalism. How did you hear about it?"

"Girl, you know rumors fly fast and far around here." Doris's dark eyes flashed with humor. "Besides Henry Simmons came in for coffee this morning. He had himself all worked up about it. Kept sayin' a woman needs a man to ease her way through the world. I about hit him over the head with a frying pan."

"You seem to have done okay without a man."

"Oh, I had one once. A long time ago." Eyes staring into the distance, Doris seemed sad, almost frail.

Tiffany reached out and touched her hand. "I didn't know you'd been married."

"Married? It never did get that far." Doris shook her head, smiling at some memory. "We planned to. I even had a white dress picked out for the occasion."

"What happened?"

"He died. Killed fighting a war that wasn't a war."

"I'm so sorry."

Doris shook her head again, the motion brusque. "No need. Like I said it was a long time ago."

"And you never met anyone else you could love?"

"Sometimes it's like that. A man is just so right, no other man will ever do."

The story was romantic and sad, a story that Tiffany would have liked to hear more about.

Doris forestalled any further questions by asking one of her own. "So, is that what's botherin' you? Man trouble? Seems to me you haven't been happy since you broke up with Doc Brian."

"That's not true. I'm very happy."

"Yeah? The frown lines you're cultivatin' say different."

"I'm fine, I just don't like salad."

"Then why eat it?"

"Isn't it obvious? I'm fat, I'm over thirty, and I'm single."

"Is that self-pity I hear? Your mother would be surprised at you, sitting here feelin' sorry for yourself when you have so much to be thankful for." Doris was right, Tiffany knew it, but knowing it didn't make her feel any better. "Besides, you may be over thirty and you may be single but you're not fat. You're gettin' downright scrawny in my opinion."

"Right."

"My opinion not good enough for you? Fine, we'll ask somebody else. Be right back."

Tiffany saw the gleam in Doris's eyes a moment too late. Before she could protest the older woman had hopped up from her seat and moved with surprising swiftness through the crowded tables.

She was back a moment later, an unmistakable figure following along behind. Doris's voice could be heard clearly above the lunch crowd din. "I sure appreciate your opinion on this, Sheriff Reed. You seem like a man of refined taste, no doubt you know more about a lot of things, what with living in the city and all."

"Miss Doris, I've lived in the city but I'm not much on art—"

"Oh, did you think I was talkin' about art?"

"You did say a picture?"

"Well, Tiffany is a picture of loveliness this afternoon, don't you think?" Tiffany watched, humiliated, as Jake's gaze traveled toward the booth. A flicker of surprise glimmered in his eyes, replaced quickly by an emotion Tiffany couldn't quite put her finger on. Regret for last night more than likely. Just thinking about the kiss and Jake's apology had Tiffany's cheeks burning with embarrassment.

"Tiffany was saying she had to force-feed herself that salad. Not much of a meal in my opinion. Especially not for someone as skinny as her. What do you think, Sheriff Reed? The girl should be eating more than salad, right?"

A smile touched the corner of Jake's mouth and Tiffany felt her face heating even more. "I'd say one of those pot pies you're famous for would be in order here, Miss Doris. Maybe a bowl of chocolate pudding with whipped cream for dessert."

"Just what I was thinkin', Sheriff. Why don't you sit down there across from Tiffany and wait for your sandwich. Won't be more than a few minutes."

Tiffany watched the exchange with amused resignation.

Doris was wily as a fox and had matchmaking down to a science. Jake had just walked into her trap.

"No, I—"

"Sit. Your other seat's already gone. This place is hoppin' today." Jake's gaze drifted across the crowded room before he reluctantly admitted defeat and slid into the booth across from Tiffany. With a nod of approval, Doris walked away.

Tiffany picked at her salad and studiously avoided Jake's eyes. He had made his position clear the night before. The kiss had been mistake. Covering his blunder with a pretense of nobility had only added to Tiffany's humiliation. Just thinking about his "there is somebody out there for you" speech brought fresh color to Tiffany's cheeks and filled her with an absurd urge to cry. Pushing the plate of lettuce away, she stood. "I'm finished. Guess I'll be on my way."

"Can you stay for a minute? I planned to stop by your house after lunch. This will save some time."

"Of course." Sliding back into the booth, Tiffany grabbed the glass of water she had been sipping and took a few gulps, still avoiding eye contact.

"Did you make it to the station this morning?"

"Yes, I was fingerprinted and I gave a list of people who visited the house last week."

"Good. We can get working on the prints I took last night. Who knows? We might get lucky."

"But you're not holding out hope."

"No. And unfortunately I can't make arrests based on speculation."

"You think you know who broke in?" Startled, Tiffany looked up and met Jake's gaze.

"I have some ideas. A few Main Street shop owners have seen a group of teens wandering around town. Mostly summer kids."

"Have you gotten any names?"

"A few. I'm going to feel Tom out today. See if he wants to give me more information now that your house has been broken into."

"I doubt he knows anything."

"We'll see. One way or another I'm going to talk to some kids and parents this evening. Let them know that we're keeping an eye on them."

"Maybe that'll take care of the problem."

Jake doubted it, but didn't say as much. "How's your head feeling?"

"Fine."

"No pain?"

"No more then I'd expect."

"Good." Jake eyed Tiffany's salad for a moment, then grabbed a cherry tomato, ate it and reached for another one. "Looks like Doris is bringing the food. I'm starving."

Tiffany eyed the triple layer club sandwich that Doris slid in front of Jake and ordered her stomach not to growl. When a second plate appeared in front of her, she had to bite back a groan. "Doris, I can't eat that."

"It's on the house. Enjoy."

Before Tiffany could argue further, Doris was gone.

The heady aroma of roast chicken and fresh vegetables drifted from the pot pie, and Tiffany's mouth watered as she eyed the golden crust. Her diet resolve crumbling, she figured the safest thing to do was leave. "I need to go. I've got a locksmith coming out in a few hours and I want to call a couple of home security companies before then."

Jake placed a hand on her arm, holding her in place when Tiffany would have stood. "I can give you the name of a guy who'll install a great system for a good price. Why don't you take a breather and eat your lunch?"

"I already had a salad." Tiffany saw Jake's gaze shift to the still-full salad bowl and felt her resolution waver even more. She'd barely touched the salad and she was hungry.

"Doesn't look like you ate much and Doris will get her feelings hurt if you don't take a few bites of that pot pie."

Tiffany sighed, settling back into the booth. "I know. She really is a softy under all the vinegar."

"Yeah, but don't let on that you know. She might stop giving me refills on my coffee when I work nights." Jake paused, eyeing Tiffany curiously as she picked up her fork and poked at the pie crust. "Doris is right."

"About?"

"You have lost weight since we met. You're getting scrawny."

"I'll never be scrawny."

"You're not *meant* to be scrawny but you will be if you keep picking at your food like that."

"I'm not picking at my food!"

"Yes, you are. You haven't eaten a bite. Look, *this* is how you eat." Jake reached across the table with his fork, stabbed a chunk of chicken and ate it. "Now you try."

Tiffany dutifully lifted a carrot to her mouth, almost closing her eyes in bliss as the creamy sauce met her tongue. A chunk of chicken followed the first bite and Jake nodded with approval and grinned over the half sandwich he held. "*Now* you've got the hang of it."

Tiffany grinned back and took another bite.

Half an hour later, she patted a hand against her stomach and groaned. "I ate way too much. You shouldn't have encouraged me."

"I only suggested that you try Doris's strawberry cheesecake. I didn't force it down your throat." Jake's eyes danced with humor and Tiffany couldn't help smiling in return.

"That's true. I guess I only have myself to blame for the extra two miles I'm going to have to run tonight."

"You're not going running alone, are you?"

"No, Bandit will be with me."

"Be careful anyway. If you can, find a friend to go with you."

Tiffany nodded; she wasn't sure she'd go out at all. The incident the night before had scared her, giving her a new sense of her own vulnerability. "I may just use my treadmill. I hate it, but for now it might be safer. Which reminds me, if I don't leave now, I'll miss the locksmith." Tiffany stood, dug through her purse and laid several dollar bills on the table.

"I'll walk out with you." A true gentleman, Jake held Tiffany's elbow as they made their way through the crowded room and out the door.

The sun had heated the air to an almost unbreathable temperature and Tiffany gasped as she left the coolness of the diner. "Today is another scorcher. I hope Tom is taking a break during the worst of this heat."

"He showed up for work today?"

"Yes. His father doesn't have a weekend run, so Tom asked if he could work. Why?"

"Just wondered if he knew about last night."

"He seemed surprised when he saw the damage, but even if he did know, it wouldn't mean much. Everyone in town seems to know what happened."

"True." Though Jake agreed, Tiffany could hear the doubt in his voice and knew he suspected Tom's involvement in her troubles.

She resisted the urge to argue on Tom's behalf. "Will you let me know if you find out anything?"

"Sure."

They reached Tiffany's car and she fished in her purse for her keys, her hand pausing in its exploration when Jake leaned in close, his fingers probing the still swollen flesh behind her ear. "This has got to hurt more than a little."

"It's not that bad. Really."

"Good. I was worried you might have done more damage than you thought."

"Nope." Tiffany's fingers clasped around her keys and she pulled them from her purse, hoping all the while that Jake wouldn't mention the kiss they'd shared.

"Tiffany, I wanted to talk to you about something besides the break-in."

"I hope I haven't committed some crime I'm unaware of."

Jake didn't respond to her jocular tone. "It's about last night—"

Raising a hand, Tiffany stopped the words before they both regretted them. "Jake, I want to put last night behind us. I enjoy your company and your friendship. I understand what happened last night was a mistake. Let's not rehash the whole thing."

Before he had time to respond, she opened the car door and closed it behind her. She could feel Jake watching as she backed out of the parking space and drove away, but Tiffany refused to do more than send a quick wave in his direction.

The kiss had affected her profoundly. She'd seen more than stars; she'd seen the future. Now she had to backtrack, accept that Jake thought he'd made a mistake, and try hard not to fall in love with a man who seemed to be everything she wanted and all that she couldn't have.

As she pulled the car onto Monroe Street and headed for home, Tiffany had a sinking suspicion it was already too late for that.

* * *

If Jake hadn't made plans to go fishing with Ben Avery, he would have spent the rest of the afternoon alone. He felt irritable and angry and wasn't sure why. The conversation he'd had with Tiffany had gone as he'd hoped. Though he hadn't expected her to anticipate his words, speak them for him and drive away before he could respond, all in all, Jake would say he'd accomplished his goal—to make sure that Tiffany understood there was no future for them aside from friendship.

He should feel relief and satisfaction. Instead he felt like ripping someone's head off. A few hours alone might have solved the problem, giving Jake time to figure out what was bugging him and put it to rest. Unfortunately, plans for the fishing expedition had been made a month in advance and he didn't want to disappoint the only fishing buddy he had. Besides, he couldn't have given a reasonable excuse for canceling.

Now, as Ben stared him down, Jake wished he had been able to come up with one. The man had a knack for sensing the moods of those around him, even if those moods were well hidden. And Jake wasn't all that sure his were. "You gonna stare at me all day?"

"Just trying to figure out what's eating you, friend. No need to get testy."

"I'm not testy."

"No?"

"No."

Silence enveloped the boat again and Jake knew Ben was waiting for him to speak. His friend's gaze remained steady as Jake selected a lure, baited the hook and cast his line.

With a sigh, Jake gave him part of the story. "There's nothing wrong with me. Just having a bad day after a long night."

"I heard about Tiffany Anderson's trouble. Is that what kept you up?"

"Partly. I have night patrol this week so I would have been up anyway."

Ben sent a look in Jake's direction as he baited his own hook with a worm. "Look, I don't want to pry." He paused, smiled and started again. "Well, actually I do. Why don't you just tell me what's bugging you? I might be able to help."

"It's complicated."

"So? Sharing might make it seem less so."

Jake considered Ben's words, knowing his friend wouldn't push for an answer as surely as he knew the man would be on his knees later, praying for the unspoken request. "I made a mistake last night. I regret it but I can't take back what's already been done."

"That's usually the case."

"Yeah. Well, I'm afraid I gave someone the wrong impression. And maybe hurt this person in the process. That's what's bugging me. I can't shake the guilt." Jake ran a hand through his hair and stared out across the lake.

"This is about Tiffany, isn't it?"

Jake glanced over at his friend and saw both compassion and curiosity in his eyes. "Yes. I don't know what it is about that woman, but she seems to have an affinity for finding trouble."

"And you always happen to be around when she finds it."

It wasn't a question, but Jake answered anyway. "More often than not. If I didn't know better, I'd think God was purposely throwing us together."

"Maybe He is."

"Not unless He's into cruel jokes."

Ben's eyebrows went up at the comment. "I don't see why it would have to be a joke. Tiffany is an attractive, intelligent woman. She no longer has ties to Brian McMath. I think she'd suit you perfectly."

"I don't think so." Jake's tone was sharper than it needed to be, but the conversation had taken a twist he hadn't intended.

"You're not attracted to her?"

"That's not the issue."

Ben reeled in his line, put down the rod, and turned to face Jake. "Something is going on here that I don't understand. If you want to enlighten me, fine. But don't use me to work off whatever frustration you're feeling."

Jake felt his anger rise and then deflate. "Sorry. I'm short-tempered and my attitude stinks."

"You can say that again." A smile took the sting out of Ben's words. "Now that we've got that out of the way, do you want to tell me what mistake you made with Tiffany? Or should I guess?"

"I kissed her." The words were out before Jake could think better of them. He watched as myriad emotions passed over Ben's face.

"I think I understand. You kissed Tiffany and decided afterward that it was a mistake. Now you're afraid you might have given her the wrong impression, that she might think you have more in mind for your relationship."

"Yes and no. I kissed her. I regretted it. I'm not worried about her thinking I want more from the relationship. I explained that the kiss was a mistake—"

"You actually told her that?" Ben's eyes were wide with amazement.

"Yes."

"And she let you live?" Ben didn't try to hide his broad smile.

Jake could feel his mood lifting, and his own lips curving

in response. "Can we stop joking about my problem and get to the part where you help me work it out?"

"Okay. Sorry. It's just that I still don't understand why Tiffany is such a problem to you. Even knowing you kissed her doesn't change my perspective much. She's mature enough to understand and put it behind her."

Jake nodded, wondering if *he* was. "I know, but I don't want her to think she's the kind of woman that a man can just toss away. After Brian's quick recuperation from their breakup, I'm afraid what happened between Tiffany and me might make her think she isn't desirable."

"It sounds to me like you care an awful lot about a woman that you say you want nothing to do with. Maybe you should get to know her better, give a relationship with her a try."

"Tiffany deserves someone who can offer her the things she wants most—marriage, children, a house filled with love."

"Jake, I don't see how what you and what Tiffany wants are mutually exclusive."

"I'm not getting married again. Ever."

"Not even if the right woman comes along?"

Jake didn't say that he was afraid she already had. "I promised myself a long time ago that I wouldn't repeat the mistake I made with Sheila. I don't plan to change my mind."

"Change is part of life. If we don't change we can't grow. If we don't grow, we stagnate and die. Part of changing is reevaluating the way we view the world. Maybe it's time for you to do that."

Jake shook his head. If only he *could* change his mind, undo the past, wipe the slate clean and start fresh. But he couldn't. "How I feel won't change. I made this decision long before I came here, long before I met Tiffany, but it's a decision I still stand by."

"When you married Sheila you were both young. Neither of you were Christians. You can't base who you are now on what you did back then."

"Maybe not, but I won't take a chance. Not when Tiffany's the one who'd be hurt."

"Just Tiffany?"

Jake sighed and ran a hand through his hair. "Both of us. But she more so. She's still got dreams. I gave up on mine a long time ago."

"That doesn't mean you can't make new ones. You're a new person, Jake. Made that way by Christ, not by your own effort or desires. Maybe it's time to start thinking about your life in view of that."

"Maybe."

Ben eyed Jake thoughtfully for a moment. "You know you're limiting God, don't you? Why not step out of the driver's seat for a while and let Him lead?"

Jake didn't respond. Ben was right. No doubt about it but Jake's heart refused to believe what his head accepted as truth. He shrugged by way of response and cast his line into the water.

"Think about it, Jake."

"I will."

"Good. So, any leads on Tiffany's intruder?"

"A few. Mostly speculation. When we finish here I'm going to interview a few teens and talk to their parents. Then I'll talk to Tom, see if he's willing to give me names."

"You think he'll be more willing now?"

"It's doubtful, but worth a try. And now that you've reminded me of my duties," Jake glanced at his watch, and at the sun hanging low on the horizon, "we'd better head back."

"Right. I've got some visits to make tonight, as well."

"Hospital visits?" Jake spoke as Ben started the boat motor.

"Yeah. Marta Reynolds had a minor stroke last night. She's doing well, but her husband is a wreck. I'm going to do shift duty so he can get some rest."

"Sounds like we've both got a long night ahead of us."

"A quiet night for me. Should be interesting to see if yours proves the same."

Jake nodded, but didn't comment. Compared to D.C., almost every night in Lakeview was quiet. Though if he couldn't find the person responsible for the break-in at Tiffany's, things might not stay that way. The knowledge spurred him on as he helped Ben tie the boat to the dock, and hurried to his truck. He'd find the kids responsible for this summer's trouble. Only then could he be sure that the break-ins and vandalism would stop.

And only then could he be sure Tiffany would be safe.

Chapter Thirteen

The last thing Tiffany wanted to do after a hectic week was attend another bridal shower. How many had she been to this year? Five? Six? The worst part being that there was no wedding in *her* immediate future.

She bit back a sigh of frustration and hefted the shrink-wrapped basket she'd prepared for the occasion. She should have ridden a bike. Then she wouldn't have had to park her car at the public dock. Now, after a half-mile walk in heels, Tiffany was hot, tired and ready to go home.

Unfortunately she hadn't even reached the party yet.

She shifted her grip on the gift and glanced at her watch. If she didn't hurry she'd be late. Worse, Joy Worther, the bride-to-be, might drive down the long gravel driveway and spot Tiffany struggling along with the bridal basket. She increased her pace.

After what seemed an eternity, she rounded a curve in

the driveway and spotted the large colonial that Joy had grown up in. Though Tiffany had visited several times in the past, the size of the house always amazed her. It stood boldly in the middle of acres of green lawn and had been one of the more prestigious addresses in the community for years.

The shower would be an all-out affair. One with games, prizes and all the trimmings. There would be cake and food and talk of the wedding and the honeymoon. Tiffany grimaced as she thought of the festivities. When she'd received the invitation a month ago, she'd been sure she would attend as a soon-to-be-wed woman. Instead she was going as the local spinster.

Not that she minded. Much.

She liked Joy. They'd been friends since college and Tiffany had no intention of letting her own sour mood ruin Joy's party. Besides, she figured the shower activities would keep her mind off Jake Reed. Though she hadn't seen him in a few days, thoughts of Jake and the kiss they'd shared took up too much of her time. Tiffany was determined to refocus her energy.

She hoisted up the package and glanced at the house. Faces peeked from behind heavy drapes and Tiffany smiled and nodded. She was wondering if one of the ladies would think to come and help her carry the basket when the sound of a car engine filled the air. The half-dozen women who watched her progress gestured wildly, pointing behind Tiffany and then to the trees that lined the driveway.

Obviously they were telling her to hide.

Tiffany took a firm grip on the heavy basket and dove behind the nearest tree, just as the sound of tires on gravel heralded the bride-to-be's arrival. Tiffany held her breath and waited for the car to pass.

It didn't.

She pressed closer to the rough bark of the tree, and wondered how long it would take for the story of how she'd ruined Joy's surprise to spread. She'd lay odds it would be all over town before she even left the shower.

"Is everything okay, dear?"

The voice held the trembly quality that sometimes accompanies age, and Tiffany peeked around the tree to see who was speaking. A shiny blue sedan had pulled up beside her hiding place, and the kindly face of Eva Murphy peered out from the passenger side window. With her white hair pinned in a prim bun and pink blush applied to parchment-thin skin, she looked every inch of the librarian she had once been.

Smiling, Tiffany stepped away from the tree. "I'm fine, Mrs. Murphy. I thought you were Joy."

"No. Joy is still at the church with her mother setting up for the wedding reception. I dropped off the flower arrangements and came straight here. Such a lovely idea, don't you think? Surprising her with a shower the day before her wedding."

"It certainly does make it easier to surprise her. She's probably so caught up in preparations she doesn't suspect a thing."

"You're right about that. Her mother is having a difficult time trying to get her to leave the church."

"I imagine I'd be the same way." *Not that I'll ever have to worry about it.* Tiffany shoved away the thought and stepped away from the tree, smiling at the woman who'd presented her with her first library card. "I'm glad I didn't ruin the surprise for her."

"You've always been such a thoughtful young lady." Mrs. Murphy's faded blue eyes lighted with pleasure. "What a lovely basket. Another one of your creative gift ideas, I suppose?"

"I'm afraid so." Tiffany grinned. She was well-known for finding creative gifts and presenting them in artistic ways.

"I can't wait to see what you've come up with this time. It looks heavy, Tiffany. Do you need a hand with it?"

"No, I'm fine." The words were said on a grunt as Tiffany's high-heeled foot skidded on gravel and her ankle twisted painfully.

"Of course you're not. Those shoes aren't made for gravel roads. You're going to kill yourself if you're not careful. Come. Get in the car. Sheriff Reed can drive us both up to the door and carry our packages in for us. You know he rents the rooms above my garage? Such a kind young man, and so helpful." Eva turned and smiled at Jake.

Tiffany took the opportunity to step away from the car. "Um, I don't think that's necessary. It isn't far to the house and..."

Tiffany's words trailed off as the driver's side door opened and Jake stepped out. "Mrs. Murphy is right. Gravel and high heels don't mix."

Before Tiffany could think to protest, Jake had taken the basket from her hands and slid it into the back seat of the car.

"Thanks, but I really can walk the rest of the way."

"Stop being stubborn and get in the car. Otherwise we'll *all* be jumping for the trees. Joy and her mother will be here any minute."

Though the words were spoken without reproach, they galvanized Tiffany to action. Stiffening her spine she marched the last few feet to the car, ignoring the ache in her ankle. "I am *not* stubborn." She shot the words over her shoulder as she slid into the back seat.

"Sure, and grass isn't green." Jake grinned down at her, his eyes both amused and wary.

"Mine isn't. I haven't watered it in a week." Grabbing her skirt, Tiffany yanked it out of the way as Jake shut the door.

Her ankle was beginning to throb and Tiffany glanced down, eyeing the swollen flesh.

"Is your ankle okay?" Jake spoke as he pulled the car up to the house and Tiffany raised her eyes, meeting his gaze in the rearview mirror.

"It's fine."

Liar. Tiffany heard the words as clearly as if Jake had spoken them aloud. But he hadn't, choosing instead to shoot a knowing smile in her direction before stopping the car.

As Jake gently extracted Mrs. Murphy from the front seat and led her up the wide verandah steps, Tiffany pulled the basket from the seat beside her. She had no intention of waiting for Jake's return. Though he seemed able to treat her with the same easy camaraderie they had shared from the beginning, she couldn't seem to forget their kiss. Avoiding the man was much easier than the effort she had to put into acting natural when she was around him.

"Don't even think about it." Jake's voice rumbled close to Tiffany's ear and she jumped, almost dropping the basket. "You've already nearly broken your ankle. There's no way I'm going to let you carry that thing up the steps."

"What about Mrs. Murphy?"

"She's in good hands." Jake gestured to the house where several women had converged on the elderly librarian and were helping her up the last step of the verandah.

"All right, I guess this *is* a little awkward." Tiffany handed over the basket, ignoring the warm tingle that traveled up her arm as Jake's fingers brushed hers. Anxious to escape the man who elicited such strong feelings, Tiffany moved toward the house, trying hard not to wince as pain shot up her leg.

Jake fell into step beside her. "I thought you said your ankle was fine."

"It is. I just twisted it a little."

"Let me see."

"No—" Tiffany started to protest but a handful of women stood watching from the open door of the house, their eyes curious. If she argued too much, she and Jake would be fodder for the gossip mill before the day ended. With a disgruntled sigh, she dropped down onto a wide whitewashed step and raised the hem of her skirt to display the injured ankle.

"That was easy. I thought you'd put up more of a fight." Jake's voice was low, his words meant for her ears alone, as he bent down and eyed Tiffany's ankle.

"And have the entire population of Lakeview discussing us?" Tiffany's whisper came out a hiss as Jake pressed a finger against her bruised flesh.

"And me looking at your ankle won't do that?" Jake put the basket down and pulled off her shoe.

Tiffany winced, sucking in a breath. "No, you're the sheriff. Everyone saw me fall. They'll figure it is your sworn duty to look after me. On the other hand, if I protest, they'll wonder what's gotten in to me and figure maybe there's something between us. After all, we've been seen together more than once already."

"Does that bother you?"

"No, I just don't want people getting the wrong idea."

Jake's eyes met Tiffany's for a moment, a shadow of something she couldn't name flashing through his eyes. Then he handed her the shoe and stood. Raising his voice he spoke loud enough for the small crowd of women to hear. "You were right, looks like you just wrenched it. Nothing's broken." Extending a hand, he pulled Tiffany to her feet. "You'd better get inside before Joy comes."

A murmur of excited voices followed the comment and Tiffany's mood turned even glummer than it had been. The last thing she wanted was to spend hours with a group of happy, enthusiastic friends. If she'd had any choice in the matter, she'd have stayed home and moped. Instead, she pasted a smile on her face and turned toward the group of chattering women.

"Tiffany?" Jake moved beside her, the basket still held in his long-fingered hands.

Tiffany turned to meet his gaze and froze at the emotion she saw there. Sadness, regret, loneliness. She recognized them all. Lived with them all. "Yes?"

"I need to talk to you about the break-in at your house. Can I stop by later? Or would you rather come to the station?"

"I don't know how long I'll be here."

"I don't go on duty until eight tonight. I can drop in at the beginning of my shift."

Clearly he wanted her to know the visit was purely business. Tiffany accepted his words with a brief nod. "That's fine. I'll be home." Without another glance in his direction she limped into the house.

She spent the next two hours laughing at jokes, conversing with other women, and fielding comments about Brian and his new girlfriend. Though she put on a good show, her heart felt as heavy and dull as mud. As soon as the cake was cut, she made her excuses and left, limping the half mile back to her car even though several friends offered to drive her.

She needed to be alone and she needed time to think.

When she arrived home Bandit greeted her with abandon, licking and jumping and grinning. Tiffany patted him on his head, but couldn't muster the enthusiasm it would take to play with him.

As if sensing her melancholy mood, Bandit settled down more quickly than usual, watching through soulful brown eyes.

"Don't worry, boy. I'm not depressed enough to forget to feed you dinner."

The dog whined and nudged her hand.

"Are you sympathizing or trying to get me to move faster?"

Bandit whined again.

"Okay, here you go." Moving into the mudroom, Tiffany dug a huge portion of kibble from the economy-size bag she'd bought and slid it into Bandit's bowl. Then, leaving him to eat his fill, she retreated to her sewing room.

Quilting had always relaxed her. Always helped to clear her mind of troubles. Tiffany figured she needed both right about now. She had several pieces to choose from, as she'd started four new projects as gifts for upcoming weddings and baby showers. She fingered the fabric of a blue-and-white double wedding ring quilt and considered completing it. Instead she pulled out another quilt, this one in shades of green.

The pattern was one of her own design, a sunburst of dark green in the center, with bright green and gold rays shooting out toward the edges of the quilt. Complete but for the verse she'd begun embroidering in the center of the sun, the piece seemed to have motion and depth that Tiffany hadn't planned. The gothic style lettering she'd chosen for its bold and intricate beauty added to the mystique of the quilt, gold embroidery thread contrasting brilliantly with the deep green of the sunburst.

Fingering the letters of the verse, Tiffany read it aloud, filling in the words she had yet to complete, "'Be still and know that I am God.'"

Simple, almost stark in its pronouncement, the verse touched Tiffany as no other ever had. In the rush and bustle of everyday life, she found it easy to lose sight of who she was and where she was headed. Sure, she had goals and desires but in the long run, nothing mattered but her commitment to God and her relationship with Him.

It had taken her a while to realize it, but her relationship with Brian had been too much the center of her life. In committing herself to being the kind of woman Brian wanted to date, she'd hustled and hurried, worried and fretted, until she'd all but lost sight of what God wanted. Then when she'd finally realized Brian wasn't the man for her, she'd slunk back to God like a naughty child who'd been caught playing hooky and complained that things hadn't turned out the way she wanted.

After a few days of praying and searching scripture she'd come upon the verse and from its simple, reassuring message had finally gained a measure of peace. As a child of God she had a place with Him and a direct line of communication. All she had to do was be still and wait for His direction. Omnipotent and all-knowing, He could handle the things she could not.

With that realization came freedom. Freedom from worry. Freedom from disappointment. Freedom from all the things she'd struggled with since she broke up with Brian.

Now if Tiffany could just hold on to that feeling.

She sighed, eyeing the quilt critically. Inspiration for the design had come shortly after her breakup, and she worked on the piece every time she felt lonely, frustrated, or worried about the future. Now it was almost finished, and she still hadn't found the peace she longed for.

Not that she thought about Brian anymore. No, she'd

been able to move past their relationship with an ease she found alarming.

It was Jake who haunted her. Or maybe not Jake so much as what he seemed to represent.

Beyond attraction, respect and friendship, she and Jake connected on a level that she and Brian never had. When she was with him, she felt...complete.

The word cut through Tiffany like a knife and she sagged into a chair, clutching the quilt in tense fingers as her mind flew from one thought to the next. Complete? That wasn't good. Not good at all.

She'd made a life for herself. She was strong, independent, able to take care of herself. She'd never relied on a man to fulfill her. Never asked Brian for anything other than companionship. Sure, she *wanted* marriage and children. But she didn't need them to be complete.

And yet, when she was with Jake she felt different. Better. More herself. As if suddenly she was exactly the person God intended her to be.

"That's insane." Tiffany stood, shoved the quilt onto the cutting table and stalked to the window.

It was the kiss. It had thrown her. No doubt about it.

Tiffany rubbed the tension from her neck and stared out at late-afternoon beauty. She imagined the soft call of bullfrogs and sweet trills of songbirds. The fragrant scent of summer grass and the moist breeze that blew across the lake.

Home. She'd made this place for herself. The faded old Victorian, slowly being transformed to its former splendor. The lawn that, despite what she'd told Jake, was green and lovely. The porch, gleaming white in the sun, thanks to Tom's diligent labor.

From her vantage point, Tiffany could see Bandit roaming the fenced yard, his nose pressed to the ground, perhaps searching for some small animal. White pickets were bright against the sun's fading glory. The lot, the house, the lake view—every piece a beautiful part of Tiffany's world.

She needed to find contentment here, in this place that God had given her. Only then would life be what it should.

If quilting wouldn't help her find solace today, perhaps physical labor would. The gazebo needed work before winter. Today was the perfect day to get started.

Hurrying, eager to put her melancholy mood aside, Tiffany wrapped her still-stiff ankle, changed into shorts, and walked out into the yard. Bandit ran to greet her, black tail high and curled.

"Hey boy, we've got some work to do. Ready?"

The dog gave a short bark and fell into step beside Tiffany. She laughed, leaning to pat his head. "You're something else, Bandit. And here I thought you were just a pretty face."

Together they shoved through thick foliage. The gazebo was in bad shape. Bad enough that Tiffany was afraid it wouldn't survive another winter. Now that the porch was complete, Tom could begin work replacing some of the gazebo's rotted floorboards.

Or maybe the roof should be first.

Tiffany eyed the structure, wondering how much she and Tom could do together, and how much work she'd need to contract out. Maybe getting rid of some of the overgrown foliage that surrounded the gazebo would give her a better view of things. "No time like the present to get a job done."

Bandit, who lay sprawled on the gazebo floor, eyed Tiffany with little enthusiasm.

"Don't worry, I won't need your help and you'll get your evening snack before I grab the clippers. Come on."

Physical labor was what she'd wanted. It was what she got. Two hours later she stood sweating, panting and eyeing what her hard labor had revealed.

Thin-trunked pines formed a half circle on one side of the gazebo. Closer in, touching the base of the structure, were a variety of shrubs that Tiffany couldn't identify, but that she imagined would flower in the spring. A tall oak dipped its branches close to the gazebo roof and an old magnolia stood sentry duty nearby. She could picture it—trimmed, overflowing with blossoms, and she smiled.

Next year the gazebo would be a welcoming spot. Just as Tiffany was sure it had been a century ago.

"Come on, Bandit. I've got some measuring to do and I don't want you knocking over that ladder while I do it."

With sunlight fading to dusk, Tiffany worked quickly, locking Bandit into the mudroom and grabbing the ladder from the garage. It was heavy and unwieldy. She considered putting it back, perhaps waiting until Monday when Tom would be on hand to help, but she had a trip to Rocky Mount planned the next day, and knew she could order the wood she needed for repairs while she was there.

Besides, idle, her mind might return to its earlier worries, and Tiffany had no intention of spending more time regretting what could never be. When Jake arrived later, she planned to look busy, productive and content with her lot in life.

Measuring tape in hand, she climbed up the ladder and began measuring. The steep, slanted roof was difficult to reach and Tiffany clambered up farther, standing on the top rung and stretching to reach the pinnacle of the roof. When Bandit began barking she paid little attention, her mind focused on the task at hand.

Then his barking became frantic and even from a distance, she could hear his big body slamming against the wood door. Startled, Tiffany turned, saw movement to the right and scrambled to glimpse what had caused it. "Who's there?"

A figure lurched from between the pine trees, lunging toward the ladder, shoving it hard.

Before Tiffany could scream she was falling, the world spinning in a kaleidoscope of summer colors. She tried to catch hold of something to slow her fall, but her hands met empty air and she crashed to the ground. Pain, sharp and brutal, ripped through her arm seconds before her head slammed into the ground.

Chapter Fourteen

Jake paced the emergency room lobby, glancing up each time the double doors to the treatment area opened. What was taking so long? Was the deep, ugly bruise on Tiffany's forehead even worse than it appeared? Perhaps her injury had already sapped the vitality and life from her.

Jake winced at the thought, his hands clenched into fists. He wanted to shove open the doors and search for answers to his questions. Questions he'd been asking himself for over an hour, the same helpless fear he'd felt when Will had been shot eating away at his gut.

At least with Will, Jake had a chance before the ambulance arrived. A chance, while Will's lifeblood seeped onto his hands, to tell him how much their friendship had meant to him.

With Tiffany, Jake hadn't had that chance. He'd found her lying still as death, a heavy metal ladder on top of her.

The bruise on her head, the obscene twist of her arm, the waxy paleness of her skin, had made ice flow through his veins.

That her pulse beat slow and steady had seemed little comfort as the ambulance crew slid her onto a gurney and took her away. She hadn't regained consciousness and that, more than anything, worried Jake.

Head injuries could be bad. Really bad.

"Sheriff Reed?"

The voice sounded familiar and Jake looked up to find Brian McMath walking toward him. The expression on his face was grim and Jake braced himself for bad news.

"The nurse told me you were out here."

"How's Tiffany?"

"She's awake. Claiming someone pushed her off the ladder. I tried to calm her down but she's distraught and very insistent that you be notified."

"I'll go in and see her."

"That isn't necessary. I'll let her know that I've contacted you and that should calm her."

"If she was pushed I need to speak with her."

"*If* is the operative word in that sentence. Head injuries often cause confusion. And Tiffany tends to be accident prone."

"Like I said, I need to speak to her." Jake bit out the words, rage coloring his voice. He wanted to grab McMath by the front of his overstarched shirt and shake some compassion into him.

Surprise flickered in the doctor's eyes, then he shrugged. "All right, but I doubt you'll accomplish much and you won't have long. She's scheduled for surgery on her arm."

"Surgery?"

"She has a compound fracture and the bone is splintered.

The sooner we can get in there and put things back together, the better."

Jake nodded his understanding, following the doctor down a long corridor filled with curtain shrouded cubicles. He could smell ammonia and antiseptic and illness. A smattering of people stood outside the curtains, anxiety and irritation floating on the waves of tapping feet and restless pacing.

His own nerves frayed, Jake spoke to the doctor's back. "Besides the arm, how is Tiffany?"

"She has a concussion, a few bruises, but she'll be fine. The way insurance companies operate, she'll probably be home by tomorrow night. And hopefully not climbing ladders any time soon." The doctor let out a bark of laughter and Jake fought the urge to drag him around and beat the humor out of him.

As if sensing his thoughts, McMath sobered and turned to look at him. "You must think I'm terrible making jokes about Tiffany's accident."

"Lacking in compassion would be a better description."

McMath's eyes hardened, his mouth pulling into a tight line. "You don't know me well enough to make that judgment, Sheriff. Tiffany and I dated for a year and I believe I know her well enough to laugh at some of her...idiosyncrasies."

"I don't call being pushed off a ladder an idiosyncrasy."

"Climbing onto a ladder to take measurements of a worthless outbuilding is a typical example of Tiffany's foibles. As for being pushed...let's just say Tiffany is highly imaginative."

"For someone who dated her for a year, you don't know her very well, do you?"

"I know her well enough to make a judgment call about this situation. Hang around her a while, you'll see that I'm right."

Jake started to argue the point, but forced himself to silence. One of the many things his friendship with Will had
taught him was to focus on the important and let go of
everything else. The jerk of a doctor standing before him
was not important. "Where is she?"

For a moment he thought McMath would continue the
argument. Then the man turned, his shoulders tense with
resentment, and stalked forward several paces. "She's in
there. Like I said, you won't have long. We'll be prepping
her for surgery soon."

Without another word he walked away. Jake was glad
to see him go, glad he'd have a few minutes to speak with
Tiffany without McMath adding his two cents in.

Besides, another minute in the arrogant doctor's presence
might have resulted in Jake doing something he'd regret.
"Pompous piece of..."

"Hold that thought, Jake. Wouldn't want Sunday's sermon to be about controlling our tongues." Jake looked up
at the sound of the familiar voice and spotted Ben Avery
coming toward him.

"Fluff. I was going to say 'pompous piece of fluff.'" Jake
moved forward to greet his friend, tension and irritation lifting as he pushed McMath from his thoughts. "What are you
doing here?"

"Mrs. Johnson had hip replacement surgery this afternoon. I was upstairs visiting and heard the nurses whispering about the commotion down here. Figured I'd come
down and get the real scoop."

"What commotion?"

"Well, first I heard Tiffany had an accident."

Jake nodded, not sure why her accident would cause an
uproar.

"Then Sue Brandon, one of the nurses, said she got a call

from a friend who saw Tom Bishop being handcuffed outside Tiffany's house."

"What?!"

"According to several people who've made a point to ask for my prayers on the matter," Ben's expression was wry, "Tiffany told Brian McMath she'd been pushed from the ladder. Tom's arrest has people adding two and two and getting ten."

"In other words, Tom's responsible for what happened."

"Right."

"Great." Jake ran a weary hand through his hair then pulled his cell phone out and dialed the station. It didn't take long for him to get the information he needed. Smiling grimly at his friend, he replaced the phone and moved to Tiffany's cubicle. "Looks like the rumors are based on fact. Tom was caught trying to enter Tiffany's house. He's being questioned now."

Ben didn't say anything, just waited for Jake to continue.

"I need to talk to Tiffany before I go to the station. Can you do me a favor? Drive to the station and keep an eye on Tom. Make sure he doesn't get in any more trouble until I get there. Henry's there, I told him you were going to play referee."

"No problem. Do you think Tom did it?"

"No. But he was there, so he knows something and I plan to find out what."

Ben nodded. "I'll try to keep Tom from getting thrown in jail for attitude. Tell Tiffany I stopped by and I'll try to get back later."

"Will do." Jake didn't wait for his friend to retreat down the hall. His time with Tiffany was limited and he needed to get information that only she could provide.

The area beyond the closed curtain was just large

enough to hold a gurney style bed, an IV pole and a chair. The overhead light had been dimmed and the darkness of the cubicle was a stark contrast to the brightly lit corridor. Closing the curtain, Jake moved toward the bed where Tiffany lay.

Her eyes were closed, her lashes forming dark crescents against skin so pale it seemed translucent. A large bruise marred her forehead, the rectangular-shaped bump reminiscent of the ladder rung that had landed there. Jake pulled the chair over and sat down, careful not to jar the bed and Tiffany's swollen, mangled arm.

He'd seen worse injuries but few that had affected him as much. Leaning forward, he brushed a stray curl away from Tiffany's cheek. "Tiffany?"

Her eyes opened immediately, deep green and startling in contrast to her pale skin. It took a moment for her gaze to focus on Jake. When it did, tension eased from her face. "I told Brian you'd want to know what happened." Her voice sounded raspy, the words slightly slurred.

"You were right. How are you feeling?"

She eyed Jake for a moment, then grinned. "Like a walking disaster area."

That she could smile after her ordeal made Jake's throat tighten with an emotion he refused to name. "More like a moving target."

"You were right about me and trouble. I've attracted more this summer than I have in my entire life." Tiffany's gaze drifted to her arm. It had been covered with sterile gauze, hiding, Jake knew, the place where bone had pierced flesh. "I've never broken a bone before." Her pale skin turned gray and she swallowed as if fighting nausea.

Hoping to distract her, Jake reached for her uninjured hand and clasped it tightly. "Want to tell me what happened?"

"You mean my version, or the one Brian probably already gave you?"

Good, she still had some fight left in her. "Yours. Brian is an idiot."

"You said that the day we met. I think I'm finally starting to believe you." Tiffany's eyes drifted closed, as if keeping them open were too much effort.

"Tell me what happened, Tiffany."

A frown line appeared between her brows as she opened her eyes again. "I was measuring the gazebo roof, trying to figure out how much wood I'd need for repairs." She paused licking dry lips. "I'm really thirsty, can you get me some water?"

"I don't think they'll let you have any before surgery."

"That's right. The nurse told me that. I forgot." Her eyes drifted shut again.

"You were measuring the gazebo, and...?"

This time Tiffany didn't open her eyes when she responded. "I put Bandit in the house. I was afraid he'd knock the ladder over accidentally."

"Is that what happened?"

"No, like I told Brian, Bandit was in the house barking and I looked around to see what had gotten him riled up. Before I could figure out what was going on someone darted out from behind one of those big old pine trees and shoved the ladder out from under me."

"Did you see the person?"

"No, just a dark blur. But I think he might have been the same one who was in my house the other night."

"Why do you think that?"

"I don't know." Tiffany opened her eyes and frowned. "Oh, wait. I remember he kind of ducked and crouched when he came out from behind the tree. The branches in the pine are pretty high. Maybe six feet. I think he was try-ing to avoid running into them."

Jake nodded. "You said the person who was in your house was tall. Your mind must have made the connection without you realizing it."

"I guess that's it."

"Did Tom Bishop work today?"

"Yes. A half day because I had to go to the shower late this afternoon and I didn't want him to be stranded at my house."

"You drove him home?"

"Yes, I dropped him off before I went to Joy's. Why?"

"Just wondering how he might fit into things."

"He didn't push me, if that's what you think." Tiffany raised her head from the pillow, wincing as she did so.

"Just relax. I don't think he did."

She subsided back onto the pillow, her eyes closing and then fluttering open again. "Sorry, I'm just so tired."

"Sleep. I've got some things to take care of at the station. Then I'll be back to see how you're doing."

Jake moved to disengage his hand from Tiffany's, but she tightened her fingers around his, and opened her eyes, anx-iety and pain clouding their depth. "Can you stay for a while longer?"

For the first time, it occurred to Jake that she might be scared. He squeezed her hand gently. "Nervous about the surgery?"

"A little. Mostly I just don't want to be alone right now."

Jake watched Tiffany trying to smile and wanted to tell her that if it were up to him she'd never be alone again.

"I know it's silly. I'm alone all the time...."

"It's not silly. I'd want someone with me, too."

"Really? I asked Brian to call my parents, but he said it would be better to wait until the surgery was over."

Her eyes had closed again, and she looked vulnerable. Fragile in a way Jake had never seen her. "I'll call them for you. What's the number?" Jake took out his cell phone, ready to dial but Tiffany didn't respond.

Eyes closed, face relaxed, she slept soundly. Jake brushed another lock of hair from her cheek, his fingers lingering a moment longer than necessary. What would he feel for her if he allowed himself to?

He refused to answer the question. Refused to think about what could never be. Instead he dialed information. Only when he'd located her parents and been assured they were on the way did he leave.

Maybe he couldn't give Tiffany the love she deserved, but at least he could be a friend she could depend on. If the thought of being only that made him feel hollow and empty, Jake didn't acknowledge it.

He had more important things to think about. Like how he was going to get Tom Bishop to give him the names of his buddies. He knew the kid had information, and Jake had every intention of getting it this time.

Anger and frustration had him pressing down on the gas pedal, speeding to the station. He didn't waste time with niceties, just shoved the door to the interrogation room open with enough force to have it banging against the wall.

Tom sat at a long table, his face set in lines of rebellion. Ben, stationed to one side of him, had a hand on the boy's shoulder, the gesture designed either to comfort or to keep him in place. Two officers sat on the opposite side of the table. Neither looked happy.

That was fine. Jake wasn't happy, either. They'd make a good team. He nodded at Ben, not bothering to try on a smile. "Thanks, I'll take it from here."

Ben must have sensed the rage behind Jake's words. He

hesitated, his normally easygoing expression hardening. "Jake—"

"Don't worry, I'm not going to give him the beating he deserves."

Ben held his gaze for a moment. Then, as if satisfied that Jake had his emotions under control, he released his grip on Tom and stepped away. "His father might. He'll be here in an hour."

"Good. Hopefully we'll have the information we need by then and Tom can go home with him."

"Tiffany doing okay?"

"As well as can be expected."

"I'll stop by the hospital. See if there's anything I can do."

"Good idea. Her parents should be there by now."

Ben walked out the door and Jake turned his attention back to Tom. "Did you give the names yet?"

"He's not talking. Says he's got nothing to say." Jeff Mallory spoke from across the table, his slightly nasal voice reminding Jake that he wasn't alone.

"No? Tell you what, Mallory. You and Simmons take a break. I'll see if I can talk some sense into Tom."

"You sure, Sheriff? We don't mind staying." Henry Simmons stood, his face creased into lines of worry.

"Go get some coffee. Come back in a few minutes and we'll go round up our suspects."

The two officers hurried from the room and Jake grabbed a chair, sliding it close to Tom. "You should have told me weeks ago. You know it."

"I've got nothing to say."

"Yeah? Tell you what. Let's go to the hospital. I want you to see what your silence has done." Jake stood, grabbed Tom's arm and dragged him to his feet. "Then you can look Tiffany in the eye and tell *her* you don't know anything."

Tom pulled against the pressure on his arm. "I'm not going anywhere with you."

"No?" Jake grabbed his handcuffs and snapped them onto Tom's wrists.

"Hey. You can't do that!"

"Yeah. I can. And more. I warned you if anything happened to Tiffany you'd be the one to pay. I'm taking you to the hospital. Then I'm bringing you back here and charging you with assault."

"But I didn't do anything!"

"We've got a witness who saw you at the scene. Might be circumstantial, but people have been convicted on less."

"But—"

"You've made your choice. I've made mine. I'll find your buddies with or without your help. Let's go."

"They're not my buddies!"

"Then why are you protecting them?"

"I'm not, I'm..." Tom's shoulders sagged, his eyes moist with something that looked like tears.

Jake hardened himself against it. "You're what?"

"I thought I was protecting Tiffany. I thought if I kept quiet they'd leave her alone."

"Too late for that, isn't it? She's already been hurt. Give me the names and I'll keep it from happening again."

"I don't know names. Not the ones you want."

"Are you trying to tell me you weren't part of the gang that's been causing trouble all summer?"

"They aren't a gang. At least they weren't. Then this new kid butted in. He's the one calling the shots now."

"Give me a name."

"I don't have one. He showed up at Tiffany's the day Dr. McMath was there. Asked me if I wanted to go have some fun."

"And you said no?"

Tom's face went deep red. "The other guys were with him. I figured we'd have a good time so I said sure. Then he started talking weird. Saying stuff about brotherhood and proving I could be trusted. He wanted me to get Tiffany's account information. Steal credit card numbers and stuff. I said no."

"So he beat the crap out of you."

Tom shrugged. "I've had worse."

"And you're trying to tell me you don't know his name? He never introduced himself? None of the other guys said his name?" Jake didn't buy it and he was done playing. "You're lying. You're as deep in this as anyone. Come on. Forget the trip to the hospital. I'm pressing charges."

"He goes by Slade. But it's not his real name. He's older. Maybe eighteen. Blond hair. Tall. Really tall. Maybe six-three."

Jake stopped cold at Tom's words. The kid had no way of knowing Tiffany's attacker had been tall. "Anything else?"

"He's got friends in Chicago. Said something about heading back there before the end of the summer. He just needs to get the money to do it."

Which was probably why he wanted the credit card numbers. "What about the other kids? You have names on them?"

Tom nodded, all the bluff and rebellion gone. "I never meant for this to happen. I've been following them around as much as I can, trying to make sure they didn't hurt Tiffany."

"That's what you were doing at her house?"

"Yeah. I heard something might be going down, but I couldn't get there in time."

Jake unlocked the handcuffs, and pointed to the table.

"Sit. You should have come to me. Should have told me this before."

"Why? So you could call me a liar?" The words were snide, but there was hurt behind them.

"I would have checked things out."

"You would have arrested me as soon as I admitted to knowing the guys responsible for all the vandalism and sh—"

"Careful."

"Stuff. You would have assumed I was involved, too."

Jake couldn't deny it. "So you sacrificed Tiffany to keep yourself out of trouble."

"No!" Tom slammed his fist down on the table. All the anger, frustration, and fear he felt bursting out in that one word.

"Then what?"

"I wanted to get proof. I wanted to be able to say I'd seen them committing a crime. Then they'd be in jail and I'd..."

His voice trailed off, but Jake could imagine what he was thinking. Tom wanted to be a hero. To somehow redeem himself in the eyes of a town that had pegged him as trouble.

If he was telling the truth then his mistake had been misguided, not malicious.

Jake eyed the teen. Saw him as he was—scrawny, scared, unsure. The body too lanky. The hands too big. The eyes guarded. And beneath the veneer of toughness, a child begging for a chance.

Was that what Tiffany had seen? Was that what she'd reached to touch? A soul not yet corrupted. A young man struggling to become something better than what the world said he would be.

Jake thought of Will. Of the time he'd spent reaching out

to gang members, giving each one a chance. Always believing that what they *could* be was something much more than what they were.

Could Jake do any less?

Not when he'd been forgiven much more than childish mistakes.

With a sigh, Jake pulled out a chair and sat down next to Tom. "Looks like we're on the same side after all. Let's get these guys."

Chapter Fifteen

An hour later they had a list of names, and had brought the kids into the station, but nothing else. Frustrated, Jake eyed the ragtag group of teens waiting to be dismissed. Parents hovered over them. Some stunned, some angry. Jake didn't bother to diffuse the emotions. Let them take it home with them. Maybe there, they'd get the answers Jake hadn't been able to.

He had to give the kids credit; they'd concocted a believable alibi and were sticking to it. Interviewed separately, they'd each said the same thing—they'd been on the lake all day. Fishing, swimming and staying out of trouble.

Without proof that they were lying, Jake had no choice but to let them go. He signaled to Simmons and watched as the older officer led the group away.

All except one.

Jake swung open the door of the interrogation room

and stepped inside. Greg Banning and his parents sat huddled together. The mother looked worried, the father angry. Greg looked smug. Jake wanted to wipe the half smile off the kid's face, but resisted temptation.

"Sorry to keep you so long. I needed to check with the other kids. See what they had to say."

Greg Sr. stood, his sharp gaze and perfectly styled hair a testimony to his confidence. "My wife and I have a house full of guests. If we could get on with things...."

"No problem. I just have a few more questions for Greg."

"Like I said, we're running short on time. Are you sure this can't be done another day?"

"Yeah. I'm sure." Jake turned to the young man. "Nice bandanna."

The kid raised his hand and fingered the black-and-red cloth tied around his head. "Thanks. I can get you one. Cheap. If you're interested."

"Shut up, Greg." The older Banning's voice stopped his son's words, but not his ever widening grin.

Jake ignored the father and focused on the son. "I made a few calls. Spoke to the principal of Rigby High. He said you got kicked out your senior year. Seems you were involved in some gang activities."

"That was never proven." Greg Sr. interrupted, his voice harsh.

"No. It wasn't. You moved a few months later, right? From Chicago to Richmond."

"Job transfer. It had nothing to do with Greg."

"Didn't it? If I had a son involved in a gang, I'd move."

"He wasn't—"

"He was. Now he's causing trouble, trying to find a way to get back to Chicago, pulling other kids into his schemes."

"We're on vacation. Greg is hanging with some buddies. If that's a crime, arrest him. Otherwise, let us go."

"Soon. So, Greg, tell me again how you were on the lake all day."

"I took my dad's boat out this morning. We were out on the water all day. We stopped to gas up at the marina before we went home. At least ten people saw us there."

"You said it was close to eight when you stopped."

"It was."

"So you gassed up the boat and went home."

"I've told you this ten times."

"So tell me again."

"We went home. I had the boat back at the dock by eight-fifteen."

"You sure you weren't on Monroe Street tonight?"

"I told you we weren't."

"Maybe you were bored and were looking for a little excitement."

"There's no excitement in this town." Greg's voice dripped with malice.

"So you decided to make some, right? What'd you do? Leave the marina and walk to Monroe Street? Was pushing Miss Anderson's ladder out from under her payback? Or was it a message to Tom? A warning that he better keep his mouth shut."

"You can't really mean to accuse my son...." Greg Sr. shot up from the chair, nearly toppling it in his haste.

"Not accuse. Ask."

"I told you. I was in the boat and at the marina. Not pushing some lady off a ladder."

"I think you're lying and I plan to prove it. When I do, there won't be a cave in the world dark enough for you to hide in."

"I'm not—"

"You're free to go. But stay out of town and stay off Monroe Street. If I see you near the Anderson property, I'll haul your butt back in here and charge you with trespassing."

Jake left them to their misery, stalking out of the room before they could respond. They followed, whispering to each other as they moved past Jake and walked outside.

"So, did you get the kid to admit anything?" Henry Simmons spoke from beside Jake, his usual puppy dog expression replaced by one of concern.

"That *kid* is an eighteen-year-old man and he knows his rights almost as well as we do."

"They came up with a good alibi. Be hard to prove they weren't where they said they were."

"Hard, but not impossible. Did you ask Bill if he saw them at the marina?"

"Everything checked out. He said they motored in around eight. Had some sodas. Filled the tank and took off twenty minutes later."

"And he actually saw them?"

"Yeah, but it was busy and he said he's not sure how many there were."

"So it's possible one or more of those kids wasn't on the boat."

"Looks that way."

"But we can't prove it. Which brings us back to square one. Our hands are tied and the punk knows it." Jake ran a hand through his hair and fought back his frustration. "Any word on the fingerprint match from the chisel?"

"None. Like you said, back to square one. So what's the plan?"

"Spread the word. A town the size of Lakeview is small

enough to have an effective community watch. Let's get the citizens involved. Eventually Greg and his pals will be caught in the act. Until then we double the patrols and keep our own eyes open."

"Will do. You finishing your shift tonight?"

"Yeah, I'll run patrol. It should be a quiet night."

"All right, then. If you need me, give a holler. I don't mind working overtime."

It was midnight when Jake drove into the hospital parking lot. He wasn't sure why he was there. By all rights Tiffany should be asleep, tucked safe and secure in an uncomfortable hospital bed. But he needed to check on her. Needed to be sure the surgery had gone well. He didn't question those needs, just parked the cruiser and stepped out into balmy air.

The parking lot was unnaturally still and the doors to the hospital swung open into an equally still lobby. The information desk had been abandoned hours ago, visiting hours long since over. Bypassing the silent lobby, Jake rode the elevator up to the third floor where he'd been told Tiffany had been moved.

Several nurses looked up from their work station as Jake stepped off the elevator. One smiled and moved toward him. "I'm sorry, visiting hours are over. Can I take a message for you?"

Jake flashed his own smile along with his badge. "I'm here to see Tiffany Anderson."

The nurse nodded. "Of course. Sorry, I didn't notice the uniform at first. She's in 313. Straight down the hall to the left."

A hush hung over the third-floor hallway, as if the building were holding its breath, waiting to see who would live and who would die. The contrast to the frenetic pace of the emergency room was striking. Here no one tapped an impatient foot or uttered a weary sigh. Muted sounds of television sitcoms drifted through closed doors. Other than that, the hall was silent.

Tiffany occupied a room at the far end of the hall. Her door was closed and Jake tapped lightly.

"Come in, Mom."

Jake wasn't Mom but he figured he'd go in anyway. Pushing the door open, he walked into the darkened room.

"You didn't have to knock. I think the nurse must have..." Tiffany's voice trailed off as she realized she wasn't speaking with her mother. "Oh, hi."

Even in the dim light, Jake could see the surprise in Tiffany's eyes. He didn't blame her. He'd surprised himself with the late-night visit. "Hi."

"I thought you were my mom." Tiffany's voice was weak, but not slurred as it had been earlier.

Jake took a seat in a chair that had been pulled up close to the bed. "And you're disappointed?"

"Only because she promised me a vanilla milkshake from Dairy Queen."

"The knock on your head hasn't hurt your sense of humor any. How are you feeling?"

"Like I can't talk to you like this." Tiffany reached over and pushed a button on the bed's rail. The bed angled up until she was almost sitting. Then she reached to drag a pillow from behind her back, wincing a little at the movement.

Jake brushed her hand away, eased the pillow out and placed it behind her head. "That better?"

"Much. Thanks."

"You didn't answer my question. How are you feeling?"

"Not too bad."

Jake flipped on the overhead light and took a look for himself. Illuminated, Tiffany's face looked even paler than it had earlier, the bruise on her head a bright slash of blue, red and black against the pallor. "Not too good either, from the looks of things."

"I've had better days. Actually, I've had better years."

To Jake's horror, a tear slid down Tiffany's cheek. "Hey, it's not that bad, is it?"

"No. Yes." Another tear escaped and she scrubbed it away with her uninjured hand. "I'm not sure."

"Want to tell me about it?" Jake's mind was shouting at him to leave, telling him he was in dangerous territory. He ignored it and grabbed Tiffany's hand, giving it an encouraging squeeze.

"I'm just irritated with everything right now."

Tiffany didn't seem the type of person to get irritated easily. Jake took a shot in the dark at the cause. "What's Dr. McMath have to say about everything?"

"*He* says if I had listened to him and not given Tom a job, none of this would have happened. According to him, I was asking for trouble and I got it."

"He said that?"

"Not in so many words, but the implication was there."

Jake bit his tongue to keep from expressing his opinion about the doctor.

"The worst part is, he's right."

Surprised, Jake met Tiffany's tear filled gaze. "How do you figure that?"

"Everyone warned me. I refused to listen. Even *you* told me Tom was trouble. You must think I'm a fool."

"What I think," Jake paused, brushing away a tear that slid down the curve of Tiffany's cheek, "is that you're one of the most compassionate people I've ever met. I also think you're tired and hurt, and now isn't the time for you or anyone else to second-guess the decisions you've made."

Tiffany's eyes widened, her tears drying, and a flash of humor appearing in their depths. "I'm disappointed."

"About?"

"I thought you were going to say you think Brian is an idiot." She smiled as she repeated words he had spoken twice before.

Laughing, Jake shook his head. "That goes without saying."

Tiffany's own soft laughter joined his and without conscious thought, Jake leaned in, catching the laugh with a kiss. He only meant to touch her lips with his, to feel the gentle breath of her joy, but somehow the kiss deepened and became more.

"Tiffany?" A hesitant voice sounded from the open door and Jake jerked back, his heart pounding as if he'd run a marathon. A petite woman and a tall, broad-shouldered man stood in the entrance. The woman held a carryout cup in one hand and a stack of magazines in the other. She stared at Tiffany as if she'd never seen her before.

The man's hands were empty. His eyes were on Jake.

"Mom. Dad. Um, this is Jake Reed. The sheriff. He's trying to find out who pushed me off the ladder."

"It looks to me like he's trying to do a lot more than that." Tiffany's father had eyes the same color as hers. Only his weren't nearly as friendly.

"Dad!"

Jake let his gaze drift back to Tiffany for a moment. Two spots of color danced along her cheekbones as she looked at her father who, Jake noted, was still glaring daggers at him.

Mentally kicking himself for putting her in such an awkward position, Jake stepped forward to greet Tiffany's parents. "Nice to meet you."

Good manners too deeply ingrained for him to ignore the hand Jake extended, Tiffany's father returned the greeting. "I'm Ed Anderson. This is my wife, Patti."

"Ma'am."

"Sheriff." Reaching out with a small-boned hand, Patti Anderson offered her own greeting. "Tiffany told me you've helped her out several times recently. I'm glad to finally have the chance to thank you."

In stature and build, Tiffany and her mother couldn't have been more different. Still, Jake could have been in a room filled with redheads and picked out Patti as Tiffany's mother. The two shared the same full-lipped smile and had the same flash of humor in their eyes.

Ed Anderson mumbled something under his breath. Jake couldn't quite make out the words but thought the man might have said something about thanking him with a fist to the mouth.

Mrs. Anderson continued to smile up at Jake as she spoke sweetly to her husband. "Ed, honey, I need to speak with you for a moment. Privately." Grabbing her husband by the arm she all but yanked him out into the hall.

Jake turned to Tiffany and had barely opened his mouth when she raised a hand and stopped him. "Don't."

"Don't what?"

"Don't even think about apologizing. It was nothing. And if we're both lucky all the dope they gave me for pain will wipe out my memory of everything that has happened in the past twenty-four hours."

Jake couldn't help it. He smiled. "That bad, huh?"

"I cannot believe my father just acted like that. Did you hear what he said?"

"Which part?"

"The part about thanking you with a fist to your mouth."

"Your father's upset about what happened to you today. He's feeling protective."

"I'm thirty-three, not thirteen." Shaking her head, Tiffany ran a hand across her eyes. Her fingers trembled slightly.

Jake placed a hand over hers, stilling the fine tremors. "You're tired. Why don't I turn off the light and leave you to rest? There'll be time enough to worry about all this tomorrow."

"My parents will be back in a minute. They'll want to talk." Tiffany's protest was only a token and they both knew it.

"They'll understand."

Tiffany knew Jake was right. Her parents would understand. But she didn't. One minute she'd been fine, happily measuring the gazebo. The next she was in the emergency room staring up at Brian and a bunch of nurses. From that point on, her life had spun completely out of control.

Who was she kidding? Her life had been out of control since the day she jumped in the lake to save Bandit. And the man standing beside her seemed to have a lot to do with that.

"You okay?" Jake's voice broke into her troubled thoughts and Tiffany tried to smile up at him.

"I was just thinking you're right. My parents will understand that I'm tired."

Tiffany could tell Jake didn't believe her. A soft knock prevented him from saying so. When her mother and father opened the door, Tiffany didn't know whether to be pleased or disappointed.

"We're back," Patti Anderson entered the room with the

same cheerful good humor Tiffany remembered from childhood, "Sorry about that. Hopefully the milkshake hasn't melted much."

"It'll be fine, Mom." Tiffany knew she sounded as tired as she felt but couldn't muster enough energy to sound any different.

"Are you okay, honey?" Her father approached, bending down to kiss her cheek.

"I'll live."

"Of course you will. I just worry about you."

"I know." Tiffany could feel Jake's steady gaze from the position he'd taken at the door, but refused to glance his way.

"Good. Now, you need to get some rest and I need to speak with the sheriff. Mind if I leave you and your mom for a bit?"

"Dad, I—"

Before Tiffany could finish her mother cut in, smoothly taking away any choice they were pretending she had. "You two go on ahead. I'll meet you downstairs after I make sure Tiffany is settled in."

Biting back further protest, Tiffany said good-night to Jake and her father, watched as they walked out the door and turned to her mother. "Traitor."

"Tiffany Lynn, how could you say such a thing?" The twinkle in Patti's eyes belied her serious tone.

"Because it's true."

"No, it's not. Your father isn't going to give Sheriff Reed the third degree. He's going to apologize."

Tiffany almost laughed but the pain medication was wearing off and she hurt too bad. "Come on, Mom. You know how Dad is."

Patti sat down in the chair next to the bed, placing the

milkshake and magazines on a small table. "Yes, I do. He loves you and he's worried."

"I—"

"Tiffany, we came in here expecting you to be asleep and saw a good-looking stranger kissing you. Your father was shocked."

"And you're not?"

"A little, but I figure you're old enough to know what you're doing."

"Thanks."

"Besides, I know I'll get all the details once you're feeling better. Right?"

"There aren't any details."

Patti didn't argue, though Tiffany could sense she wanted to. "All right. You look really pale again. Are you sure you're okay?"

"I'll be fine. I just need to sleep."

"Then I'll go and leave you to it."

"Thanks. I love you, Mom."

"Love you, too, Tiffany."

Tiffany watched her mother walk out the door and wished she could leave with her. The antiseptic smell of the hospital made her slightly queasy, and being confined to bed made her feel vulnerable. She wanted to sleep, but anxiety kept her awake staring at the door.

She'd lived through some bad days in her life, but none could compare to the one she'd just survived. In a list of the top ten things she'd rather not repeat, Tiffany figured the last twenty-four hours ranked number one.

Except for maybe the kiss.

And that was something she refused to think about. Instead she pictured the quilt she was making, and tried to grasp hold of the peace she felt when she worked on it.

"Be still and know that I am God." Tiffany spoke the words aloud, embracing the message and trying to let it soothe her. After a few moments she began to relax and, despite the pain, let sleep carry her away.

Chapter Sixteen

Three days later, Tiffany sat in silence at her kitchen table, enjoying the solitude of her empty house. Though she'd been released from the hospital with strict orders to rest, the past few days had been filled with visitors and an endless stream of phone calls. Now, early Monday morning, Tiffany hoped her friends and family would be too busy with hectic work schedules to stop in and check on her. She needed some time alone.

With her feet up on a chair and a cup of coffee in her hand, Tiffany watched dust motes swirl in the first rays of morning sun. Tom would be arriving shortly and Tiffany had a list of small jobs for him to do. She didn't even want to think about the growing list of jobs she had to accomplish herself. Though owning her own business had many advantages, it kept her busy. Sometimes too busy.

And, if the number of messages on her work line were

any indication, the following week was destined to be one where she barely had time to breathe, let alone rest.

For now though, she had a few minutes to herself and planned to enjoy them. With the windows open and the sweet smell of summer drifting in on a warm breeze, Tiffany nursed her coffee and thought over the weekend with all its twists and turns. Certainly having a broken arm and a concussed head didn't seem a blessing, but the outpouring of love and friendship had reminded her of all she had to be thankful for.

And, of course, there had been the kiss. If Tiffany was honest with herself she'd admit Jake's kiss had been on her mind a lot the past few days. She knew he offered nothing but friendship, and it was a good thing she did, as his sweetly passionate kiss had hinted at commitment and love. Two things Jake had said he could never offer.

Running her hand through hopelessly tangled hair, Tiffany pushed thoughts of Jake out of her mind and focused on more important things. Like how she was going to fix her hair one-handed. Though the pain in her left arm was tolerable, it still ached and throbbed. A soft cast had been applied, and once the stitches were removed from her forearm, it would be replaced by a hard cast. For now though, Tiffany was careful not to bump or jostle the arm and kept it in the sling the hospital had provided.

Glancing at her still-swollen appendages, Tiffany wondered if it would be safe to use the hand, then wiggled her fingers, winced and gave up on the idea. She'd brush her hair the best she could and leave it down. Forcing herself to action, she pushed to her feet and went to get ready for the day.

Tom arrived earlier than she'd expected, the doorbell and Bandit's bark announcing his arrival as Tiffany searched through her closet for a pullover blouse to wear with the only skirt she owned that didn't have a button to contend with. Grabbing the first thing her hand touched, she threw on the shirt and rushed down the stairs to open the door.

She knew immediately that something was wrong. "Tom. What is it? Are you okay?"

"Yeah. I'm fine."

"You look like your best friend just left town. I thought we agreed that wearing a smile was part of the job description."

Tiffany's attempt at levity fell on deaf ears. Tom's expression remained solemn, his gaze darting away as he spoke. "I need to talk to you about that. The job, I mean."

"Come in. I have juice in the fridge and some bagels if you're hungry."

"No. No thanks." Tom scuffed a toe against the porch floor. "Look, I really appreciate you giving me the job and everything but I can't work for you anymore."

"What? Why?"

"I told my dad I'd help with his deliveries. He asked before but I didn't want to be on the road so much."

"What's changed your mind? Not this I hope." Tiffany pointed at her arm.

"No. I just think my dad could use some help."

"Tom, I—"

"I need to go. My dad's waiting."

The young man turned to walk away but Tiffany reached out and touched his shoulder. "This is about what's happened to me. I know it is and I feel awful about it."

Tom turned back and looked Tiffany in the eye. "Don't. Don't feel bad. You've been kinder to me than anyone else I know. Nothing that's happened is your fault. Things just got out of hand this summer and I need to get away for a while until things cool off."

Tiffany swallowed a lump that was two parts joy and one part sorrow. "You're a wise young man, Tom. I'm proud of you."

"Not wise yet. But I'm learning. Thanks for giving me a chance."

"You proved yourself and if you decide you want your job back when school starts give me a call. We can work out the details."

A horn blared loudly and Tom glanced at his father's truck parked at the end of the driveway. "Dad's waiting. I gotta run. Maybe this fall though, I'll be back."

Tiffany watched Tom run down the porch steps and along the driveway. She felt empty, depressed by the thought that, to protect her, Tom had quit a job he enjoyed. Bandit stood beside her and whined softly as the truck drove away. "Don't worry, boy. He'll be back when school starts."

Suddenly Tiffany was tired. Too tired to think about driving around town updating computer systems and answering well-meant questions about her health. Shivering despite the warmth of the morning, she walked back into the house and went into her office. Though she handled most of her business alone, she had several contractors lined up, waiting for overflow jobs. Two of them had worked for Tiffany on other occasions and she called them, then faxed over lists of jobs and addresses for the week to come.

An hour later she had called her most pressing clients and informed them of her week's vacation. Most knew what had happened and didn't question her. The few who did were satisfied with Tiffany's explanation and the replacement contractors she'd lined up.

Pacing the floor of her office, Tiffany felt at loose ends. Though she knew taking a week off was the right decision, she couldn't imagine how she would spend her free time.

One-handed quilting might be possible, but she doubted the finished product would be worth her effort. She supposed she could tackle some of the smaller renovation projects for the house, but could muster little enthusiasm for the idea.

Shrugging off her restlessness, Tiffany grabbed a copy of a computer magazine off her bookshelf along with a quilting book she'd been meaning to read, shoved her feet into a pair of neon-pink sandals and headed for the door. "Hey, Bandit. Wanna go outside?"

Her companion raised his huge head and looked at her a moment, as if trying to decide if getting up was worth the effort. Then he lumbered to his feet and followed her outside.

Tiffany supposed she should be nervous about leaving the house, but she figured Bandit would bark if a stranger got too close. She also figured it would be too easy to give in to fear and stay hidden inside. She wouldn't give her assailant the satisfaction.

Besides, the sky had turned to the purest summer blue, the heady aroma of blossoms lay heavy on the warm air and Tiffany couldn't imagine spending the day indoors. Walking across her backyard, she approached the old gazebo warily. The ladder still lay on the ground, though someone had propped it against the gazebo. The same person had removed the piles of clipped foliage from the surrounding area and Tiffany was able to access the old structure with little difficulty.

Her heart beat a little faster as she made herself comfortable on the swing. It seemed a thousand hostile eyes followed her movements, and she had to force herself to stay put. All around her, birds chirped and insects chattered, playing a symphony in the overgrown grass.

Surely they would fall silent if someone lurked behind a

tree. Tiffany glanced at Bandit. He'd made himself comfortable in the shade of the swing and seemed completely at ease. She needed to follow his example. After a few calming breaths she opened the magazine and began to read.

She was bored to tears in minutes.

The book proved more interesting and Tiffany's fingers itched for paper and pencil to jot down ideas. She was mentally piecing a Jacob's Ladder patterned quilt when Bandit lifted his head and barked. Startled, Tiffany dropped the book, her heart pounding frantically as she looked around. She didn't see anyone, but Bandit's second bark and his joyfully wagging tail, told her someone was coming. And that the someone was a friend.

A moment later Jake rounded the corner of the house and started across the yard. Tiffany watched his progress, thought about getting up, and decided she was just too comfortable to move. Instead she waved her hand and called out to him. "Over here."

Jake waved back, his long-legged stride quickly eating up the distance between them. Dressed in a T-shirt and shorts, his hair slightly mussed, he looked comfortable and at ease. As he climbed the two steps up into the gazebo, he smiled, motioning toward Tiffany's feet. "Nice sandals."

"A gift from my niece."

Jake's gaze moved from the sandals to the book lying on the ground and then to the discarded magazine. "Sorry to disturb you, but I had a few questions to ask. I rang the doorbell. When you didn't answer, I thought I'd check out here."

"No problem. I was just relaxing. Doctor's orders."

"I'm surprised you're following them. The last I heard, you were bound and determined to ignore Brian's advice and head off to work today."

Curious, Tiffany sat up straight, moving her legs so Jake

could join her on the swing. "Who have you been talking to?"

Jake sat down. "I stopped by Becky's Diner this morning and ran into your mom and dad. Your mom told me you kicked them out of the house so you could get ready for work. Were they here all weekend?"

"Yes. My parents and half the population of Lakeview."

"Doesn't sound very restful."

Tiffany thought about the past few days, then shook her head. "Nice, but definitely not restful. I finally put my foot down and told my parents they needed to go home so I could get back to my normal routine."

"And once they were gone you decided to play hooky from work?"

"No, I actually planned to work until Tom stopped by. After talking to him, I realized I was more tired than I thought."

"What happened with Tom? I noticed he isn't working today."

"He quit."

"Did he say why?" Jake's gaze sharpened, his demeanor changing from friendly and relaxed to alert in the space of a heartbeat.

"More or less. He told me things had gotten out of hand this summer and he needed to get away for a while. He plans to help his father make deliveries."

"I'm sorry. I'm sure that must disappoint you."

Tiffany had expected Jake to be happy with Tom's decision and to tell her so. His words surprised her and she looked away, hoping he wouldn't notice the sudden moisture in her eyes. "Yeah, I guess it does. I really like Tom. He's a good kid."

"I'm beginning to believe that."

Tiffany turned and met Jake's steady gaze. "That's a change."

Jake shrugged, his shoulder brushing against Tiffany's. "I judged him harshly. I realize my mistake. I still say most kids like Tom can't or won't change, but he's one of the few that really wants to."

Jake's assessment made Tiffany smile. "I guess I shouldn't say I told you so."

"But you will?"

She laughed, a weight she hadn't realized she was carrying suddenly lifted. It felt good to be with Jake. "No. Not this time."

"You're assuming there'll be other times when I'm wrong?"

"I'm sure this is a once-in-a-lifetime thing for you."

"Maybe twice in a lifetime, but not much more." Jake's grin did something to Tiffany's stomach and she looked away, afraid he'd see how much he affected her.

"You said you had a few questions to ask?"

"Right. Sorry. Can you remember anything else about your attacker? You said he was tall. Did you see hair color? Clothes?"

Tiffany tried to force her mind to see more than a hazy memory. "I think his clothes were dark, but his hair might have been light. Blond or light brown."

"And you didn't see if he was Caucasian or had a darker skin color?"

"No. It happened too fast."

Jake nodded. "Don't worry about it."

"Do you know who it is?"

"I've got a good guess. But guessing doesn't put criminals behind bars."

"Too bad. I'd feel a lot safer knowing whoever did this to me couldn't come back."

"You and me both." Jake leaned back and stretched, the length of his arm ruffling the edges of Tiffany's unbound hair. He glanced at the rioting curls and smiled. "I like your hair like that."

"Yeah? You're into the windstorm-survivor look?"

"On you, anything would look good."

Tiffany knew his words were a harmless flirtation but warmth spread across her cheeks. She stood and moved away, hoping distance would force some sense into her. "It's getting hot. I think I'll get some lemonade. Would you like a glass?"

"Sounds good. Why don't I come in and help you with it?"

The coolness of the house helped drain some of the rioting color from Tiffany's cheeks. Relieved, she grabbed two glasses from the cupboard and filled each with lemonade and ice, handing one to Jake. He took a sip of the cool liquid, watching over the rim as she did the same. "You manage pretty well for a one-armed woman. So, how are you feeling?"

"Better."

"That's a relative term. You were so miserable the other night, better might still be terrible."

His words surprised Tiffany and she stared at him for a moment before speaking. "You're good at that."

"What?"

"Hearing the truth instead of what makes you comfortable. I think in the past two days a hundred people have asked me how I am. I've told them all the same thing I just told you. You're the only one who questioned me further."

"Most people take things at face value. It makes life less complicated."

Jake's assessment sparked Tiffany's curiosity. She was about to ask what he meant when the shrill sound of the phone cut into their conversation. Tiffany planned to ignore it but after two rings, the answering machine picked up and the gruff voice of one of her clients filled the room.

"Tiffany? This is Matt Culver. I tried to reach you on your office phone with no luck. We've got a problem here. I think a hacker has accessed our database and is flooding it. We're having problems with the system and we need it up and running...ten minutes ago."

Matt ran a dental clinic in Lynchburg, offering free and reduced-rate dental care for pediatric patients whose parents couldn't afford regular dental care. Tiffany grabbed the phone. "Matt?"

"Tiffany. Glad I caught up with you. I know you're recovering from some injuries...the grapevine's been spreading the news...but we've got a serious problem here. Our system is locked tight and we can't access our Web site or our files. When I called your contractor he couldn't promise immediate service, and to be honest, the clinic can't afford to pay for someone to come out. Got any suggestions?"

Though Tiffany offered her services to the clinic free of charge she had always treated them like a paying customer. This was no exception. "I'll be there within an hour."

She hung up before he could protest. "Jake, I hate to cut our chat short, but I've got to drive to Lynchburg."

"Lynchburg? That's a forty-five-minute drive."

"No problem. I go out there a few times a week." Tiffany grabbed her keys and purse.

"Yeah? Not with a concussion you don't."

"I feel fine."

"What did McMath say about driving?"

"He said I should take it easy. I'm not sure he mentioned driving," Tiffany hedged, fairly sure she had heard something about not driving for a week.

Jake stared her down.

It only took a minute for Tiffany to cave. "All right. He did say I should avoid driving for a few days. But it's been three days and I feel fine."

Jake shook his head. "Not good enough. Head injuries are unpredictable. What if you black out at the wheel?"

The thought of doing just that, and inadvertently hurting or killing someone made Tiffany capitulate. "You're right. I can't risk it."

Frustrated she slammed her keys down on the counter and ran a hand through her curly hair. "I'm going to have to make some calls, see if I can find someone willing to do the work."

"Or I could drive you."

"You'd drive me to Lynchburg?"

"Why not? I still want to discuss a few things about the case with you and this will give me the opportunity to do that."

"I'd hate to put you out."

"It's no problem."

Tiffany could see Jake meant it and she shrugged her acceptance. "All right. I'll just get my stuff."

"Let me help."

It was only after Jake followed her to the office, helped her load supplies into his truck and gave her a boost into the cab that Tiffany started to worry. She enjoyed his company too much, and was letting him become an important part of her life. Those things wouldn't have bothered her if he hadn't made it clear that he wanted nothing more from her than friendship.

Not that Tiffany minded being just a friend. Friendship was great. The problems began when one friend fell in love with the other. And, as Jake slid into the driver's seat and smiled in her direction, Tiffany had a sinking suspicion that she was about to fall hard.

"You sure this isn't going to be too much for you? You're starting to look a little green around the gills."

"I'm fine. Just wondering where Bandit disappeared to."

"He's in the back of the truck. Hiding behind my cooler."

"You're kidding, right? The cooler is about the size of his head."

"Yep. I went to put your stuff in the back and saw him curled up as small as he could get. His head is behind the cooler and everything else is sticking out. Guess he wanted to come with us."

Tiffany glanced out the back window and spotted Bandit in exactly the position Jake had described. Laughing, she shook her head and turned back to Jake. "Well, we don't want to disillusion him. Let's just pretend we didn't notice."

Chapter Seventeen

Jake didn't mind the drive and he didn't mind the company. Tiffany kept him entertained with stories about her sisters, her parents and her nieces and nephew. The forty-minute drive seemed to take only minutes, and when Tiffany pointed out the five-story glass building that housed the clinic, Jake felt a jolt of surprise that they had reached their destination so quickly.

"There are quite a few shops in the area if you want to take a look around. I'm not sure how long I'll be."

Tiffany had her hand on the door handle, ready to step out in the summer heat. When she turned to look at him, Jake almost winced at the sight of the bruise that covered her forehead and spread down along her temple. No way did Jake plan to let her out of his sight. "I'll just come in with you."

"You'll be bored."

"Why do you say that?"

"Computers aren't the most exciting things in the world and it might take me hours to fix the problem."

"Today's my day off. I have plenty of time."

Tiffany's eyes shone with questions Jake knew she wouldn't ask. Questions he wasn't sure he could answer. "All right. If you're sure."

"I am. What about Bandit?"

"He can't come up to the clinic, but the security guard won't mind keeping an eye on him for us."

Tiffany got out of the truck before Jake could go around and help her. He did manage to convince her that she'd be more useful keeping Bandit in line than she would be trying to carry her heavy tool kit. They walked into the building together and, as Tiffany had predicted, the security guard was more than happy to keep Bandit down in his office.

It didn't take long for Jake to understand why Tiffany had been adamant about getting to the clinic. The office space was large, the equipment state-of-the-art, but the children were what grabbed Jake's attention. Some wore braces, some had noticeable gaps in their mouths where teeth should have been but weren't, several had cranial-facial deformities that Jake assumed needed special orthodontic care. And, according the receptionist Jake spoke to, none of them had to pay more than what they could. The clinic was free to those who qualified, and reduced-rate programs were available for those who didn't. The receptionist also informed Jake, as Tiffany made her way to a room where the main computer was housed, that Tiffany never charged a cent and always provided prompt, courteous service. Though the program was funded by state and government grants, Tiffany's contribution freed several thousand dollars a year that the clinic could use to help more children.

Jake followed Tiffany into the small computer room and

watched her work. She tackled the computer as she did most things, with enthusiasm. He let time pass in silence, watching as Tiffany's brow furrowed and then cleared, only to furrow again. "Is it a big problem?"

She looked up distractedly. "Not too bad. It's fixable, anyway."

"You must really love computers to have made such a successful career out of them."

Tiffany's hand stilled and she shook her head. "You know, I don't. Not really. Computers are practical. I'm good at them. I make a good living fixing them. But I don't love them."

"So this isn't your first career choice?"

"No, if I could choose just for pleasure, I'd be a quilter."

"So why don't you do it?"

"I haven't thought about it much. I guess I went to college thinking it was more important to do something I could support myself with than to do what I enjoy. How about you? Do you love what you do?"

Jake noticed her eagerness to turn the conversation away from herself, and he let her. "Yes. I do, actually. Though if you'd asked me fifteen years ago, I would have told you a cop was the last thing I'd ever be."

"What changed your mind?"

Jake spent the next several minutes giving Tiffany a tame version of his misspent youth. When he finished they fell silent, speaking only occasionally as Tiffany worked.

That she didn't push for more conversation, that she didn't demand Jake's constant attention, was a stark contrast to the way things had been when he was with Sheila. Though Sheila had been tough to the point of aggression, she'd also been needy, clingy and unsure of who she was. She'd never been silent. Never been content to sit and dream.

In the end it was her dissatisfaction that had broken them apart. Bored, restless and unhappy she'd drifted from one lover to another, leaving a trail of evidence for Jake to find.

He hadn't been angry. He'd been relieved.

"I'm done." Tiffany's voice drew Jake from the past.

He forced himself to push thoughts of Sheila from his mind. "That didn't take long."

"It wasn't too bad. But admit it, you were bored out of your mind."

"Nope. Not at all. I find it fascinating to watch someone do something she's really good at." He paused, grabbing the tools out of her hand. "Of course, that doesn't mean I'm not happy to be out of here."

Tiffany laughed, the sound tugging at Jake's heart. Together they walked through the clinic and onto the elevator. In the lobby Bandit lay at the guard's feet, chewing a fat rawhide bone. He thumped his tail in greeting but didn't rise.

The guard glanced up from some paperwork he was doing, his eyes clear blue and sparkling. "Hey Tiff, sure you don't want to give the dog away? I'm gettin' kinda fond of him."

"Sorry, Hank. Bandit is family."

"I could be family, too. If you'd let me." The guard raised white eyebrows in a Groucho salute.

Jake felt his eyes narrow at the blatant flirtation. He wanted to tell the man to keep his innuendoes to himself, but managed to hold his tongue.

Tiffany didn't seem to mind at all and smiled at Hank as if he were her best friend. "I don't know, I think you're a little old to be adopted. Besides, what would your children think if their father ran off with a dog? I don't think your wife would care much for the idea, either."

Hank laughed. "Darlin', my wife would probably jump for

joy if someone adopted me. She's always saying that I'm worse than all five boys combined."

"That I believe. Thanks again for watching Bandit."

"Any time. Take care of yourself. I don't want you coming in here all bruised up again."

The guard waved them on their way, and Jake tried to shrug aside his irritation. The man was old enough to be Tiffany's grandfather. He was also married. Apparently happily. So why did Jake feel on edge because of a bit of flirtation?

"Hank's a piece of work, isn't he?" Tiffany interrupted Jake's thoughts and he turned his attention back to her.

"You know, he and his wife have been married for thirty years. They raised five sons and then," Tiffany paused as she slid into the passenger seat and waited for Jake to put Bandit in the back of the truck, "when Dorothy, that's his wife, was fifty-one she got pregnant."

"You're kidding."

"Nope. Hank was fifty-five, just retired from the government and ready to travel with Dorothy. Imagine his surprise when instead of Hawaii, they were going to Lamaze classes."

"I imagine it was a mixed blessing." Jake put the truck in gear and pulled out of the parking lot, hoping Tiffany hadn't picked up on his lukewarm response to the man.

"Yes. God gave them a little girl. She's seven now and Hank said she's sweeter than grapes picked from the vine."

"He did not say that."

"He did and his eyes misted over and everything. I almost cried myself."

"Almost?"

"Okay, so a tear or two fell, but it was a beautiful story."

"Yeah, it is. I wish everyone could have a story like that."

Jake could feel Tiffany's gaze slide his way and he knew she wondered about his life. About his marriage. About his choice to be alone.

To her credit she didn't ask, respecting his privacy and choosing another topic of conversation. "What did you think of the clinic?"

"I was impressed. Not only does it offer dental care to children who wouldn't get it otherwise, but the staff treats clients with respect and understanding."

"That's what I liked about it. When Matt approached me about doing pro bono work for him I was a little leery but once I visited a few times I knew I had to help."

Tiffany's words ended on a yawn and Jake glanced her way. The deep shadows under her eyes seemed more pronounced and the tinge of color he'd seen earlier had leeched from her skin, leaving her looking pallid and ill. "Are you all right? You look beat."

"I'm a little tired. I guess it's a good thing I'm taking the rest of the week off."

"Why don't you close your eyes for a while? We've got another forty-minute drive ahead of us, so you have time for a quick nap."

"You don't mind?"

"I'll be upset if you don't." Jake smiled in her direction to let her know he was kidding.

Tiffany didn't argue further. Her eyes were nearly crossing with fatigue and she doubted she could keep them open if she wanted to.

Closing her eyes, Tiffany let the low purr of the engine and the warmth of Jake's presence lull her to sleep.

Chapter Eighteen

Jake could tell by Tiffany's deep, rhythmic breathing that she was asleep. As he drove, he felt his eyes drawn to her again and again. Leaning against the window, her left arm cradled close to her body, she looked fragile and defenseless. The vitality and enthusiasm that made her such a strong force while awake, drained from her while she slept and Jake had the absurd urge to pull her close and protect her from whatever life might throw her way.

The urge worried him. He'd never doubted his decision not to marry again. He'd known from the moment he and Sheila separated that being single suited him. He liked his alone time. Enjoyed his solitude. More than that, he liked knowing that the only person he was responsible for was himself. Without responsibility, there could be no guilt. And guilt was something Jake wanted to avoid.

He'd had enough of it in the past few years. Enough of

the gnawing, persistent what-ifs. What if he'd paid more attention to Sheila? What if he'd been able to love her a little bit more? What if he'd refused to divorce her, despite her infidelity, and had insisted they seek counseling?

Would she be alive today?

Probably not. His partner, Will, had convinced Jake of that, even as he'd shared his belief that there was something beyond the here and now. A Creator who loved, who forgave, who provided.

As Jake embraced that knowledge, he'd finally been able to let go of the guilt that had eaten away at his joy, robbed him of contentment, and threatened his very soul.

What he hadn't let go of was the belief that marriage, family and love were for other people. Not for him.

Maybe Ben had been right when he said that Jake wouldn't *allow* himself to have those things. Maybe the guilt that he'd thought he'd let go of still haunted him. Or maybe he was just afraid. Afraid that what he wanted most was something he'd never be able to achieve.

He eased the truck along Tiffany's driveway and pulled to a stop in front of her house. What was it about Tiffany that made him wish for things he'd given up on years ago? He glanced at the woman beside him, his heart aching with a longing he refused to name. Then he reached out, brushing away the soft curls that fell against her cheek.

She stirred, her eyes opening slowly, a soft smile curving her mouth as she focused on him. "Jake?"

He let his hand fall away, wishing he didn't have to. Wishing he had the right to thread his hands through her hair, and kiss the sleep from her lips. "You're home. I'll help you get your stuff in. I think Bandit just made a run for the backyard."

Tiffany allowed him to escort her to the house, then

waited on the love seat while Jake brought in the computer equipment. She still looked pale and he saw her wince as she leaned back against the pillows. "Headache?"

"No, but my arm is making up for the pain I don't feel in my head."

"That bad, huh?"

"Either that or I'm a wimp."

"Any woman willing to go after an unknown man with a pint of Ben & Jerry's is definitely not that."

Tiffany smiled at the comment, looking up at Jake with eyes still misty from sleep. "You're never going to let me live that down, are you?"

"Nope." He almost sat down beside her, not willing to give up the companionship they shared. "I have a meeting with Ben Avery tonight. I guess I'd better go get ready for it."

"All right." Tiffany rose and walked with him to the door. "Maybe I could make you dinner sometime. To thank you for all your help."

"That would be nice." He'd refuse when the time came. What choice did he have? It was that or risk her heart. And his.

Jake stepped out onto the porch, anxious to put distance between himself and Tiffany, but she put her hand on his arm, stopping him before he could retreat. "You never asked me those questions about my attacker."

She was right, he hadn't. "It can wait another couple of days. Just be sure to keep your windows and doors locked. And use the security system."

"I will."

Bandit lumbered up the porch stairs and collapsed near Tiffany's feet. "I need to get this brute some food. He eats more than three dogs should."

Jake knew he was being gently dismissed and he knew

he should be glad. Instead he wished he had a reason to stay. "All right. Take it easy and call if you have any trouble."

"I doubt I'll have to. You always seem to show up right around the time I'm getting myself into a mess. Say hi to Ben for me."

Jake nodded and stepped down into late-afternoon sun. "I'll do that."

Tiffany watched him get into his truck, then slowly closed the door blocking out the sight of him driving away. She'd been dreaming on the way home from Lynchburg. Dreaming that she and Jake were married, driving toward some honeymoon destination. Just thinking about the silly romance of it made her blush. When she'd woken up to the gentle touch of his hand on her hair, she'd believed, for one heart-stopping moment, that the dream had become reality.

Thank goodness Jake wasn't as good at reading her mind as he was at rescuing her from all the trouble she'd fallen into lately.

Tiffany sighed and walked down the hall and into the kitchen. There were plenty of things to do. She scooped food into Bandit's dish, cleaned the counter of crumbs left from lunch, heated a cup of tea. All the while trying to ignore the truth. But even keeping busy couldn't prevent her mind from whispering its knowledge—Tiffany was falling in love with a man who could not love her in return.

Jake didn't have an appointment scheduled with Ben, but he did plan to meet with him. He needed his friend's advice and he knew Ben would make time for him. Grabbing the cell phone he punched in the number to the church and waited for the secretary to connect them.

"Hey, Jake, what can I do for you?" Ben's cheerful voice greeted him.

"I was wondering if I could stop by the office for a few minutes."

"Anything wrong?"

"No, I just need some advice from a friend."

"That's one thing you can count on. Me having advice to give. When did you want to come by?"

"What's convenient for you?"

"Any time between now and six. I'm going on hospital visitation then."

"I'll be there in ten minutes."

"You sure everything's okay?"

"Yeah. I'll tell you about it when I get there."

True to his word, Jake made it to the church in ten minutes. Bypassing the office, he moved down the hall to the pastor's study. Ben greeted him at the door. "I grabbed a pitcher of tea from the kitchen. Or we can do coffee."

"Tea is good."

They moved into the room, a cozy area where built-in wall shelves housed books and a small desk held Ben's computer. The carpet was a well-worn green, the shelves freshly painted white and the large window overlooked the backyard playground. Usually bustling with activity, the playground was empty. "It's quiet around here today."

Ben nodded, motioning for Jake to sit down. "Summer lull. The preschool doesn't operate during the summer, so we've got a fairly quiet building for most of the day."

Ben grabbed two brightly colored paper cups from a small stack and poured iced tea from a plastic pitcher. "So, what brings you my way? I guess it's too much to hope you're here to volunteer as cleanup day coordinator."

Though the words were spoken lightly, Ben looked tired, his eyes shadowed. Concerned, Jake leaned forward and eyed his friend. "If you need a coordinator I can fill in. What's up with you? You don't look your usual cheerful self."

"Just some family trouble. I can't go into all the details right now but I may need your help with that more than I need a cleanup day coordinator." Ben tried to smile but it didn't reach his eyes.

"What kind of help are we talking? Professional?"

"Maybe. Like I said, I can't talk about it now. I'm not even sure of all the details myself."

Jake stared Ben down for a minute, but couldn't imagine what kind of trouble his friend might have that required police help. "Ben..."

Ben raised a hand and shook his head. "Don't worry, it's not about me. At least not directly. I just might need some help finding someone."

Jake nodded, satisfied with the answer. "All right. Let me know."

"Now let's talk about you. I'm thinking this has something to do with Tiffany Anderson."

"Why would you say that?"

"I ate at the diner today. Jessica Ann swore she saw you and Tiffany heading out of town in your Chevy."

Disgruntled, Jake picked up his tea and swallowed deeply before answering. "So this is what small-town life is like."

"Yep. What's going on with you and the lady in question?"

"Nothing. Yet. I just keep imagining what it would be like if I could offer her the life I think she deserves. And I wonder if you were right. Maybe my decision not to marry again is a knee-jerk reaction to a bad first marriage. Like you said, I've got a new life in Christ. I shouldn't be dwelling on the past. And maybe I am taking too much responsibility on myself."

"Meaning?"

"Meaning, I need to figure out where God is leading me, not where I think I should go. I'm just not sure how to go about that."

"And you're hoping I can tell you?"

"Well, you *are* the Bible scholar." Jake grinned, relaxing now that he'd shared his troubles.

"Maybe not a scholar. But I did have a feeling you might need this." Ben passed a sheet of paper across the desk. "I printed out a list of some verses I think might help."

Jake took the paper, glancing down at the neatly typed page.

"I think, if you spend some time looking up the verses and studying what they say, you'll be able to answer your own question. If not, we can get together again and talk things through."

Nodding in agreement, Jake folded the sheet of paper and slid it into his wallet. It seemed too simple, too easy, but he trusted Ben's judgment. "Thanks. Now that that's out of the way, why don't you tell me what you were doing at the diner talking to Jessica Ann." The young woman was a part-time receptionist at the station. Bright, ambitious and attractive, she also seemed to have a good heart. Jake wasn't surprised that Ben had noticed her.

"Jessica is a kid. We just happened to be in the same place at the same time." Ben's laughing protest invited Jake to argue the point.

"She's not a kid. She's twenty-nine. And you're all of what? Thirty-three?"

"Thirty-five, but who's counting?"

"You, apparently, if you're calling a twenty-nine-year-old a kid."

"Give me a break, Jake, just because the love bug's bitten you..."

"Who said anything about love?!"

The two argued companionably until the phone rang, cutting their conversation short. Ben answered, spoke briefly and hung up. "I hate to do this, but I'm afraid I'm needed at the convalescent center."

"Is someone ill?"

"Worse. Mavis and Jasper Harvell are arguing. They've been married fifty years and Mavis has it in her mind that it's time to have a little freedom. Jasper isn't too happy about it. Every couple of weeks he threatens to divorce her, and she calls me."

"You've got to be kidding."

"Nope. I don't really mind. By the time I get there, they've mended their fences and we have a nice chat."

Both men stood and walked to the door.

"Make sure you read those verses. And let me know what you think."

"I will."

Later, Jake sat at home, eyes skimming the verses Ben had given him. Thumbing through his Bible he looked up one after another until he reached the fifth chapter of Galatians. Ben had noted the thirteenth verse and Jake read it. Then read it again. "You, my brother, were called to be free."

Free. Jake didn't feel free. He felt choked by the past. Unable to let go. Or maybe, more to the point, unwilling to let go. He read the verse again, then the chapter, then the entire book of Galatians. When he was done, he closed the leather cover of his Bible and sat in silence, listening.

Though he heard no audible voice, the scripture spoke clearly to him. Nothing Jake could do would make up for or change the past, yet in Christ he was a new creation. Because of that he had freedom from what had come before and hope for something better. Ben had been right: the mistakes Jake had made before had no claim on him. He belonged to God and God would create the perfect future for him.

For the first time in years, Jake allowed himself to dream of a life shared with someone else. And there was no denying whom he wanted to share it with. Even sitting alone in the two-bedroom garage apartment he rented, he could almost smell the berry shampoo that Tiffany used and feel the silky softness of her golden-red hair. He thought of her laughter and indomitable spirit, and he knew he could spend the rest of his life with her and it still wouldn't be enough.

The thought terrified him.

Even with Sheila Jake hadn't imagined forever. He'd never thought about her in the context of a lifetime.

Tiffany was different. When he looked at her he saw the future. He imagined raising children with her, imagined seeing her face aged and wrinkled, her hair gray, her bright eyes dulled with time, and he imagined loving her always.

Jake rose on shaky legs and walked outside. A white-gold gibbous moon shone bright against the midnight sky, night creatures sang the glory of creation and in the moments beyond night and before dawn broke the sky, Jake poured his heart out to God, giving the burden of the past, the present and the future to Him.

It was time to let go of yesterday and move on to tomorrow. He was finally ready to be free.

Chapter Nineteen

Jake began his campaign the next day.

First he drove to the diner and picked up a bag of fresh pastries. Then to the hardware store where he purchased several lengths of treated wood. Tiffany would be surprised to see him. He'd use that to his advantage.

He planned to woo her. And he planned to do it right. A smile tugged at the corner of Jake's mouth, as he remembered Tiffany scoffing at the old-fashioned word and at the idea that any man would go to the trouble to pursue her.

Jake was about to prove her wrong. Candy, flowers, moonlit walks—Tiffany was going to get all the wooing a woman could ever want. And, when she'd finally had enough, he'd tell her the only way she could get him to stop would be to marry him.

Grinning a little at the thought, Jake pulled up in front of

Tiffany's house and got out of the truck. Pastry bag in hand, he walked up the steps and onto the porch.

Tiffany heard the doorbell ring as she got out of the shower. With her soft cast still wrapped in a plastic trash bag, she had a difficult time pulling on the cotton pullover she'd picked from her closet. She managed to yank it on and pull on drawstring shorts before the doorbell rang again. With her wet hair dripping down her back, she raced downstairs, fumbled with the security code for the alarm system and finally managed to open the door on the third ring. She didn't know who she had expected, but it wasn't Jake. Lifting a hand to smooth her soaked hair, she tried to act like having Jake on her doorstep first thing in the morning was a natural occurrence. "Jake. I wasn't expecting you."

"I hope you don't mind. I've been suffering guilt pangs and I decided to clear my conscience."

"Guilt? About what?" Tiffany hoped he wasn't going to say the kiss. She'd been trying hard to put it out of her mind.

"I think Tom quit because of the fear I put into him the other night. Since it's my fault you don't have hired help anymore, I thought it only fair that I pitch in with the gazebo renovations."

"That isn't—"

"I thought you might argue, so I brought these." Jake held up a white bag. "They're Danishes. I hope you don't mind eating pastries for breakfast."

"I'll eat a Danish anytime."

Jake's grin sent Tiffany's heart skittering into overdrive and she turned away quickly, hoping to hide her blush.

Jake followed her into the house. "You look rested. Good night sleep?"

"Yes, having an alarm system makes me feel pretty safe." Tiffany led the way into the kitchen.

"When I was growing up we had a security system. It never made me feel safe."

Surprised, Tiffany looked up from the plates she was setting on the table. "Really? Was there a lot of crime in your neighborhood?"

"Some. But I think the system was designed to keep me and my mom in as much as it was to keep others out."

"Keep you in?"

"Only my father had the code. He liked to control the people in his life."

"That's terrible."

"Yes, but it was a long time ago."

"Are you and your father close now?"

"My father has been dead for years. If he were alive, I doubt we'd be friends."

Tiffany met Jake's gaze. His blue eyes were steady, pain and regret shining from their depth. Reaching out, Tiffany touched his hand. "Jake, I'm so sorry."

"Like I said, it was a long time ago."

"Not so long ago that it doesn't still hurt."

"True, but I'm trying to move on. It's past time for me to forgive my father and forgive myself."

"Forgive yourself? For what?"

Jake ran a hand through his hair and rubbed the base of his neck. "I've made mistakes. One of them was my first marriage. Sheila was...lovely. Very sweet when we first met, but demanding. I didn't know how to handle that. I'd been raised to take care of myself and had no idea there were people who didn't know how to do that."

"Did you marry young?" Tiffany couldn't stop the question. Jake hadn't talked about his past before, and she wanted to know everything.

"Not so young that I could use that as an excuse. I was

twenty-six. She was a year younger. I'll tell you more. But not now. Now I want to sit down, eat breakfast and enjoy the company of a beautiful woman."

Tiffany had to bite her tongue to keep from asking more questions. She had so many things she wanted to know, but pushing for more information seemed nosy and rude, especially since Jake had called her beautiful. Smiling, she grabbed the bag from his hands and looked inside. "All right. Did you bring any cheese Danish?"

They discussed Jake's offer of help over breakfast, Tiffany explaining that she didn't need to have the gazebo finished any time soon, and Jake arguing that one more winter might be too much for the old structure. In the end, unable to think of any compelling argument against it, Tiffany let him have his way. "I guess I can't turn down free help."

"I was hoping you'd see it my way." Jake stood and grabbed the empty Danish bag, tossing it into the trash can as he made his way to the mudroom. "I've got some treated wood in the truck. I'm going to bring it out and leave it in the garage."

"You already bought wood?" Tiffany tried to curb her irritation but wondered at the presumptuousness of his actions.

"Not much. The garage apartment I'm staying in has a little deck off the back. It needs some work and I told Mrs. Murphy I could do it for her. I stopped by the hardware store and picked up enough wood to finish the project."

"Shouldn't you bring it to your place, then, instead of using it here?"

"I could, but if I need wood for your project it'll be nice to have some on hand. You can reimburse me for the cost if I use it."

Mollified, Tiffany nodded her head. "Okay. That's fair. Let me just go run a brush through my hair and I'll come out and help you."

She was sure Jake would argue and was prepared to stand firm, but he surprised her by quickly agreeing. "Great. I'll see you in a few minutes."

Not sure what to think of Jake's presence, or his sudden offer to lend a hand, Tiffany stood up, threw the remainder of her Danish to Bandit and hurried up the stairs.

Her hair, impossibly curly and thick on the best of days, clumped together in masses of tangled curls in the aftermath of her one-handed shampoo. Spraying on a detangler, Tiffany tried to work a comb through her hair, gave up and tugged a brush down its length. With a little finesse, she was able to twist her hair into a clip that would keep most of it off her face and neck. She might not look great, but at least she wouldn't swelter under the weight of her heavy hair.

A few gentle pulls at soaked tape released the bag from her broken arm and Tiffany shrugged on the sling, wincing a little as she moved her arm into it. She considered putting on makeup, decided against it, and shoved her feet into sneakers, not bothering to tighten the laces. Calling to Bandit, she rushed down the stairs and into the kitchen. The big dog was waiting beside his empty food and water bowls, dark eyes faintly accusing.

Tiffany quickly replenished his water and scooped food into his bowl. "Sorry, guy, I haven't forgotten you. It's just been a busy morning."

Bandit licked her hand and turned his attention to breakfast.

By the time Tiffany made her way across the yard to the gazebo, Jake had propped the ladder up against the side of the roof and was jotting measurements into a notebook.

Sunlight glinted off his dark hair, causing it to glow with fiery warmth. As she approached, he glanced her way and smiled, the blue of his eyes so intense Tiffany felt the breath catch in her throat.

"Hey, I was hoping you'd show up about now. I need a steady hand on the ladder while I climb. Think you can manage?"

"Sure." Tiffany grabbed hold of the ladder and held it as Jake climbed.

While he measured, he asked Tiffany a few questions about her attacker, prodding for details Tiffany was unable to give. She felt frustrated by her inability to give a more detailed description and said as much.

"You're no different than most people who witness a crime. Things happen so fast, it's hard to remember the details afterward."

"I still wish I could."

"The knock you took on your head probably dulled some of your memory. Maybe in a few days you'll remember more details." Finishing a last measurement, he backed down the ladder and stood beside Tiffany.

"Even if you don't remember anything else, we'll catch the person."

"You sound pretty confident."

"I am. I know who it is. I just need to prove it. Or catch him next time."

"You think there's going to be a next time?"

"There's no doubt in my mind. The kid is cocky and has something to prove. He'll make more trouble before he leaves."

The thought of someone lurking around waiting to strike again made Tiffany's heart do a nervous jig.

As if sensing her concern, Jake hurried to reassure her.

"I don't think you have anything to worry about. Tom's buddies got what they wanted. Now that he doesn't work for you, their focus will shift."

"I hope you're right."

Jake reached out and tugged at a curl that had escaped Tiffany's clip. "Relax, I won't let anything else happen to you."

His hand slid from her hair and brushed against her cheek, making Tiffany's heart dance for an entirely different reason other than fear. Suddenly Jake wasn't just the friend he claimed to be. Nor was he simply an acquaintance. Instead, he looked at her as if she had immeasurable beauty, as if he wanted something only she could give.

Startled by the transformation, Tiffany opened her mouth to ask what was going on, but Jake turned away and the moment was lost.

"I don't think I'll need to replace much of the roof. A few nails, some sanding and refinishing should do it."

Tiffany blinked, confused by the turn in conversation and not entirely comfortable with her response to Jake. "Maybe I'll go back to the house. I don't think there's much I can do to help with the roof."

"All right. I'll check in when I'm done."

"Be careful."

"You, too." Jake sent a grin in her direction and Tiffany hurried away, determined not to ruin their friendship by falling in love with the man.

Unfortunately, she was afraid it might already be too late.

She lectured herself on the folly of her emotions as she mixed a pitcher of lemonade. Just because Jake's smile seemed softer, just because heat seemed to simmer between them, was no reason for Tiffany to lose sight of the big picture.

And the big picture was that Jake didn't want commitment. He didn't want another marriage. And he more than likely didn't want her.

That firmly in mind, Tiffany carried the lemonade outside. Jake stood on the ladder sanding off layers of chipped, gray paint. The hum of the electric sander muffled the sound of her approach and Tiffany stood for several minutes, watching him work. What was God's purpose in bringing them together time after time? Surely He had a reason Tiffany couldn't imagine.

Jake glanced down, saw her and turned off the sander, a warm smile curving his lips. "I didn't expect to see you out here again."

"It's getting hot. I brought you some lemonade."

"I was just thinking a drink might be good." Jake stepped down off the ladder and took the pitcher. "Do I drink out of the pitcher?"

"Nope, I came prepared." Hoping Jake wouldn't notice how nervous she suddenly felt, Tiffany reached into the pocket of her shorts and pulled out a small plastic cup. "Here you go."

"Cute trick. You're getting too skinny if you can fit a cup in your pants pocket."

"It's a small cup."

Jake snorted and poured himself a drink, taking a long swallow before passing the cup to Tiffany. "It's great. Have some."

"Thanks." Tiffany took the cup and sipped the refreshing liquid, smiling as Jake grabbed the cup before she could drink more. "You're greedy."

"No. I just don't know how to share."

Tiffany laughed at that, watching as he sat on the bench, put the pitcher down on the floor, and stretched his legs out in front of him. He seemed completely comfortable and at ease, a fact that made Tiffany unreasonably happy.

Tugging at her hand, he pulled her down beside him, and offered his cup again. She eyed it dubiously. "I thought you said you didn't know how to share."

"I learn fast with the right motivation."

"What would that be? Fear that I won't offer you lemonade again?"

"More like fear you'll go back in the house to get your own and leave me here alone again."

Flustered, Tiffany turned from him and gestured at Bandit. "You weren't alone. Bandit's been out here all morning."

"He's a guy. He doesn't count as worthwhile companionship."

"You're full of it."

"That's what my mom used to tell me."

Tiffany grabbed the cup Jake still held out to her and took a swallow. "Do you see your mom often?"

Now it was Jake's turn to look away, his gaze leaving Tiffany and staring into the past. "She's been gone for years. Cancer. Though I've always said she died of a broken heart."

"She couldn't accept your father's death?"

"Actually, she passed away before he did. All those years of loving someone who couldn't love her back destroyed her spirit long before the cancer destroyed her body."

Appalled at the picture of family life Jake painted for her, Tiffany set the cup down and reached for his hand. She could think of no words of comfort, nothing that would take away the painful memories and so she kept her peace.

They sat silently in the warm summer air, the scent of pine heavy around them, connected by clasped hands and heavy hearts. Finally Jake turned to look at Tiffany, his eyes sad, his hand squeezing hers lightly. "For a long time I thought I'd done the same to Sheila. Broken her heart and destroyed her the way my father did my mother. When she died that feeling was reinforced. I thought if I'd just loved her more she wouldn't have turned to drinking for solace."

"Jake—"

"I know." He smiled, but sadness lingered in his gaze. "She made her choices. She partied before we met, partied while we were married. The pattern was there. I just didn't see it."

"Did you love her?" The question was out before Tiffany realized she was going to ask it.

"I thought I did. But if I had, I think I would have fought for the relationship more."

"So she asked for the divorce?"

"She didn't ask. She just made it a point to let me know she'd found other people to be with." Jake's tone was wry.

"No wonder you don't want to get married again."

"Partly. Mostly it's fear. Fear that I'll never have what I've always wanted—a wife, children. Family. I screwed it up once. I don't want to do it again. Lately, though, I've wondered if I'm worrying too much and not trusting enough. God has a plan. Maybe it's time I relax and let Him work it in my life."

Tiffany's heart began a slow, heavy throb, and her mouth went dry. If she didn't know better, she'd think Jake was telling her he'd changed his mind about marriage and family.

"I'm beginning to see that God can do anything. And He will if we let Him. Tiffany, I..."

Bandit stood up and barked, interrupting his words. Jake turned to look at the house, then shook his head. "Looks like we have company."

Tiffany followed the direction of his gaze and saw her parents at the gate. Bandit rushed toward them barking happily. At least someone was thrilled to see them. Tiffany loved her parents, but their timing stunk. Still, she managed to smile as she stood up and waved to them. "We're over here."

Her parents opened the gate and stepped into the yard, each carrying several grocery bags. Jake rushed to help, taking the bags from Tiffany's mother and walking with her father into the house. Watching them with trepidation, Tiffany barely noticed when her mother stepped into the gazebo.

"Well, you two were looking cozy. I wish we'd gone for lunch before coming over. Sorry, honey." Patti stretched up to give Tiffany a peck on the cheek.

"We weren't cozy. Jake was helping with the gazebo and I brought him some lemonade." Giving her mother a one-armed hug, Tiffany tried not to worry about the conversation Jake and her father were having.

"Okay. If you say so."

"Mom..."

"Don't worry, I'm not getting my hopes up. But Jake is an awfully nice man."

"You said that about Brian, too, and look where that ended up."

"Actually," Patti paused, digging through the purse she carried on her shoulder and pulling out a brush, "I said Brian was a good catch. Not a nice man. There's a big difference."

"So you don't think Jake is a good catch?"

"I didn't say that. I just think he's a nice man, too. Sit down, I'll brush through your hair and braid it for you."

Tiffany did as her mother suggested, thankful for help with the curly mess. "He is a nice guy. He always seems to be around when I need him."

"Your father likes him, too."

"Really?" Tiffany turned to look at her mother, wincing a little as the brush was pulled through tangles. "Dad's usually pretty hard on men he thinks are interested in me."

"Yes, well according to your father, Jake has his head screwed on straight. That's a high compliment, you know. Of course, I don't know why it matters. You aren't interested, right?"

"I'm not even going to bother lying. You already know the truth. I just wish he were as interested in me."

"What makes you think he isn't? I saw him kissing you, remember?"

"How can I forget? I was humiliated." Tiffany sent her mother a wry grin before continuing. "I know he's not interested because he's told me he wasn't."

"I don't believe it. That man would have to be blind not to be."

"You have to say that, Mom, you're my mother."

"I don't have to say anything. It's true. And I'm not going to argue with you, even though you're looking better today." She finished brushing Tiffany's hair and quickly braided it. "Looks like I've finished just in time. The men are returning."

Tiffany turned her head and caught sight of Jake and her father walking toward them. Though Jake's low voice didn't carry, her father's words were clearly audible. "So, Jake, I suppose law enforcement pays a pretty good salary."

Mortified, Tiffany jumped to her feet and opened her mouth to put a stop to her father's third degree.

"Honey, let Jake fend for himself. He may as well get used to your father." Her mother spoke at the same instant Jake glanced Tiffany's way. His eyes held hers for a moment before he winked and turned to answer the question.

Tiffany didn't hear what he said, but her father chuckled and patted him on the back. Not sure how her life had come to a point where, at thirty-three, she still had her father questioning a potential beau, Tiffany sat back onto the swing. "I cannot believe Dad just asked him that."

"Don't worry about it. Jake didn't seem to mind."

"Mind what?" Jake moved up the steps and into the gazebo, his gaze on Tiffany.

"Mind that my father is being nosy." Tiffany shot her father a reproving look. He didn't even try to look penitent.

"I'm just curious about the man's job."

"Dad, don't even try the innocent routine. We all know what you were doing."

"*I* wasn't quite sure about it. Maybe you could explain." Jake spoke as he leaned against the rail, smirking in Tiffany's direction.

She glared back, trying not to grin. "You're a rat. And so is my father."

"Yeah, but we're cute rats."

Tiffany shook her head and gave up. "Fine, I'll keep my nose out of the male bonding ritual. But don't blame me when Dad gets even more intrusive. Next thing he'll be asking for is your stock portfolio."

"How do you know I haven't already?"

"Dad—"

"All right, children, enough." Patti cut into the good-natured ribbing, linking her arm through her husband's as she spoke. "We actually came for a reason, besides dropping off groceries and giving you a hard time. Did you finish your entry for the quilt show? They want them at the church by Wednesday night so they can get things ready for Saturday's fair."

"I'm glad you reminded me. I did finish the piece. I guess I'll drop it off later this week."

"Why don't your dad and I bring it now? We're heading in that direction and I can fill out the paperwork."

"I'll get it for you."

"We'll walk with you. We've got to be on our way."

"I'd better go, too, I've got the night shift."

Tiffany felt like a band leader as she led her parents and Jake to the house and into the sewing room. The quilt sat where she had left it, spread across the table. Flicking on the light, Tiffany reached out and touched the gold lettering, pleased with the effect against the dark green sun. "I'm calling this *Stillness*."

The name seemed opposite of the piece, whose streaks and swirls of vibrant color seemed to possess energy and motion. However, the midpoint of the quilt was the sun, which stood still and motionless in the midst of the fiery background. A metaphor, Tiffany thought, of God's steadfast presence even during life's most chaotic times.

"I think that's the best you've ever done." Patti moved up beside Tiffany and leaned in close to eye the tiny stitches. "Did you use the machine?"

"No, it's all hand-stitched."

"Well, it's gorgeous. Are you going to sell it?"

"No, I don't think so."

"Too bad." Jake moved up behind Tiffany and placed a hand on her shoulder, leaning over to look at the quilt. "I'd have bought it."

His hand felt warm against her shoulder and Tiffany fought the urge to lean back against it. "Maybe if you do a good job on the gazebo, I'll give it to you as a Christmas gift."

"I'd rather have it as a wedding present."

Jake's words were so shocking, Tiffany dropped the quilt she'd been trying to fold with one hand. Her mother quickly retrieved it. "Don't get it dirty. You don't want to wash it before the show."

Swallowing down her surprise, Tiffany tried to focus on the task at hand. "I've got a label somewhere. Do you mind sewing it on for me, Mom? I can probably manage, but the stitches won't be as even as I'd like."

She felt Jake's gaze as she fumbled through her sewing basket and pulled out a label, placing it on top of the neatly folded quilt her mother was holding. A wedding present? Jake said he never planned to marry and yet this was the second time he had hinted that he had changed his mind.

She didn't dare ask him what he meant, not with her parents there. Not at all. Instead she smiled and nodded and talked as the four of them moved from the sewing room into the hall and out the front door. Jake lingered on the porch for a moment after her parents left but didn't mention his earlier comment.

"I really need to go. I'll be back tomorrow to finish some of the work."

"All right."

"It's your turn to provide breakfast." Jake's voice was playful as he turned to walk down the steps.

"I only have one good arm."

"You're resourceful. I'm sure you'll think of something. See you tomorrow." Not giving Tiffany a chance to respond, Jake got in his truck and drove away.

Chapter Twenty

True to his word, Jake arrived the next morning ready for breakfast. When Tiffany opened the door, he smiled charmingly and handed her a bouquet of wildflowers. The purple, pink and orange blossoms were fragrant, the bright colors intoxicating. Charmed by their simple beauty, Tiffany ushered Jake into the kitchen and placed the flowers in a leaded crystal vase.

"That's a fancy vase for a bunch of wildflowers," Jake teased as Tiffany arranged the bouquet.

"I think it's perfect."

Jake eyed the arrangement critically before nodding his head. "You're right. It is. There's only one problem." He paused, his gaze roaming the kitchen. "I don't smell anything cooking."

"You will." Tiffany gestured to the counter where a shallow dish filled with thick slices of egg-soaked bread sat.

"French toast?"

"Yep. And bacon, once I get it out of the fridge."

"Sounds good. Sit down and I'll cook."

"It's my turn. Remember?" Tiffany took out a heavy skillet and placed it on the stove.

"I was kidding. You're supposed to be resting, not cooking breakfast for me." Jake opened the refrigerator and took out the package of bacon.

"I think I can manage a few pieces of French toast and some bacon. Besides, I feel much better."

"In that case, I'll start the coffee. I need some caffeine."

"Did you just finish your shift?"

"An hour ago. Tonight's another night shift, then I'll be working days for a couple of weeks. I trade off with the other full-time officers."

Tiffany turned on the stove and began cooking the bacon. "There aren't many officers, are there?"

"No, only eight. In the winter that's plenty. In the summer we could use a few extra people. I hired a couple of part-timers. That's helped."

Tiffany listened as Jake described some of the people he worked with, and finished cooking breakfast as he related some of his scary moments as a D.C. police officer. They ate slowly, enjoying each other's company and conversation until Jake stood and brought his empty plate to the sink. "I could talk to you all day, but I promised I'd get some work done on the gazebo. You coming out?"

The idea was tempting and Tiffany considered it for a moment before shaking her head in regret. "I'm afraid not. I've got a ton of paperwork that needs to be filed and invoices that have to go out today. One of the drawbacks of owning my own business is that even during my weeks off there's work to do."

"Too bad. How about I take you to lunch later, after we've both gotten some work done?"

"Flowers and lunch all in one day. Better be careful or people will talk." Tiffany attempted a flip tone, while her heart began its familiar dance.

"I'm willing to risk it. How about you?"

"Sure."

"Good. See you later." Jake leaned toward her, and to Tiffany's surprise, planted a kiss on her cheek.

She watched him go, bemused and pleased by his display of affection. Having Jake for a friend eased the loneliness she'd been feeling for months. Now if only she could rein in her errant emotions and stop hoping for more. Not that Jake made it easy with his flowers and invitation to lunch.

Sighing, Tiffany scraped leftover French toast and bacon into Bandit's bowl and retreated to the office. The stack of mail and paperwork was more daunting than she'd remembered and Tiffany spent an hour sorting through the pile. She'd almost finished the task when the phone rang; expecting it to be a business call, she let the machine pick up.

"Tiffany, this is Gracie Sheridan. Your mother told me you're feeling better. I'm glad. Listen. My daughter Jackie was signed up to supervise the setup and cleanup for the quilt show Saturday. Well, wouldn't you know it, she had her baby three weeks early. A beautiful little girl. Anyway, there's no way she can fulfill her responsibilities and I wondered if you could fill in."

Tiffany grabbed the phone, picking up before Gracie finished. "Hello, Mrs. Sheridan. Congratulations! What is this? Jackie's third?"

"Oh, Tiffany. You *are* there. This is her fourth, actually."

"Wow."

"Yes. My thoughts exactly. So, do you think you can lend a hand?"

"Unfortunately I only have one. Did my mom tell you I broke my arm?"

"Yes, and I know you're still recovering but we're desperate. The group is small and we've all got jobs already."

"Mrs. Sheridan—"

"It really won't be a lot of work. We're setting up the quilts and the table for our bake sale. All you have to do is make sure everyone is where they're supposed to be, doing what they should be doing."

Gracie paused before pushing home her point. "We made it as easy as possible because Jackie insisted on participating even though she was so pregnant and swollen and had those three little boys to care for."

Tiffany knew she'd never live it down if she refused a job that a pregnant mother of three sons had felt capable of doing. "All right. I guess I can help."

"Great. How about if I fax over all the information?"

"Sure." Tiffany reeled off her fax number, said goodbye, and sat wondering how she had been outmaneuvered by a woman who handed out homemade chocolates every Christmas and baskets filled with goodies every Easter.

"A woman that sweet shouldn't have a devious bone in her body," Tiffany muttered under her breath as she tapped a pen against her desk and waited for the fax. The machine hummed and spit out several sheets of paper.

The list of people and tasks looked daunting but after a few minutes of careful perusal, Tiffany could see that Gracie had been right. Every woman in the group had a specific job and, if all went well, Tiffany wouldn't need to do much more than show up.

"You look frustrated." Jake's voice sounded from the open door.

Startled Tiffany jumped, dropping the papers on the desk. "You scared the life out of me!"

"Sorry. I knocked at the back door but you didn't answer."

"It's okay. What's up?" Tiffany glanced at her watch. "It's not lunchtime yet, is it?"

"No. And I'm afraid I'm going to have to cancel. I got a call from Jessica Ann at the station. Someone stole one of Amos Mirrah's prize sows. He's insisting I come and talk to him."

"Someone stole a pig?"

"He says so." Jake shrugged, his broad shoulders pulling at the T-shirt he wore. "Two months ago he insisted someone took his goat. I found it munching on grass about a mile up the road. Amos had left the gate open and Gertrude wandered out."

"Amos sounds like a character. I'm surprised I haven't met him."

"He lives quite a ways outside of town and he keeps to himself. Sorry about lunch. I was looking forward to it."

"Me, too." Tiffany stacked the papers she'd dropped and stood. "But I understand. Come on, I'll walk you out."

After Jake left, Tiffany finished her paperwork and made a few calls confirming the job list for the quilt fair. With that done, the afternoon stretched before her, empty of any but the most menial tasks. She picked up a quilting magazine and leafed through it, but was unable to focus. Every creak of old wood, every sigh of leaves brushing against the house, sent Tiffany's heart skittering with fear. Even Bandit's large body pressed close to her feet did little to comfort her.

Finally, Tiffany had enough of being alone and she stood, grabbing her purse and keys. "Come on, Bandit. Let's go for a walk."

Bandit rushed to get his leash and sat patiently while Tiffany fumbled to attach it to his collar. They walked out the front door together.

The heat hit Tiffany like a warm, wet blanket and for a moment, she couldn't breathe. Luckily, the sun had retreated behind a layer of dense clouds and the pavement wasn't hot enough to burn Bandit's feet. They'd walked a half mile when the first drop of rain fell. Grabbing a plastic bag she'd shoved into the pocket of her shorts, Tiffany quickly covered her cast. The sprinkling of raindrops grew heavier, falling with increasing intensity.

One good thing about the rain—it drove most summer residents indoors. With any luck, the beach would be deserted. Smiling in anticipation, Tiffany tugged at Bandit's leash and began a slow jog, ignoring the slight ache in her head and the annoying, itchy pain in her arm.

Jake found the pig behind Amos's barn, cheerfully snuffling at a bag of trash. It didn't take long to get the animal back in its pen, and Jake arrived at the station before noon, ready to file his report.

The phone rang as he typed the information. He picked up on the second ring. "Reed, here."

"Hey, Jake, how's it going?"

The voice, though he hadn't heard it in months, was easily recognizable. "Pete?"

"Yep. The one and only. How're things in Smallsville?"

Jake didn't respond to the jibe. "Good. Things so slow in the city you got time to call me?"

"Actually, just the opposite." The teasing had gone from

Pete Bradshaw's voice and Jake wondered if his old boss was in trouble.

"You okay?"

"Yeah, just busy. The summer is too hot and too humid. People are getting edgy. Crime rate's up and I'm supposed to do something about it."

"So you're calling me?"

"I'll get to the point, Jake. I want you back."

Jake's fingers clenched on the phone but he didn't speak.

"Look, you're a city guy. I know it and you know it, too, if you're honest with yourself. We all understood you needed some time to regroup after Will's death. No shame in that. But it's been a year and a half. It's time to come home."

Jake could picture Pete's dark, expressive face. The man could convince an elephant that it liked mice, but Jake didn't plan to be talked into anything. "Sorry, Pete, this is my home now."

"Okay, I won't argue that point with you. I'll just lay the offer out for you and you can make your own decision. I need two detectives for homicide. I want one of them to be you."

"Detective?"

"Right. And I've been authorized to offer you ten grand more than you were making when you left."

"That's a lot of money." Jake heard a noise and looked up to see Jessica Ann hovering in his doorway. He mouthed the word *later* and motioned her to close the door.

"Yeah, well, the department is willing to pay for the best."

Jake laughed. "They'd pay for anyone willing to take on the job. Anyway, like I said, it's a lot of money, but I'm not interested."

Pete was silent for a moment as if considering how

worthwhile pressing the issue would be. Finally, he sighed loudly and conceded. "You know where to reach me if you change your mind."

"Right."

Jake hung up the phone, shaking his head at Pete's attempt to pull him back to D.C. A few months ago, he might have considered it, but Lakeview had grown on him and Jake preferred the quiet, slower-paced life to the hustle of city living.

And, of course, there was Tiffany to consider. Even if he'd been tempted by D.C., he couldn't leave Lakeview without knowing if she was a part of his future.

Smiling at the thought, Jake quickly finished the report.

Tiffany sat on cool sand, enjoying the soft drops of rain beading her shoulders and head. As she had predicted, the beach was empty, though a few fishing boats still floated lazily on the gray-green water of the lake. Cocooned in the warm rain, Tiffany watched Bandit prance along the shore, and enjoyed the peace and solitude.

"Tiffany!" The voice pierced the silence, putting an end to Tiffany's quiet time.

She let out a muffled sigh and stood to face the interloper.

Henry Simmons rushed over, an umbrella clutched in one hand and a jacket in the other. "What are you doing out on a day like today? It's raining cats and dogs."

"I needed some fresh air."

"Well, you're gonna soak that cast through if you're not careful."

"I'm fine, Henry, thanks."

"I'm riding patrol today. Saw you sitting here and thought maybe you could use an umbrella." He thrust the umbrella at Tiffany and she had no choice but to take it.

"Thanks, but—"

"Wish I had time to stay and chat, but there's something up at the station and I'm heading over there now to get the scoop."

"What scoop?"

Henry glanced around, then leaned in close. "You didn't hear this from me, but according to those who are in a position to know, Sheriff Reed is going back to D.C."

"What?"

"His boss called today. Offered him a huge pay raise. And, get this, he's going to be a detective."

"That's...great."

"You think? I like having him around. He's been handling these summer troubles like a professional. There's a lot to be said for that."

Tiffany tuned out the rest of what Henry said, her mind struggling to come to terms with the news.

"How about if I give you a ride back to your place? You look a little peaked."

"No. I'm fine." She smiled to prove her point, hoping Henry would be on his way.

He hesitated a moment, then nodded. "Okay. As long as you're sure. Just be careful."

"I will."

Henry walked away and Tiffany turned back toward the lake. The water looked gray, choppy and uninviting. It matched her mood perfectly. She felt empty and sad, though she knew she shouldn't be. Jake hadn't made her any promises. He'd even told her what she could expect out of their relationship. She had been a fool to build dreams on a friendship that was never meant to be anything more.

And the worst part was, Tiffany knew Doris had been right. Some women were meant to fall in love one time.

And when they did, that love ruined them for any other relationship.

Jake was that love for Tiffany. The one by which she would judge all other relationships and find them lacking.

Heart heavy with the knowledge, Tiffany left the lake and headed back to her empty house.

Chapter Twenty-One

$\sim$

Jake traded shifts with Henry so he could spend Thursday with Tiffany. Unfortunately, judging by the way she'd avoided him, she didn't appreciate the effort. Watching her now as she moved across the lawn, a tray balanced in her good hand, he couldn't help wondering what had happened to change things. The companionship and laughter they'd shared had all but disappeared. Jake wanted it back.

He stepped close as Tiffany deposited the tray on the gazebo floor. "I brought some lunch for you. You've been out here for hours."

There was one sandwich and one glass. Apparently she didn't plan to join him for lunch. Giving in to temptation, Jake placed a finger under her chin and tilted her face up toward his. "What's wrong?"

Tiffany looked at him, her eyes dark and troubled. "Nothing. I'm just tired today, and not very good company."

Jake didn't believe her, but he let it go, motioning toward the swing. "Sit down for a while and rest. I'll even share my tea with you."

Tiffany's smile seemed forced. "No, I'd better not. I've got to finish some last minute details for the quilt fair."

"Is there a lot of work to do?"

"Not for me. Not really, anyway. I just have to make sure everyone else is prepared to do their jobs."

Jake poured tea from the pitcher and held the glass out to Tiffany, smiling as she took it. Grabbing the sandwich, he sat down and waited for her to do the same. She didn't disappoint him.

"I really am tired. I wish I hadn't agreed to help with the fair."

"So, why did you?"

Tiffany sipped from the glass and then turned to look at Jake, a glimmer of the old amusement in her eyes. "The woman who volunteered for the job before I got it had three sons and was eight months pregnant. I figured compared to that, a broken arm and concussion were nothing."

"What happened to supermom?"

"She had the baby."

"Oh. So, if you sprout another arm will they let you off the hook, too?"

Tiffany's eyes widened and she laughed, tension easing from her face. "I guess that would solve the problem."

Jake watched as she leaned back in the swing, her head falling against the old wood. Her unclipped hair hung over the edge in a shimmering mass of curls. Unable to resist, he ran his hand along its length. "You have beautiful hair."

Tiffany turned toward him, a half smile on her face. "Thanks. It was the bane of my existence all through high school."

"Why?" Jake twisted a curl around one finger, then let it go, watching as it sprang and bounced.

"Straight hair was in. Nice, smoothed-behind-the-ears styles." She flicked her hair self-consciously. "Mine wouldn't cooperate. Then there was the color. It was a lot more orange when I was a teenager. I really stood out in a crowd."

"You still do."

Jake could tell from the blush on Tiffany's cheeks that she understood the comment for the compliment it was. He reached over and cupped his hand on the curve of her jaw, urging her to face him. "Tell me what's bothering you, Tiffany."

"I...was talking to Henry yesterday and..."

"Anybody back there?"

Perfect timing again, Jake thought as he and Tiffany turned to see Patti Anderson walk through the gate.

"Oops. My timing stinks again. Sorry."

Jake couldn't help smiling. "The more the merrier."

"Sure." Her eyes twinkled with the same amusement he'd seen so often in Tiffany's. "I tried to call but no one picked up. Jenna's kids are sick. I promised I'd run by with some medicine and comfort food. Tiffany, I should be back to take you to your appointment, but if I'm running late, don't worry. I haven't forgotten."

"No problem, Mom. I can actually drive myself."

"No. You can't. The doctor said no driving for a week."

"I'm fine. And I don't want you to rush. Jenna might need you to stay a while."

"I already promised you—"

"I'd be happy to drive Tiffany to her appointment."

Both women looked at Jake as if they'd forgotten he was there. "That would be perfect."

"I'll drive myself."

"Tiffany, you're having stitches taken out and a cast put on. What if you start feeling sick? If you won't take a ride with Jake, I'll have to skip seeing Jenna."

Jake saw Tiffany hesitate, and decided to help her make the choice. He slid an arm across her shoulder, and pulled her close. "Don't worry, Mrs. Anderson. I'll make sure she gets there and back."

"All right. I guess I'll go get the medicine for Jenna. See you later, Tiffany. Sheriff Reed."

As soon as Patti Anderson cleared the gate, Jake turned to Tiffany. "Where are we going and what time do we need to leave?"

"Jake, I really can drive myself."

"Maybe so, but I promised your mom I'd get you there safely and that's what I plan to do."

"The appointment's at one. Dr. Hartland is in the new professional building off of Main Street."

"We better get moving then."

"Jake, I—"

"Get what you need and let's go. I'm not above hog-tying you and carrying you out to the truck."

"You wouldn't dare."

"Wouldn't I?" Jake stepped close and satisfied the urge to press a kiss to Tiffany's lips. Then he slipped an arm behind her back, one under her knees and swept her off her feet.

He had the satisfaction of seeing her mouth drop open and her eyes go wide, before she squealed and squirmed against his hold. "Put me down! I'm too heavy! You'll break your back! What are you doing?!"

Jake pushed open the gate and strode to the truck. "Sweeping you off your feet."

Tiffany went still. Then laughed, the sound tickling against

Jake's chest. "You really are too much. Now put me down. Mr. Fitzsimmons is watching us from his window."

Jake complied, lowering Tiffany to her feet, and unlocking the truck door. "Good fodder for the gossip mills. Get in. I'll run in the house and get your purse."

That she didn't argue spoke volumes. "It's hanging on the coatrack near the front door."

Jake found the purse and returned to the truck within minutes. During his time away, Tiffany had transformed, turning from the happy, laughing woman he'd carried to the truck, into a somber, sad-eyed stranger.

He wanted to press for answers. Find out what was bothering her. But she leaned her head back against the seat and closed her eyes.

"You okay?"

"Yes."

Jake reached over and cupped his hand against the warmth of her neck, kneading the tight muscles there. "Anything I can do to help?"

She turned toward him, her eyes open again and vivid with something that looked like dreams. "Jake." She paused, then shook her head, the shadowy dreams in her eyes disappearing behind a veil of indifference. "You've already helped me. Besides, I'm just tired. A concussion will do that to a person."

Though she tried to joke, Tiffany knew the words fell flat. She closed her eyes against Jake's questioning look and tried to relax as they drove to the doctor's office.

She couldn't. There were too many questions clamoring in her mind. Too many thoughts spilling along her nerves. She grabbed her purse and rifled through the contents, grabbing out the comb and a hair clip. With the clip between her lips, she twisted her hair with her good hand, then tried to finesse the clip into the mass of curls before it all dropped back to her shoulders.

Jake reached over while she struggled, and flipped open the vanity mirror.

"Thanks." Tiffany's reflection did little to improve her mood. Though she'd managed to contain most of her hair, loose tendrils tumbled against her cheeks and neck. Lack of sleep showed in the dark circles that rimmed her eyes and in the pallor of her skin. With the huge bruise on her forehead turning various shades of green and purple, Tiffany figured she was the last woman in the world to entice a man to stay.

Which was fine, because she had accepted that she couldn't keep Jake from leaving, and that she shouldn't even try. God had a plan for each of their lives. It had been nice to fantasize that somehow those plans involved each other, but Tiffany knew fantasies seldom mimicked reality. Her situation with Jake was just one more example of that truth.

Giving her mirrored image one last glance, Tiffany closed the vanity mirror and turned to gaze out the window.

Thankfully, the drive to the medical building was short and Jake didn't push for answers to Tiffany's silence. She was glad. Her answers made little sense even to herself. Her mood, half irritation, half depression, refused to lift no matter how much she lectured herself.

"This is it, right?" Jake gestured to a two-story brick building that housed the doctor's office.

"Yes. Thanks. You can drop me off. I'll call Mom and have her come pick me up when I'm finished."

The look Jake shot her way told Tiffany exactly what he thought about her suggestion. She didn't argue further. Just allowed him to escort her into the office, his hand resting on her waist as she checked in. She liked having him at her side. Enjoyed the warmth of his presence and the comfort of knowing he was there.

The thought of him leaving brought a fresh wave of sadness, and tears pricked her eyes. Luckily the doctor who was removing her stitches thought the tears were due to pain. He wrote her out a prescription, applied the hard cast and sent her on her way.

When Jake offered to stop for ice cream on the way home, Tiffany politely refused and was proud of her response. It was better to put distance between them now than to be devastated when he went back to D.C. At least that's what Tiffany told herself as she faced another evening alone.

When the phone rang at a little after six, Tiffany rushed to answer it, her heart racing with anticipation. Maybe Jake was calling to check on her. Maybe he was on patrol and wanted to stop by. Maybe *she* should be committed for delusional thinking.

"Hello, Tiffany?" Gracie Sheridan's voice was a splash of cold reality, and Tiffany forced away her disappointment.

"Hi, Mrs. Sheridan, what can I do for you?"

"I hate to bother you, dear, but Lilith Parker was supposed to pick the quilts up at the church yesterday and bring them over to the elementary school so we can hang them in the auditorium."

"Right, I saw her name on the list."

"Well, she's down with food poisoning. She went to a family reunion over the weekend, and says she's been sick as a dog ever since."

"That's terrible."

"Yes, I feel so sorry for her."

"What can I do to help?"

"Lilith volunteered to drop off the quilts and to make copies of the quilting pamphlet we've put together. She got permission from the school's principal to use the copy machine. I know it's a lot to ask but the setup crew will be at the school tonight, setting up tables and booths. We'd really like to hang the quilts tomorrow...."

Tiffany almost groaned aloud. She hated photocopying. Then again, she hated the idea of spending the evening at loose ends. "Do you have a copy of the pamphlet?"

"I'll leave it at the church with the quilts. We don't need many copies. Maybe three hundred. Thanks so much, Tiffany."

Tiffany said goodbye and hung up the phone, calculating in her mind the amount of time it would take to run several hundred copies of the pamphlet. At the rate the school's old copier worked, she figured she'd finish sometime before her birthday in the spring.

"Oh, well, Bandit." Tiffany leaned down and scratched the dog on his head. "It's not like I had anything more exciting to do."

And who knew? Maybe she'd run into some friends while she was out and about. It would be fun to catch up on the town gossip. It seemed forever since she'd had a nice long chat with anyone but Jake.

When she arrived at the elementary school, it was teeming with eager quilters and crafters all setting up for the weekend fair. Tiffany glanced around, looking for a familiar face, but was disappointed. Shrugging away self-pity, she found the school office and began copying the multipage pamphlet.

By the time she finished, the school had grown silent and her footsteps echoed eerily as she crossed the empty lobby. Darkness hung heavy and silent outside the door and Tiffany hesitated on the threshold, wondering if she should call for an escort.

She felt silly for the thought. Weak in a way she'd never been before. Forcing back the fear, Tiffany stepped out into the night and moved briskly toward the side of the building. She'd parked on the side lot, away from the back area where tables and booths had been set up, but too far away from the front door for her own comfort.

She should have planned better.

Tiffany scanned the shadows as she walked, her nerves on edge. Despite the stars that sprinkled the sky with light, and the moon adding its own bright display, the night felt sinister and Tiffany hurried toward the Cadillac, anxious to be safe inside its doors.

She'd rounded the corner, had the Caddy in sight, when the sound of breaking glass shattered the stillness. Tiffany didn't wait to hear more. She ran.

A dark figure lurched from the shadows beside the car and Tiffany veered away, her feet sliding on pavement as she tried to switch direction. A hand grabbed the edge of her shirt, tugging her sideways, and Tiffany screamed, jerking away, her feet tangling with one another as she turned too quickly.

She fell in slow motion. Her arms and legs flailing for purchase. Her body twisting as she tried to cushion her fall. She landed hard on her broken arm, felt something give as white hot pain slashed through her.

And the world went black.

Chapter Twenty-Two

Jake sat at his desk, plowing through paperwork and wondering why things had been so quiet in town lately. He liked to think his talk with Greg Banning had convinced the kid to lie low.

His gut said there was another explanation. Like maybe Greg had decided to pull something big before his departure from Lakeview. With summer quickly drawing to an end, there were several craft fairs and celebrations planned. Any one of them provided an opportunity for Greg and his gang to cause trouble.

Jake was prepared, paying overtime for officers to patrol the most likely targets. Unfortunately, nobody could be in two places at one time. Eventually, there'd be a lag in the patrol, and then the trouble would start.

He thought of the craft and quilt show being held at the elementary school. Several thousand people had attended the previous year, and there was no reason to believe this year would be any different. If Greg wanted to cause trouble, that would be a good place to do it.

Jake pushed aside his paperwork and grabbed a pen, quickly jotting down the names of men he could count on to keep an eye out for trouble during the fair. When he was done, he glanced at the clock and wondered if Tiffany was still awake.

He needed to talk to her, find out exactly what had put the sadness in her eyes. Unfortunately, eleven o'clock at night didn't seem like the time to do it.

He stood, stretched and was ready to get back to the paperwork when the call came in.

Jake's blood ran cold as he heard the details—the sound of shattering glass and a woman's scream heard by a man walking his dog near the elementary school.

Jake's first thought was Tiffany, and though he tried to tell himself she was home safe in bed, he couldn't shake the feeling that she was in trouble.

The drive to the school seemed to take longer than the five minutes Jake knew it to be. As he pulled around to the back of the building, the headlights of the cruiser highlighted broken glass and scattered pieces of paper. Tables and booths that had been set up for the craft fair were overturned, but the amount of damage was minimal.

Jake wasn't reassured. Heart pounding frantically, he jumped from the cruiser and began searching for signs that Tiffany had been there. It didn't take long for his worst suspicions to be confirmed. Lying on the ground, just a few yards from the front door, was Tiffany's purse.

He lifted it, his mind going blank with fear and rage. He'd find Tiffany and then he'd make whoever had taken her pay.

* * *

Tiffany woke in pitch-black darkness. At first she thought she might be blind. Then she noticed faint pinpricks of light and the oily smell of exhaust. She was worse than blind, she was in the trunk of a car.

The hum of the motor and the gentle bounce of tires reassured her for a moment. At least she hadn't been abandoned in some desolate area. Then the car jerked to a stop and the trunk popped open. Before Tiffany could think of a plan she was dragged from her prison and yanked to her feet.

They were near the lake. Tiffany could see the water and hear the gentle swish as it touched the shore. That gave her little comfort. Not when five young men surrounded her. One much taller than the others, his cold eyes fixed on Tiffany with a look that made her shudder.

She thought about running, but she felt dizzy with pain, her arm throbbing with every movement. She stood still instead, straightening her spine and forcing authority into her voice. "What's going on?"

The tallest of the five stepped forward, the sneer on his face apparent even in the dim moonlight. "You just don't know how to give up, do you? Everywhere I go this summer, I gotta deal with you."

He grabbed Tiffany by the arm and dragged her to the water's edge where a motorboat waited. "Get in."

Tiffany dug her feet in and pulled back. "I've never even seen you before."

"I've seen you. And I'm sick of it. Come on, guys. Help me get her in the boat."

The others boys surged forward but didn't touch Tiffany. One of them shifted uncomfortably and spoke. "Why do you want her in the boat?"

"I told you, we're gonna stash her somewhere. Keep her quiet until I leave tomorrow. By the time anyone finds her, I'll be back in Chicago. My boys'll hide me until things blow over. You come when you can. You've earned your place in the brotherhood."

"You're gonna stash her on the lake?"

"You just worry about getting her in the boat, and let me worry about the rest."

"I don't know, Slade. This doesn't seem right."

"Coward! Go home. All of you. I'll take care of this problem."

Before Tiffany realized what he was about, Slade grabbed her broken arm and yanked hard. She screamed, falling into the boat, and swallowing back the bile that rose in her throat. He didn't give her a chance to right herself, just pushed off shore, and started the motor.

Tiffany forced herself to her knees, then eased onto the seat. She could jump overboard, swim to shore. It was her best chance, but still not a good one. Pain throbbed deep in her arm, stealing her breath and threatening to do the same with her consciousness.

She forced her mind to calm. Forced herself not to panic. "Where are you taking me?"

"You'll find out soon enough. But you try to move again and I'll bash you over the head with this." He picked up an oar and thrust it toward her. "And knock you into the water."

"That would be murder."

"Only if you die." He grinned, the expression skeletal in the moonlight.

Fear. Panic. Pain. Tiffany fought against them all, struggling to think of a way to stop what she knew was about to happen. "Why are you doing this?"

"Because I can."

Tiffany shuddered at the words, the cold, hardness of them a stark reminder that she was at his mercy. She glanced around, hoping for escape, but saw only the inky blackness of the lake. In desperation she screamed for help.

Slade laughed, prodding her with the paddle he still held. "You think anyone can hear you way out here?"

Tiffany straightened her spine and looked him in the eye. If she couldn't escape, maybe she could scare some sense into him. "God does."

"Yeah. And so does the moon, and it's a lot more likely to help." Slade grinned at his joke.

"You don't believe in God?" Now didn't seem the time for evangelism, but at least if they were talking she had time to plan an escape.

"God? Yeah. I believe in God. He's me."

With that he swung the paddle hard, his movements quick. Too quick for Tiffany to jump out of the way. She ducked instead, taking the force of the blow on her shoulder instead of her head.

She rolled with the pain, slid into the water, and dove low, praying all the while that God would give her strength she knew she didn't have.

They'd been searching for half an hour with no luck. Jake banged his hand against the steering wheel, and thought through what he knew. Tiffany had been at the school. Now she was gone and so was her car. Greg Banning was missing, too. His parents unable to account for his whereabouts.

Jake didn't like where his thoughts were leading him. He liked even less that they hadn't found Tiffany yet. He had every available officer searching, but trying to find the Cadillac was like searching for a needle in a haystack. Almost impossible. There were too many back roads. Too many places a car could disappear.

He'd been promised a helicopter by the state police. God alone knew when it would arrive.

For now they were reduced to rudimentary search and rescue. He prayed as he sped through town. If Tiffany was to be found, Jake needed help to do it.

He'd just passed the town limits when a figure appeared, running hard and waving frantically. Jake pulled to a stop and jumped out, nearly colliding with the hurtling form. "Whoa. Slow down."

"There's no time. We've got to get to the lake. Jon Murray called me. He said something weird just went down. Slade took Tiffany out on the lake. Jon doesn't think he's bringing her back." Tom Bishop spoke rapidly, the words spilling out one on top of the other.

"You know where they are?"

"Down Jasper Road. Where it dead ends. There's a little dock there. I was on the way, but the truck stalled. I couldn't get it running again."

"Get in." Jake didn't wait for Tom to close the door. He sped down side roads, rounding curves at a dangerous speed, his mind conjuring images that made his blood run cold. "You call for help?"

"Yeah, but I was afraid they wouldn't get there fast enough."

"Did Jon call 911, or just you?"

"He called me. He's afraid. He said Slade went crazy and he doesn't want any part of it."

It was too late for that. Every one of the kids involved was going to pay. And Greg Banning, aka Slade, would pay the most.

Jake slammed on the brakes as he neared the end of the road. His high beams illuminated the Cadillac, its trunk and doors open. Several boys bolted for the shadows as Jake jumped from the cruiser. He didn't bother to stop them. He knew who they were.

Sirens blared and a cruiser screeched to a halt beside Jake, several cars sliding to a stop beside it. Henry Simmons leaped from the cruiser, his expression strained. "That her car?"

Jake nodded; it was hard to speak past the lump in his throat. He'd watched Will die. Would the same happen with Tiffany?

Not if he could help it. "We need a boat."

"I think there's one on the way."

Henry was right. The sound of a motor echoed across the water, and a shadowy boat moved toward shore. There was one person in it. It wasn't Tiffany.

Jake splashed into the water as Greg neared the dock and grabbed the kid's shirt, dragging him from the boat and into the lake. "Where is she?"

"Let me go. I don't know what you're talking about."

"Tiffany Anderson. Where is she?"

"What? Did you lose your girlfriend? Too bad. Maybe she'll turn up. Sooner or later."

Jake raised his fist, started swinging, but a hand landed on his arm stopping the motion. "Don't waste time, friend."

Ben stood beside him, his hand hard and unyielding. His eyes knowing. "Take the boat and go. She's out there. She's alive. Go."

Jake released Greg and jumped into the boat. Tom slid in after him. "I'm coming."

Jake nodded, focusing on the darkness of the lake. Was Tiffany out there? Was she alive as Ben believed? Jake refused to think anything else.

* * *

Tiffany liked to swim. She really did. But not in the dark with a water-logged cast dragging her left arm down. Her bruised shoulder cramped as she struggled toward shore, her eyes straining to catch a glimpse of the flashing lights she'd spotted in the distance.

They never got any closer, no matter how tirelessly she swam. Tiffany groaned as pain shot through her arm, then coughed against water that seeped into her mouth.

People were searching for her. She knew it. So where were they all?

Was Jake with them? She imagined him, mouth hard with anger, worry lining his face. He'd keep searching, she knew, even if others gave up. If she had the breath, she'd call his name. But all her energy went into staying afloat. And even that was becoming difficult.

"God, you can do anything so I know you can get me back to shore. I'm counting on it 'cause there is no way I can make it back on my own."

As if in answer to her prayer, the soft chug of a boat engine drifted across the lake. Tiffany treaded water, listening, straining to find the direction of the sound.

"Tiffany? Tiffany, can you hear me?"

The words were whisper-soft, barely penetrating her fatigue-numbed brain.

"Tiffany!" This time the shout was unmistakable, the rumble of the engine growing closer.

"Here, over here." Her voice sounded weak and frail, and she tried again, shouting for all she was worth and wondering if she could be heard over the sound of the motor.

Jake had been on the boat for twenty minutes, praying fervently and calling Tiffany's name.

Other boats were beginning to join the search. He could see the bright lights attached to the helms. They were distant, but comforting. More manpower meant more area searched in a shorter period of time. Switching on the boat radio, Jake called in his location.

"Anybody see anything yet?"

"No sign of her, Sheriff. Could be the kid dropped her off on the opposite shore."

"He's still not talking?"

"No, he denies any knowledge of Tiffany."

"How about the others?"

"They say he had her, but don't know what happened after he put her in the boat."

"They're covering their tails. Trying to distance themselves. Keep working on them. They might know more than they're saying."

"Right."

Jake stared out into the darkness. If Tiffany was okay she'd be swimming for shore and someone would see her.

If she was okay.

Without warning, the boat engine sputtered, coughed and purred back to life. In the split second of silence Jake thought he heard something. He turned to Tom who stared into the darkness. "Did you hear something?"

Jake cut the engine, not waiting for Tom's reply, and tried to listen past the pounding of his own blood.

"Help! Over here!" The voice, strained and distant, was unmistakably Tiffany's.

"Tiffany, it's Jake and Tom. We're coming. Just keep calling." Jake's voice shook with emotion, his hands trembling as he handed an oar to Tom. "We've got to paddle toward her. We won't be able to hear if we use the motor."

Together they turned the boat toward the sound of

Tiffany's cries. Within moments Jake spotted her in the distance.

"Tiffany, listen to me. I see you. Just lie on your back and float. Don't waste your energy. If you go under I'll never find you in this darkness."

Jake's fear was palpable, and Tiffany responded, lying on her back and floating in place when every cell in her body demanded that she swim toward the boat.

Within moments, the soft tap of oars against the water reached her ears, and then a strong hand grasped hers.

"Tiffany, thank God."

She looked up into Jake's face and tried to smile, but her teeth were chattering and she couldn't quite manage it. "Can you get me out of here? I'm a little sick of water at the moment."

"You bet, just relax and let me do the work, okay? Tom's going to steady the boat while I pull you in."

Tiffany nodded her understanding, felt Jake loop his arms under hers, and before she could blink, was inside the boat with Jake's arms wrapped firmly around her.

"Are you okay?"

Huddled close to Jake's warmth, Tiffany felt better than okay. "Yes."

"Greg didn't hurt you?"

"Greg? You mean Slade?" Tiffany's teeth chattered so hard, she could barely get the word out.

"You're in shock. Tom, strip off your shirt." As Jake spoke he pulled off his own shirt and tugged it over Tiffany's head. Tom's followed a moment later. Jake pulled her close and spoke over her head. "Can you drive this, Tom?"

Tiffany didn't hear the answer. Pressed close to Jake's heart, she had fallen asleep.

Later, after Greg had been taken to the station to be

booked and the spectators and reporters had gone back to their beds, Tiffany sat in Jake's cruiser nursing sweet, hot coffee and waited while Jake gave final orders to several officers.

It didn't take him long to return to the car and when he did, the concern in his eyes was obvious. "How's the arm?"

"Better."

"You should have gone to the hospital earlier. Gotten an X ray."

"I wanted to be here. I also wanted to put off more pain for as long as possible. I figure once I get there they'll do more damage to me than Slade did." Tiffany was only half joking.

Jake seemed to sense it. He smoothed a hand over her hair, and let it rest against her neck. "Don't worry. Whatever they do won't be so bad. I'll make sure of it."

Tiffany smiled at his words, reaching up to brush half-dry hair from her cheek. "I'll count on it."

Jake stared down at her, his eyes assessing. "You've got another bruise."

Tiffany shivered as he traced gentle fingers along her cheek. "I'll be fine."

"If I'd been with you tonight this wouldn't have happened."

"Jake, you can't know that. Besides, being with me every minute of the day would be impossible."

"Yes, but—"

"It wasn't your fault." Tiffany cut him off, not liking the regret she heard in his voice.

"Maybe not, but if anything had happened to you I never would have forgiven myself."

"Jake—"

This time it was Jake's turn to interrupt, his warm lips silencing Tiffany more effectively than any words could. When he finally pulled back, Tiffany was too bemused to speak.

In Jake's eyes she could see everything she had ever hoped for—love, acceptance, passion—and Tiffany was sure she was dreaming. Then he reached out and tugged a curl, smiling into her eyes. "If anything had happened to you I wouldn't have forgiven myself for never telling you how much you mean to me. I love you, Tiffany. Knowing you has changed me. You've made me believe in all the things I gave up on after my first marriage."

"You love me?"

"Yeah, I do." Jake threaded his fingers through hers and brought her hand up for a kiss.

"But aren't you going back to D.C.?"

"D.C.? Why would you think that?"

"Henry said..." Tiffany paused, realizing what she should have known all along. "It isn't true. You're not leaving."

Jake shook his head. "How could I? I'd have to leave my heart behind."

Tiffany laughed; she couldn't help herself. The sound pealed through the quiet night, filled with joy and hope and all the love she felt. "That is the silliest, most romantic thing anybody has ever said to me. And you know what? I love you, too."

"Good, then share my life with me. Be my wife."

Tiffany looked into Jake's eyes, dark with longing and with hope, and for a moment was so full of love she couldn't speak. Then she pulled his hand close, kissing it in the same way he had kissed hers moments before. "I can't imagine a life without you, Jake. I'd love to be your wife."

At her words, Jake pulled Tiffany to her feet and held her

close. She let his warm embrace envelop her, smiling against his chest as she said a silent prayer of thanks.

In His own time and in His own way, God had given her the desire of her heart.

Epilogue

✦

She stood at the door of the sanctuary, listening for the first strains of the bridal march. Yards of white silk cascaded to her feet, a long train of the same material flowing behind her. In her hands she held a bouquet of fall blossoms—hyacinth and mums, mixed with tiny red and yellow roses.

A dog barked and Tiffany smiled, patting Bandit on the head and adjusting the bow tie attached to his collar. Mom had complained about the dog being part of the wedding ceremony, but Tiffany had insisted. After all, God had used him to bring Jake into her life.

"Your turn, guys." Tiffany's father motioned to Tom who stood tall in his rented tux. Tightening his grip on Bandit's leash, he flashed Tiffany a smile, and walked through the door.

Then the music changed, slowing, gaining in depth, as the bridal march began. She felt her father's hand tighten on her arm and she looked up into his green eyes.

"It's time. I love you, sweetheart."

"I love you, too, Dad."

Friends and family filled the church, smiling their happiness as Tiffany and her father walked through the door. Tiffany barely noticed. She smiled, gazing down the aisle, longing to meet her beloved's eyes.

Jake stood waiting, tall and dark-haired, his eyes glowing with love. He moved forward as she approached, linking arms with her, leaning close to whisper in her ear. "I have never seen anyone as beautiful as you. I'll remember you like this, always." He brushed his hand against the soft lace of her veil and Tiffany's heart thundered with happiness.

Bandit barked again. This time, Tiffany didn't notice.

* * * * *

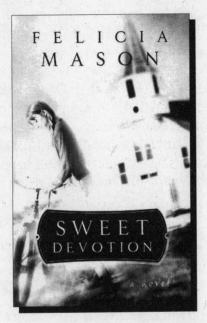

Love Inspired

TRUE
DEVOTION

BY

MARTA
PERRY

Pregnant and widowed, Susannah Laine needed
answers about her husband's death, and only
Nathan Sloane could provide them. But the truth
they learned threatened their budding romance.
Could God now give Susannah the strength
to overcome her past and embrace this
second chance at happiness?

Don't miss

TRUE DEVOTION
On sale February 2004

Available at your favorite retail outlet.